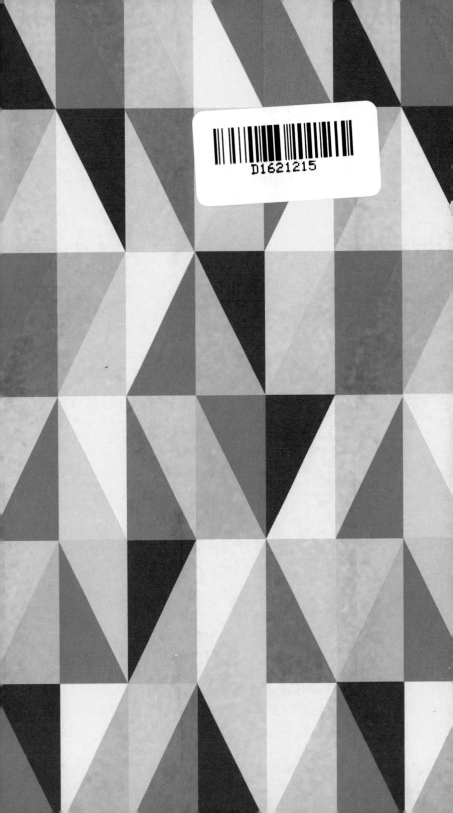

D1621215

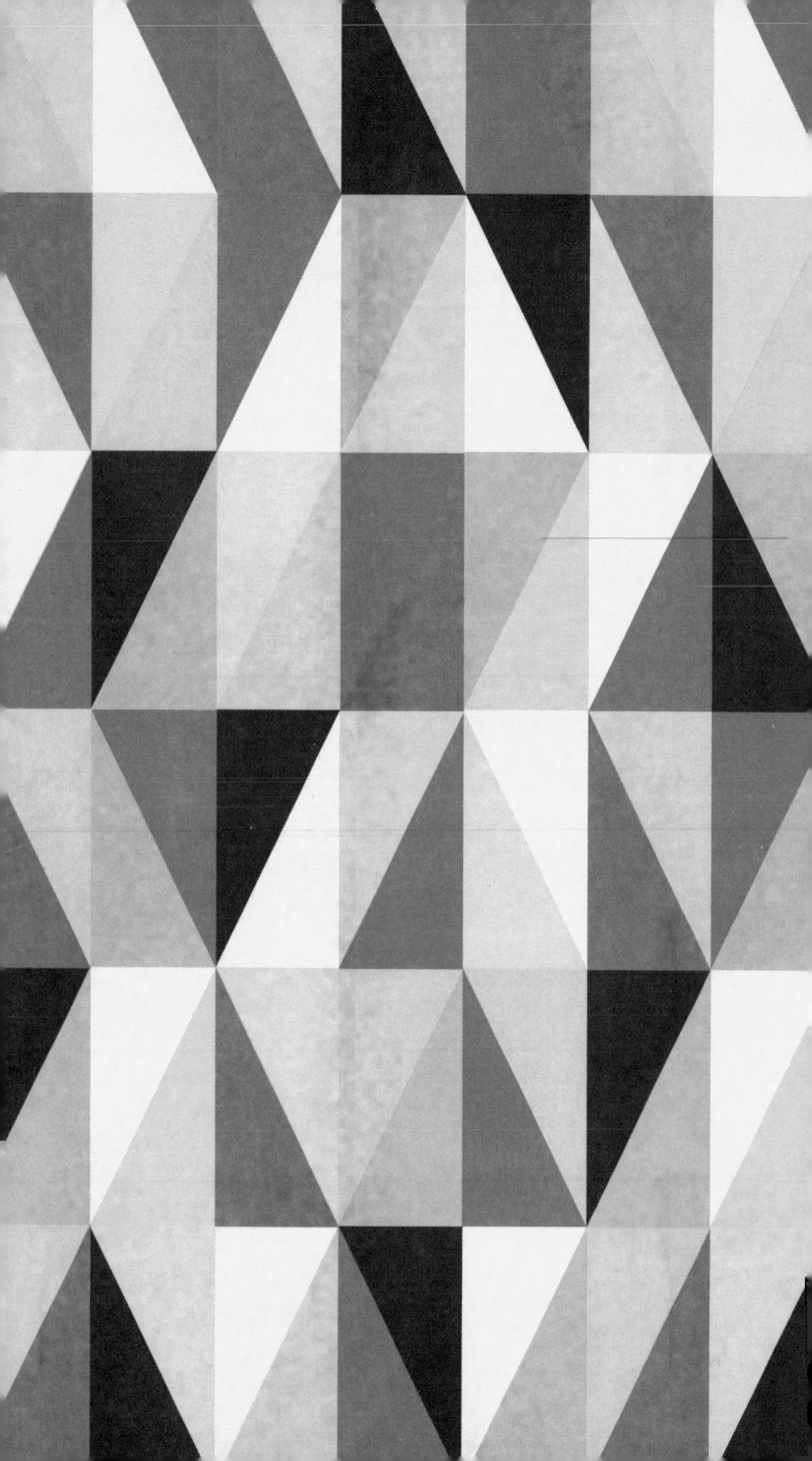

MAMIE PHIPPS CLARK
CHAMPION FOR CHILDREN

MAMIE PHIPPS CLARK
CHAMPION FOR CHILDREN

BY **LYNNETTE MAWHINNEY**, PhD

ILLUSTRATED BY **NEIL EVANS**

MAGINATION PRESS • WASHINGTON, DC
AMERICAN PSYCHOLOGICAL ASSOCIATION

**Books for Kids From the
American Psychological Association**

Magination Press is a registered trademark of the American Psychological Association. Order books at maginationpress.org, or call 1-800-374-2721.

Book design by Christina Gaugler

Printed by Sonic Media Solutions, Inc., Medford, NY

Library of Congress Cataloging-in-Publication Data

Names: Mawhinney, Lynnette, 1979- author. | Evans, Neil, illustrator.
Title: Mamie Phipps Clark, champion for children / by Lynnette Mawhinney; illustrated by Neil Evans.
Description: Washington, DC : Magination Press, 2024.
Series: Extraordinary women in psychology series | Includes bibliographical references. |
Summary: "Mamie Phipps Clark and her husband, Kenneth Clark, conducted the famous "black doll/white doll" studies that eventually contributed to the Brown v. Board of Education decision"—Provided by publisher.
Identifiers: LCCN 2023029537 (print) | LCCN 2023029538 (ebook) | ISBN 9781433830488 (hardcover) | ISBN 9781433843655 (ebook)
Subjects: LCSH: Clark, Mamie Phipps—Juvenile literature. | Social psychologists—United States—Biography—Juvenile literature. | African American psychologists—United States—Biography—Juvenile literature. | Women psychologists—United States—Biography—Juvenile literature. | Segregation in education—United States—Juvenile literature.
Classification: LCC HM1031.C53 M39 2024 (print) | LCC HM1031.C53 (ebook) | DDC 150.92 [B]—dc23/eng/20231018
LC record available at https://lccn.loc.gov/2023029537 LC ebook record available at https://lccn.loc.gov/2023029538

Manufactured in the United States of America
10 9 8 7 6 5 4 3 2 1

With all my love to Gabrielle and
Enoch, may this book give you hope
as we strive to be a better world for
Black children to grow up in. You
are both my Black joy!—LM

TABLE OF CONTENTS

DEAR READER

This is the story about one remarkable woman, Dr. Mamie Phipps Clark. She was a woman of many firsts and changed many lives in the United States. You will read about Dr. Clark and hear about her childhood, her research studies that exposed the negative effects of racial segregation on children and helped desegregate schools in the U.S., the Northside Center that she founded to support children with special needs in Harlem, and importantly, her legacy of activism and advocacy work that continues today.

Dr. Clark's time growing up in the U.S. South was supported by a warm and nurturing Black community, but there was one hard, pivotal moment that changed everything for her. You will see in this story how that event impacted her life and work, how she thought about herself and others, how this influenced her research and pursuit of answers, and how all that created an unstoppable force in her to be a champion for Black children.

During Dr. Clark's time, life was different for Black people, but it was also different for women. Oftentimes, women would work outside the home until they had children, and then careers were put on the back burner. Dr. Clark had to work extra hard to balance work and home life. And on top of all that, she was often not given credit for her work and efforts. It is my hope that this book will bring her hard work and influence to light instead of letting it be forgotten or never mentioned.

At the end of each chapter, I'll challenge you with a bit of extra information called *Did You Know*, so you can go a little deeper into her story. Then you'll have a chance to apply what you've learned in the *Try This* so you too can champion for yourself and others in your community.

Just a heads up as we are on the journey together—if you come across a phrase that you don't know or remember, please look at the glossary in the back of the book. Since we are going back in time, there are some words like *Colored* or *Negro* that are seen as disrespectful and hurtful today but were once commonly used to describe Black people by themselves and others. Language is fluid and words referring to people have evolved over time to be more considerate, fair, and appreciative. Words used during Dr. Clark's lifetime are included here for historical accuracy, even though we do not use them today.

I am pleased to tell you about Dr. Mamie Phipps Clark's life and legacy. She was a great advocate for children and is a true inspiration. I hope you'll feel her spirit as you read through this book.

—Dr. Lynnette Mawhinney

CHAPTER ONE

Growing Up in Jim Crow South

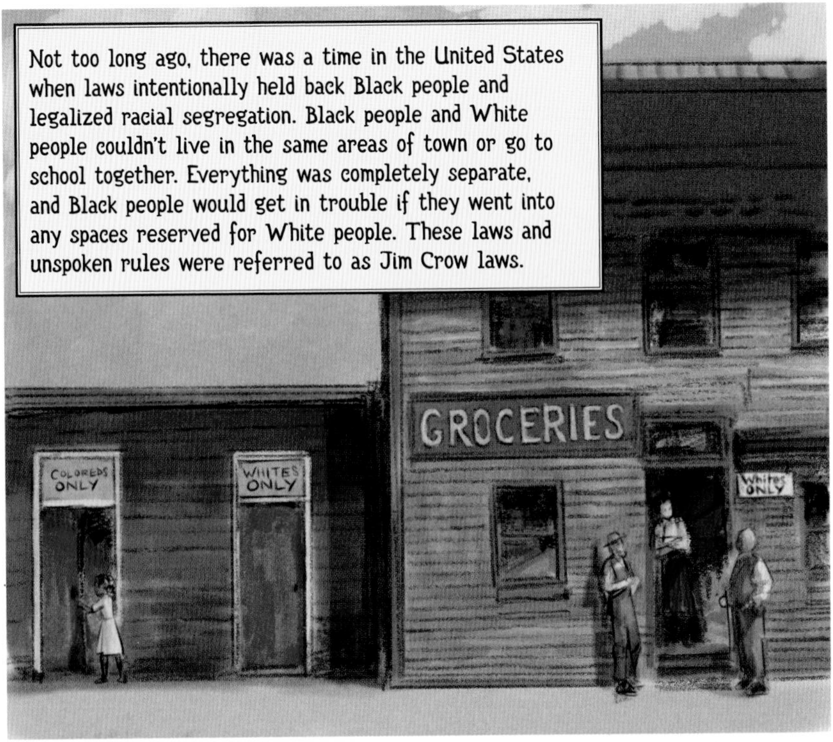
Not too long ago, there was a time in the United States when laws intentionally held back Black people and legalized racial segregation. Black people and White people couldn't live in the same areas of town or go to school together. Everything was completely separate, and Black people would get in trouble if they went into any spaces reserved for White people. These laws and unspoken rules were referred to as Jim Crow laws.
COLOREDS ONLY
WHITES ONLY
GROCERIES
Whites ONLY

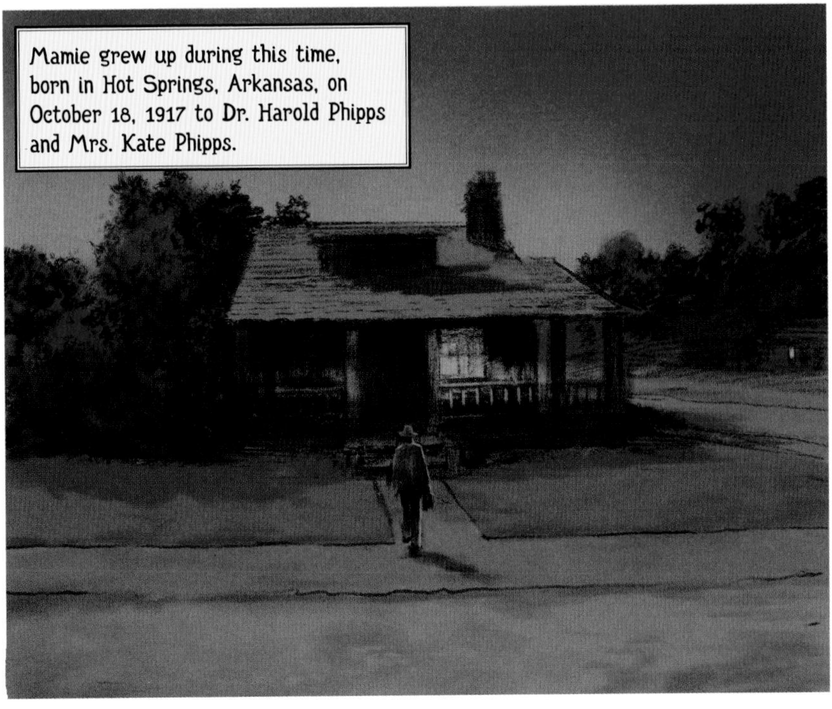
Mamie grew up during this time, born in Hot Springs, Arkansas, on October 18, 1917 to Dr. Harold Phipps and Mrs. Kate Phipps.

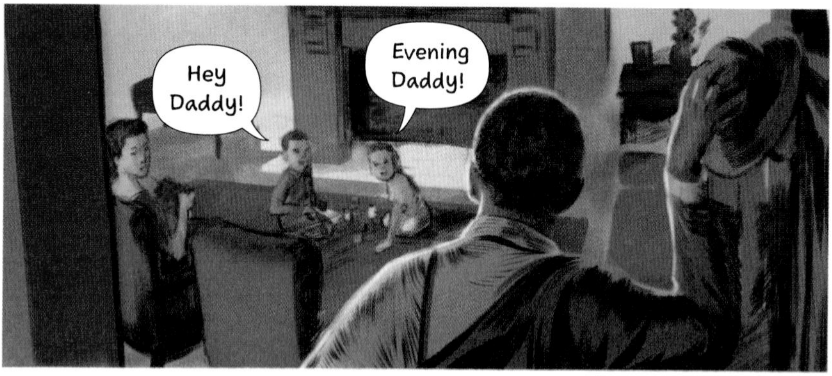
Hey Daddy!
Evening Daddy!

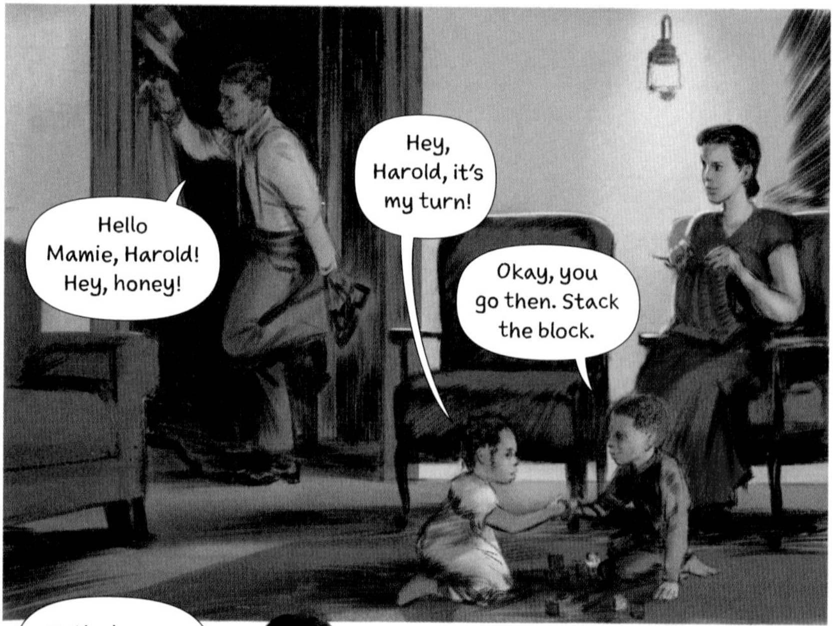
Hello Mamie, Harold! Hey, honey!
Hey, Harold, it's my turn!
Okay, you go then. Stack the block.

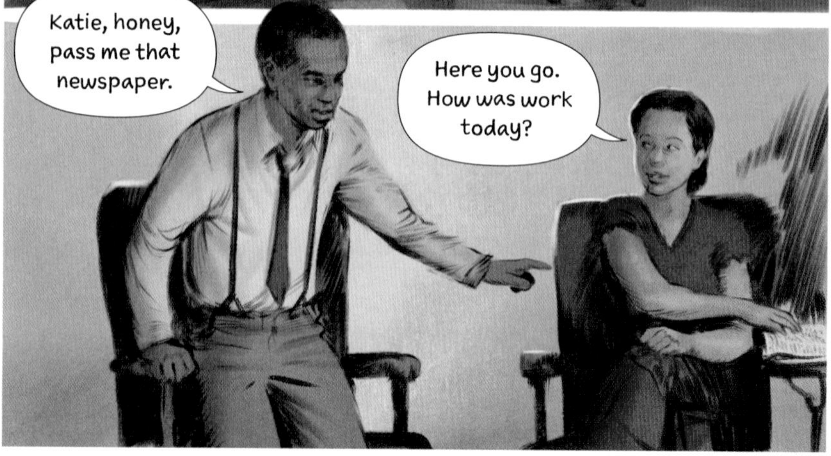
Katie, honey, pass me that newspaper.
Here you go. How was work today?

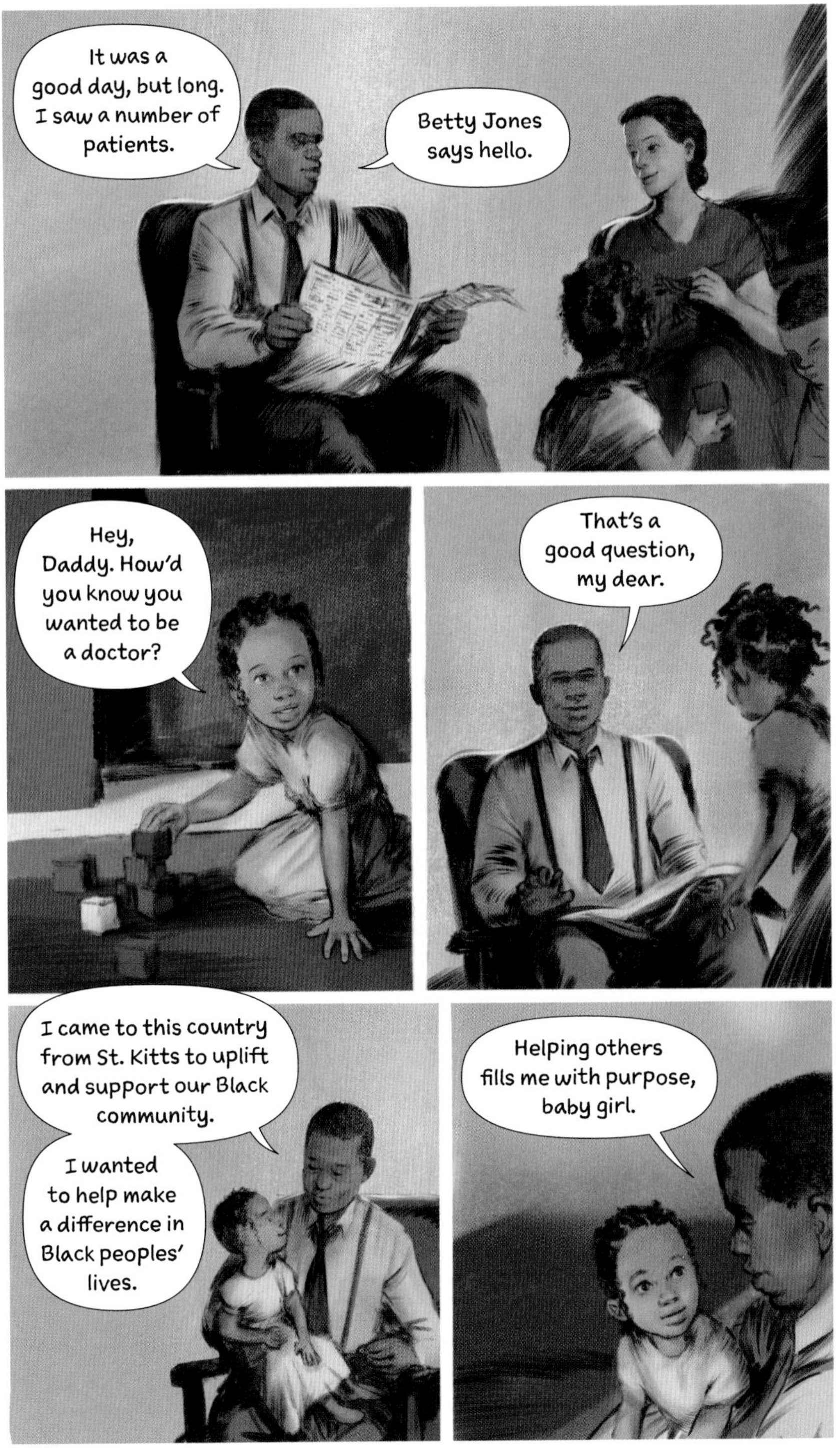
It was a good day, but long. I saw a number of patients.
Betty Jones says hello.
Hey, Daddy. How'd you know you wanted to be a doctor?
That's a good question, my dear.
I came to this country from St. Kitts to uplift and support our Black community.
I wanted to help make a difference in Black peoples' lives.
Helping others fills me with purpose, baby girl.

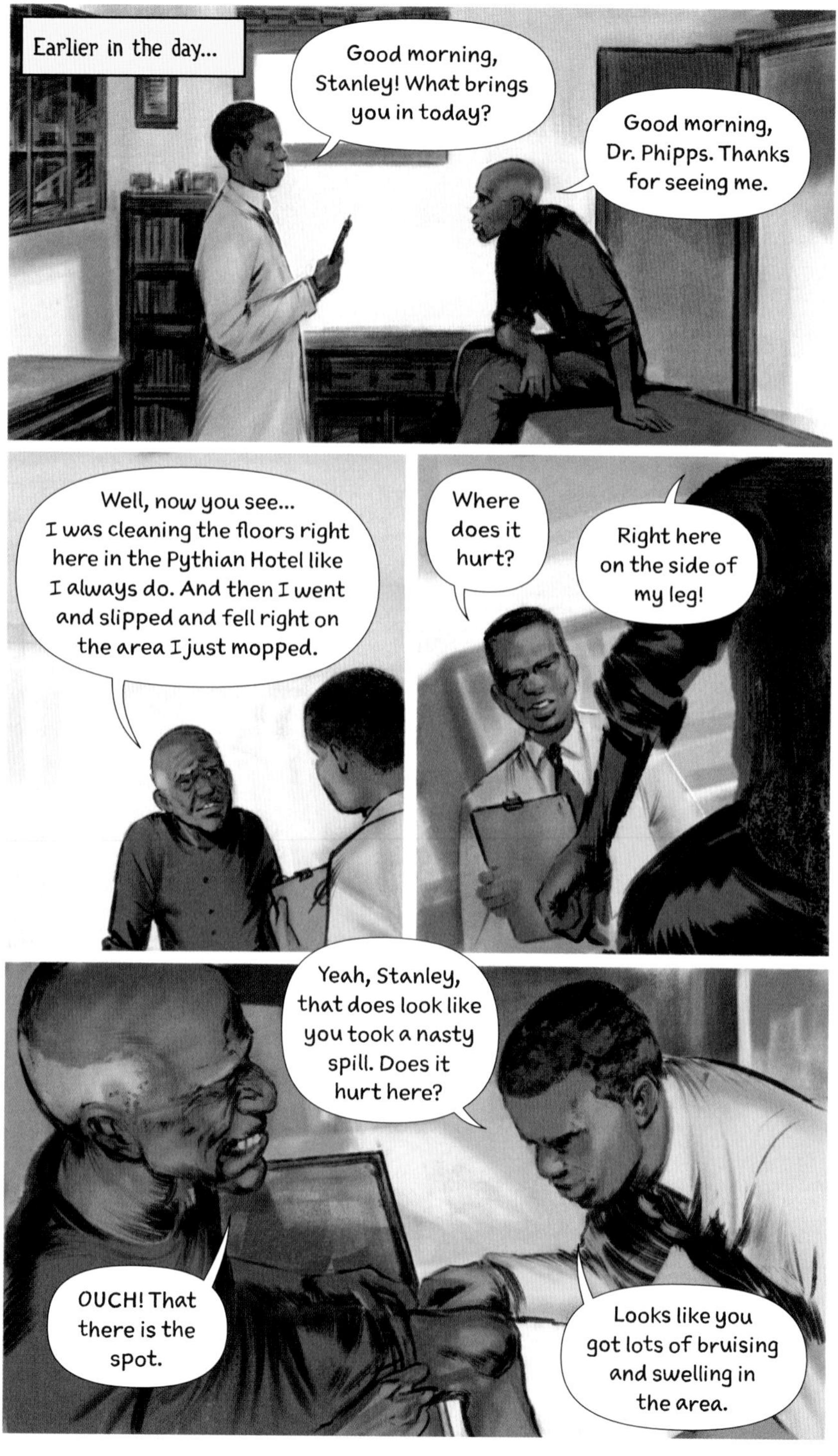
Earlier in the day...
Good morning, Stanley! What brings you in today?
Good morning, Dr. Phipps. Thanks for seeing me.
Well, now you see... I was cleaning the floors right here in the Pythian Hotel like I always do. And then I went and slipped and fell right on the area I just mopped.
Where does it hurt?
Right here on the side of my leg!
Yeah, Stanley, that does look like you took a nasty spill. Does it hurt here?
OUCH! That there is the spot.
Looks like you got lots of bruising and swelling in the area.

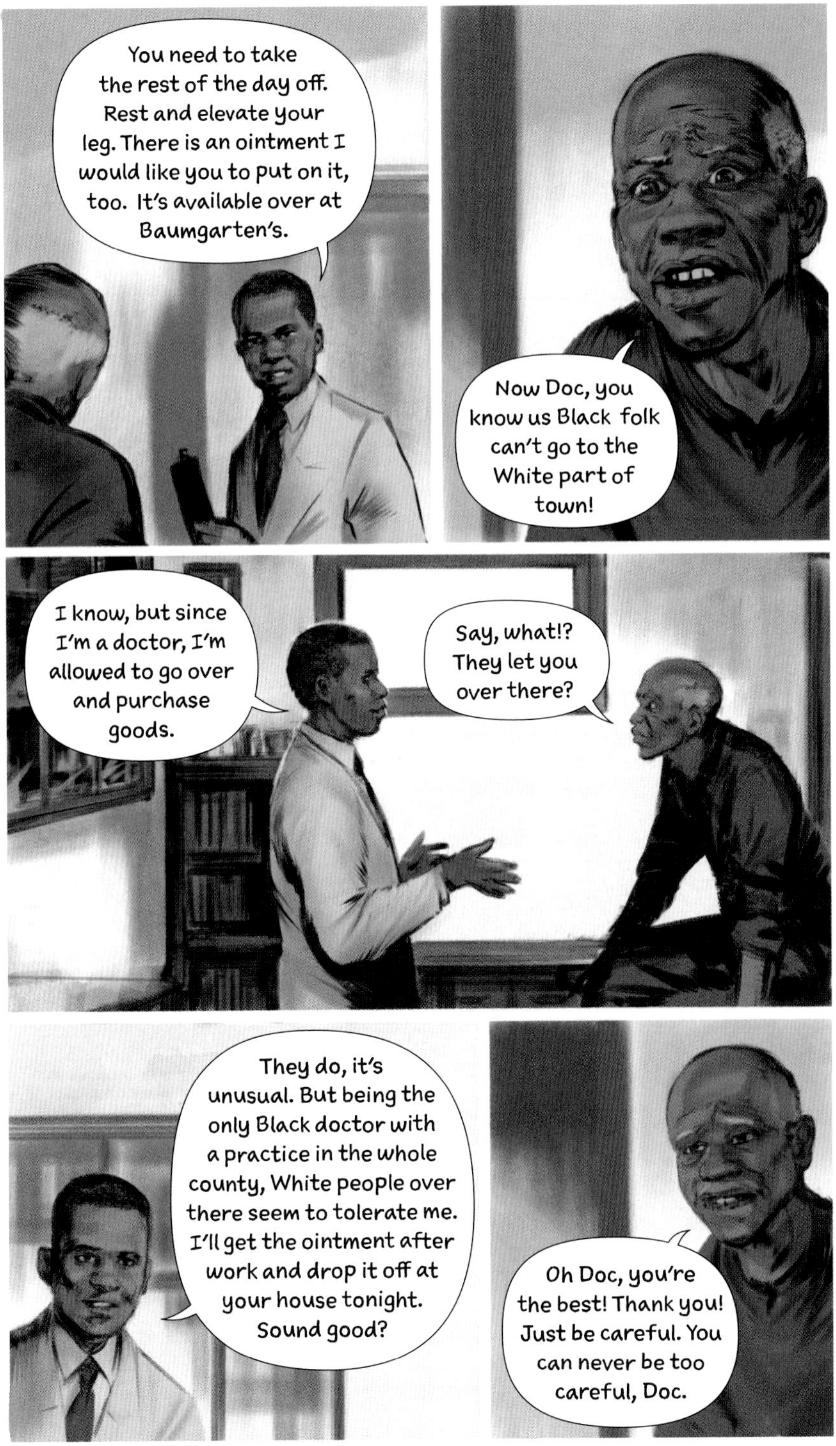
You need to take the rest of the day off. Rest and elevate your leg. There is an ointment I would like you to put on it, too. It's available over at Baumgarten's.
Now Doc, you know us Black folk can't go to the White part of town!
I know, but since I'm a doctor, I'm allowed to go over and purchase goods.
Say, what!? They let you over there?
They do, it's unusual. But being the only Black doctor with a practice in the whole county, White people over there seem to tolerate me. I'll get the ointment after work and drop it off at your house tonight. Sound good?
Oh Doc, you're the best! Thank you! Just be careful. You can never be too careful, Doc.

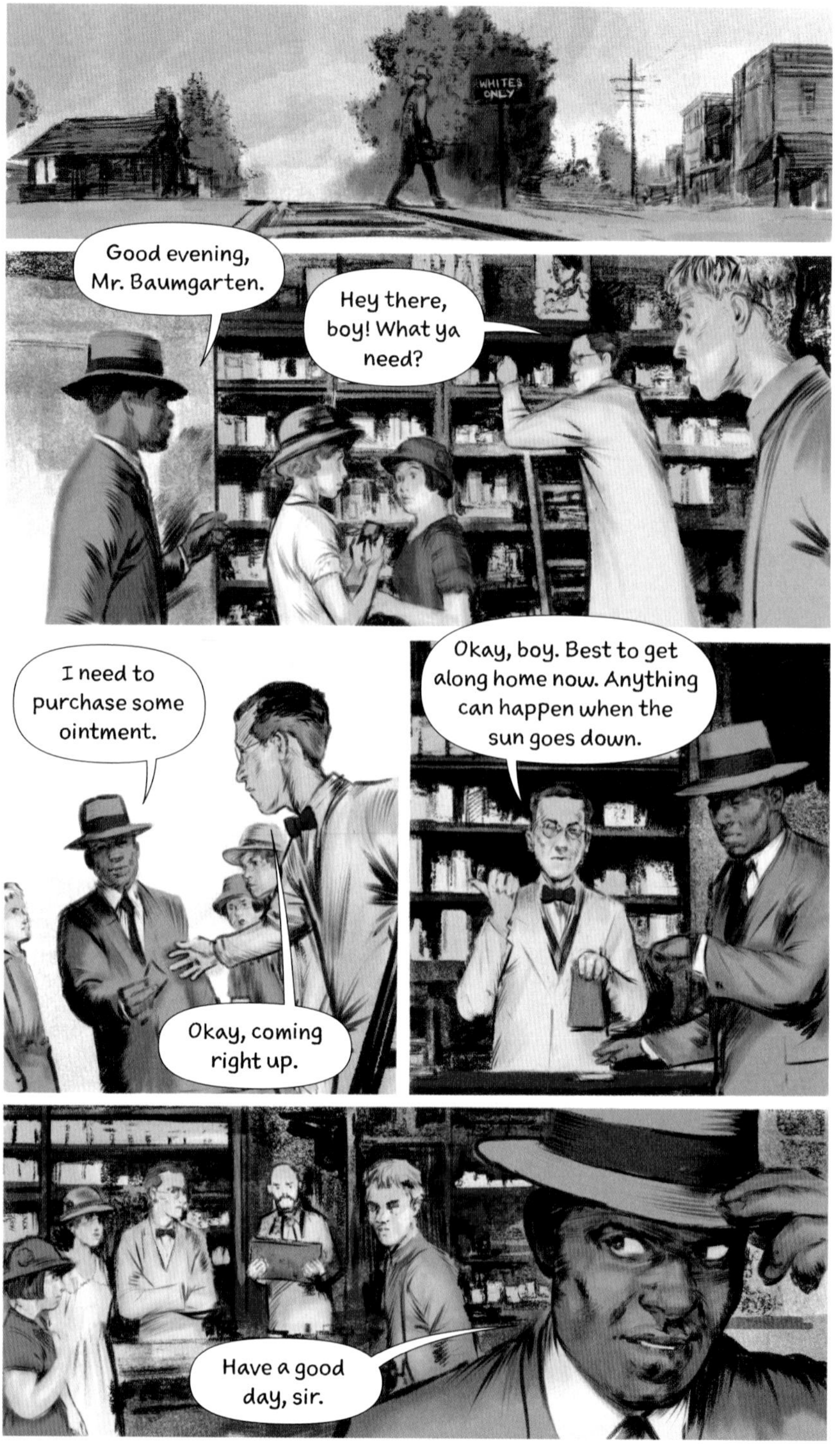
WHITES ONLY
Good evening, Mr. Baumgarten.
Hey there, boy! What ya need?
I need to purchase some ointment.
Okay, coming right up.
Okay, boy. Best to get along home now. Anything can happen when the sun goes down.
Have a good day, sir.

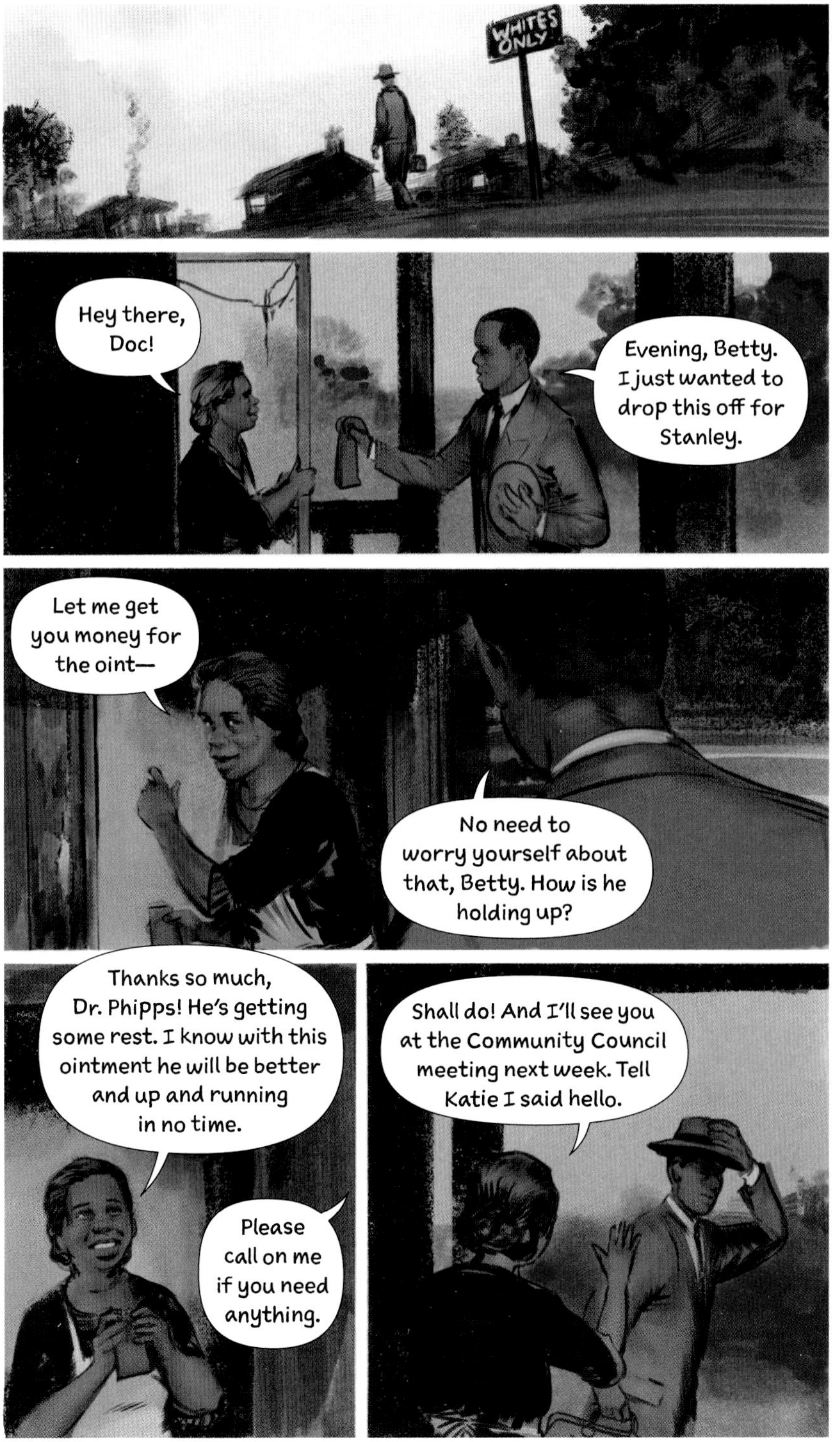
WHITES ONLY
Hey there, Doc!
Evening, Betty. I just wanted to drop this off for Stanley.
Let me get you money for the oint—
No need to worry yourself about that, Betty. How is he holding up?
Thanks so much, Dr. Phipps! He's getting some rest. I know with this ointment he will be better and up and running in no time.
Please call on me if you need anything.
Shall do! And I'll see you at the Community Council meeting next week. Tell Katie I said hello.

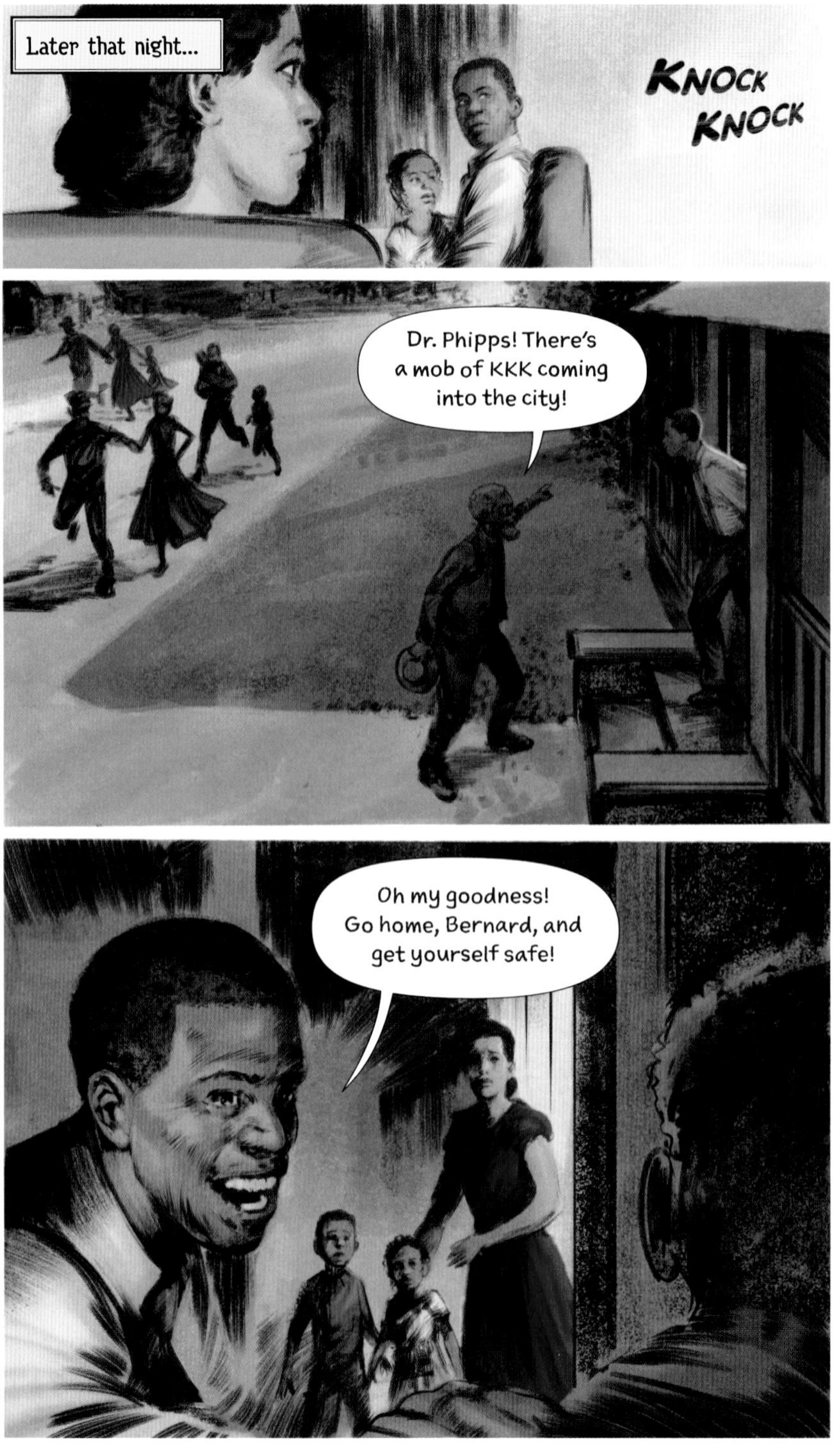
Later that night...
KNOCK KNOCK
Dr. Phipps! There's a mob of KKK coming into the city!
Oh my goodness! Go home, Bernard, and get yourself safe!

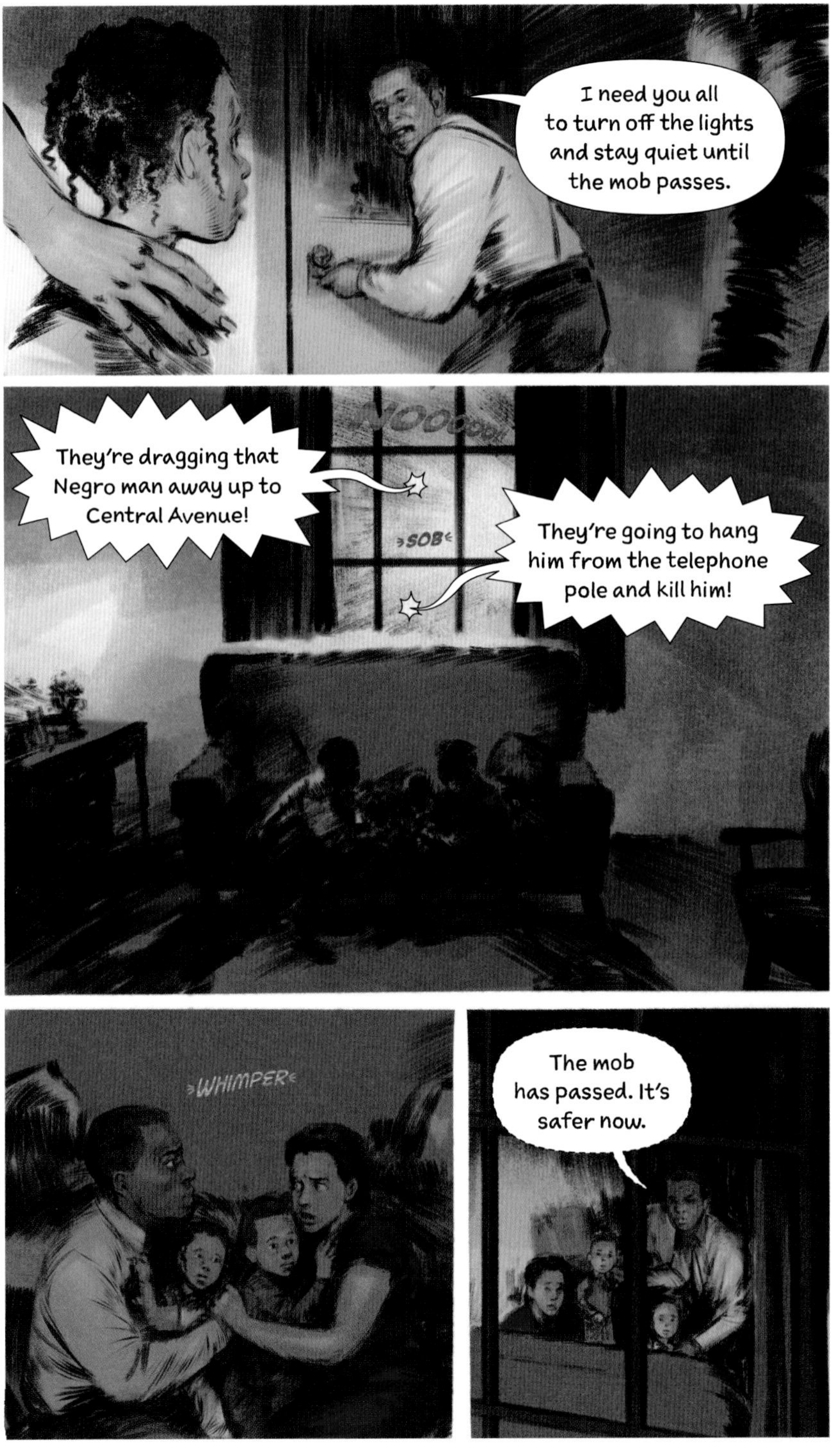
I need you all to turn off the lights and stay quiet until the mob passes.
NOOooo!!
They're dragging that Negro man away up to Central Avenue!
SOB
They're going to hang him from the telephone pole and kill him!
WHIMPER
The mob has passed. It's safer now.

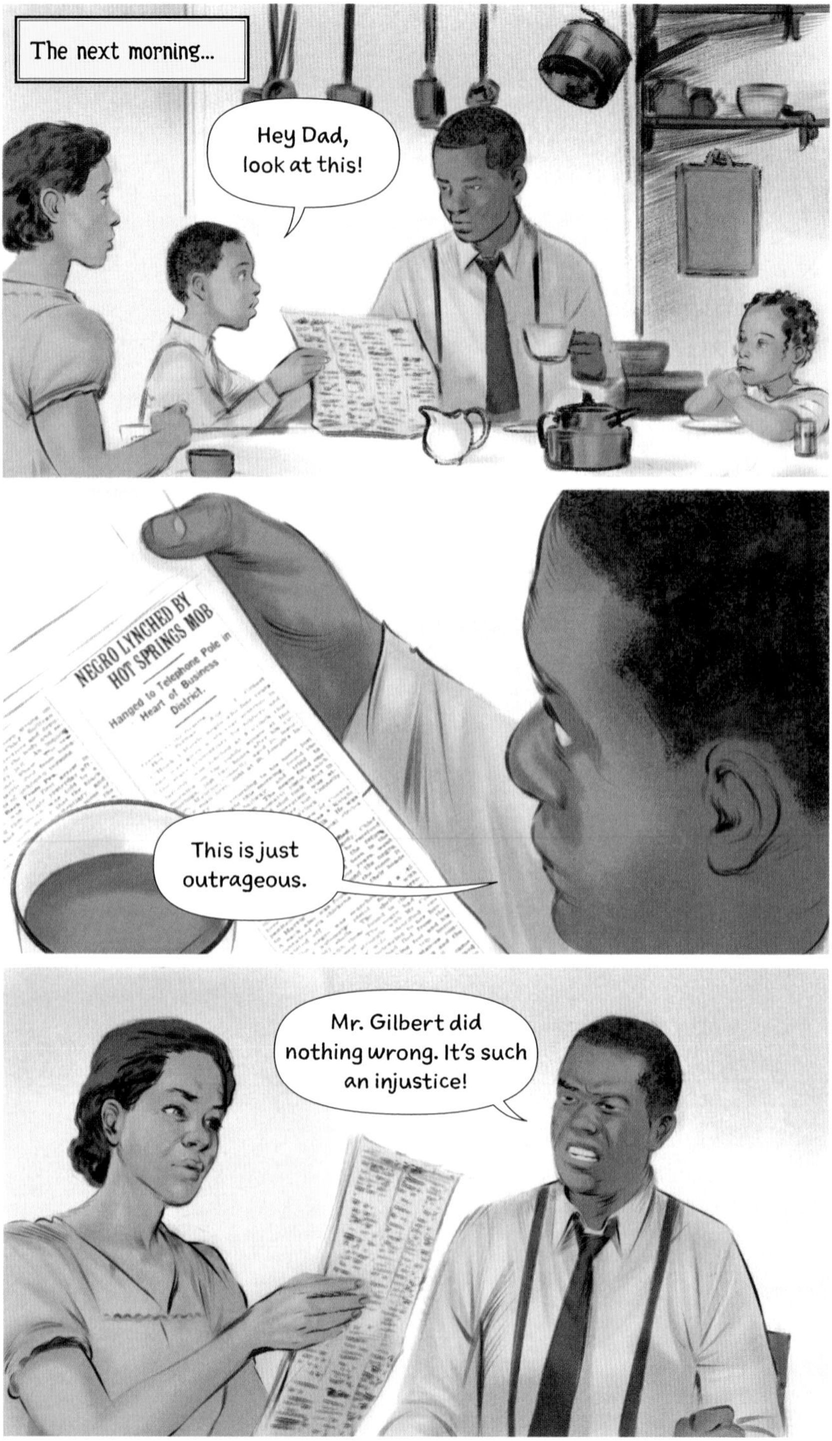
The next morning...
Hey Dad, look at this!
NEGRO LYNCHED BY HOT SPRINGS MOB
Hanged to Telephone Pole in Heart of Business District.
This is just outrageous.
Mr. Gilbert did nothing wrong. It's such an injustice!

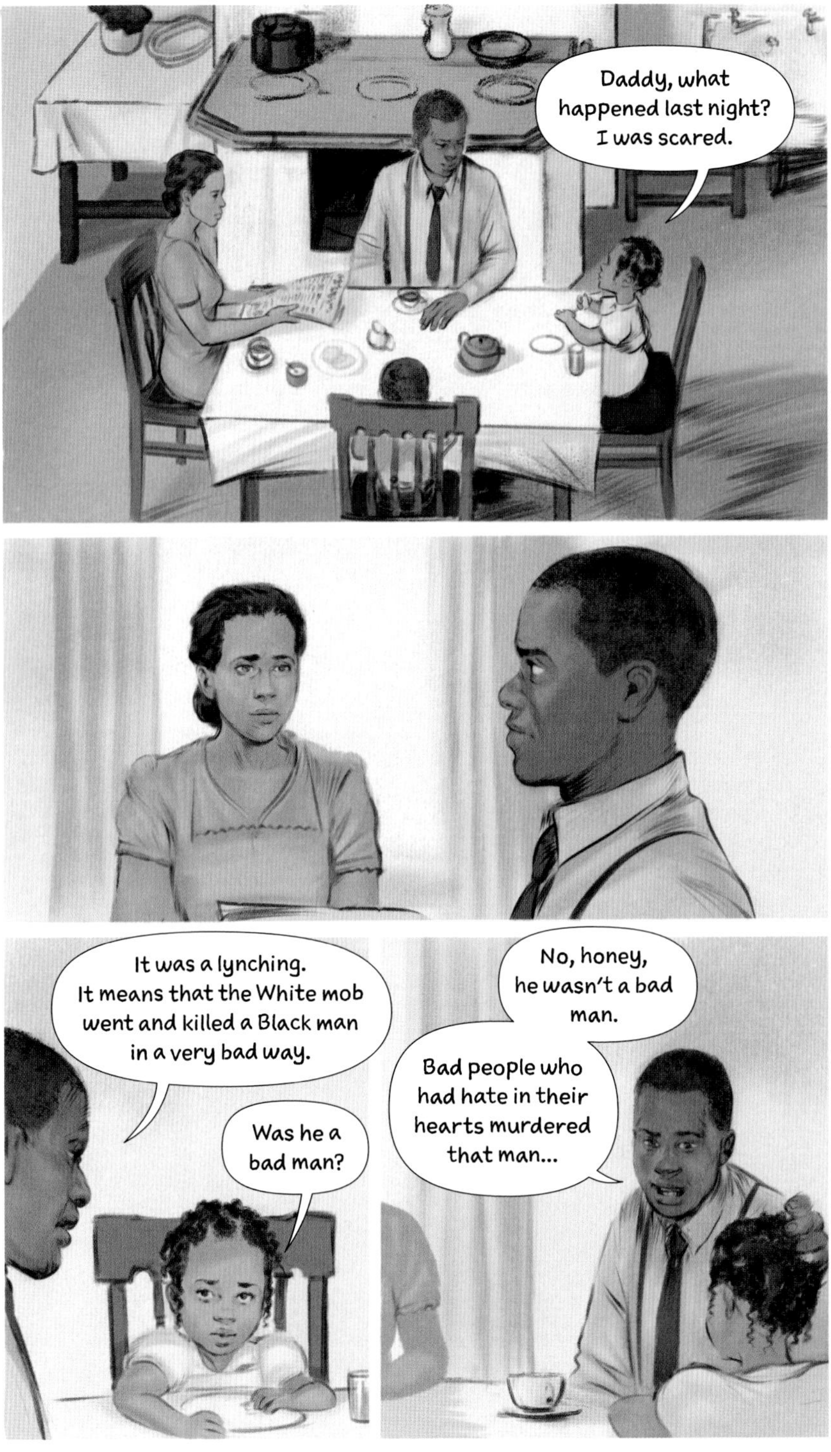
Daddy, what happened last night? I was scared.
It was a lynching. It means that the White mob went and killed a Black man in a very bad way.
Was he a bad man?
No, honey, he wasn't a bad man.
Bad people who had hate in their hearts murdered that man...

Will they come after us? Does that mean they'll hurt me, Daddy?

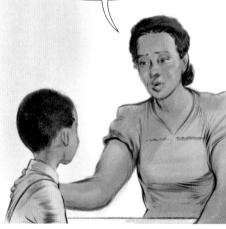

Black people always have to be careful. But, Harold, I don't want fear to lead your life. What we need to do is love each other, and do good work for our community.

KNOCK KNOCK

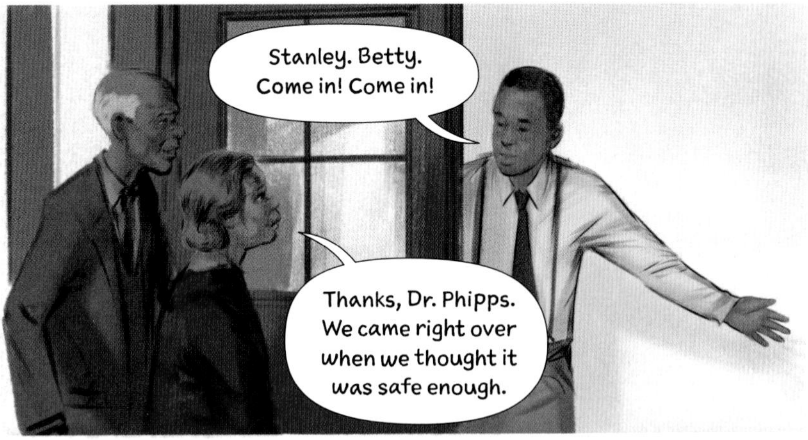
Stanley. Betty. Come in! Come in!
Thanks, Dr. Phipps. We came right over when we thought it was safe enough.

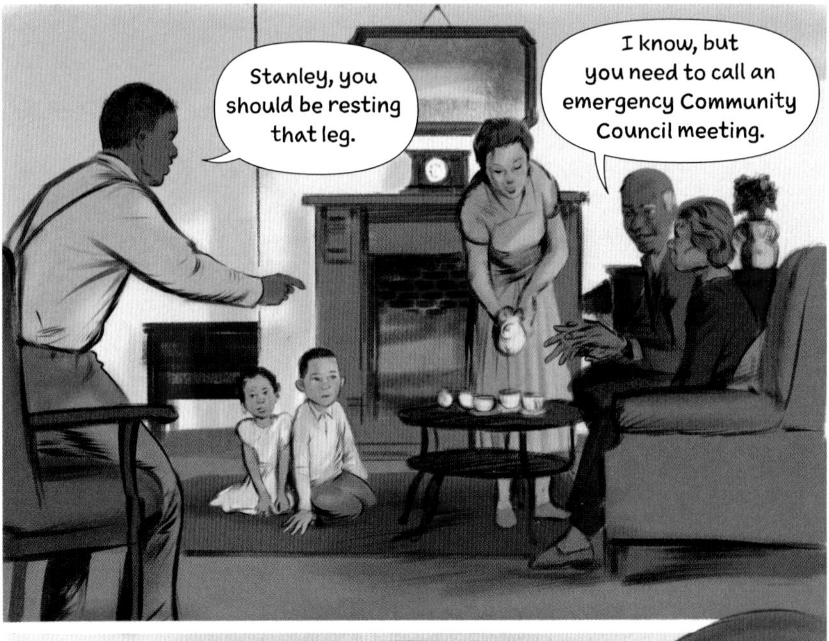
Stanley, you should be resting that leg.
I know, but you need to call an emergency Community Council meeting.

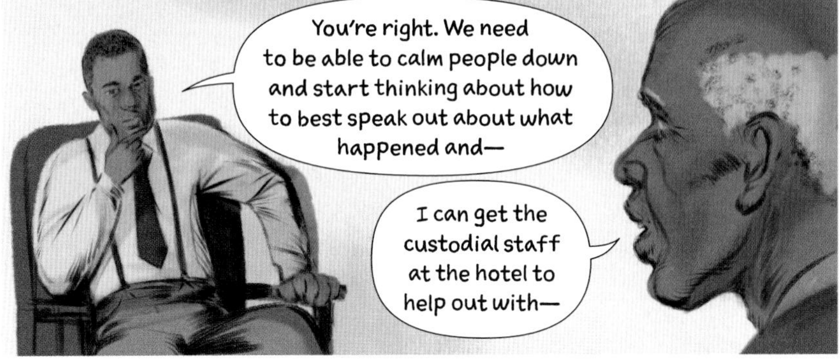
You're right. We need to be able to calm people down and start thinking about how to best speak out about what happened and—
I can get the custodial staff at the hotel to help out with—

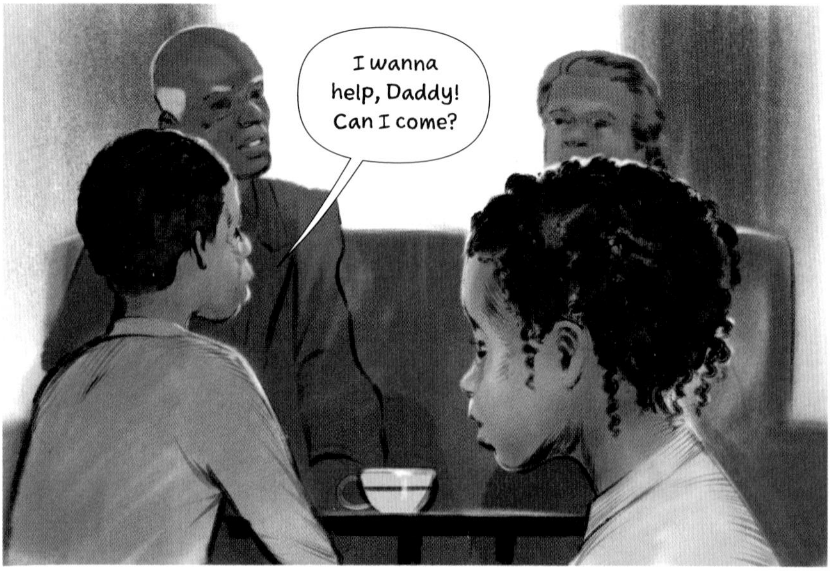
I wanna help, Daddy! Can I come?

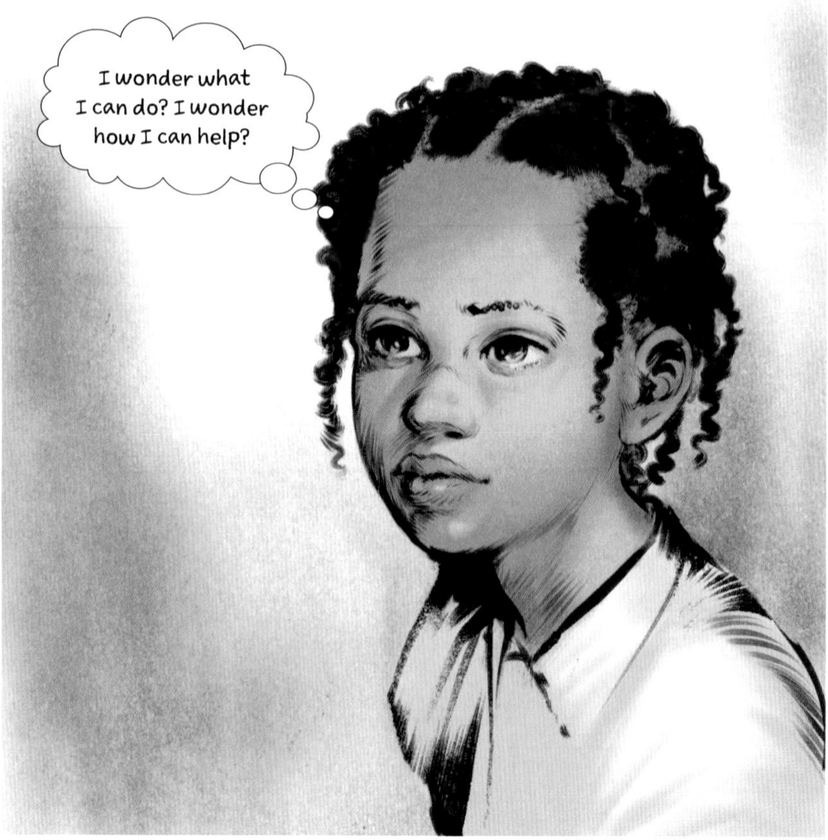
I wonder what I can do? I wonder how I can help?

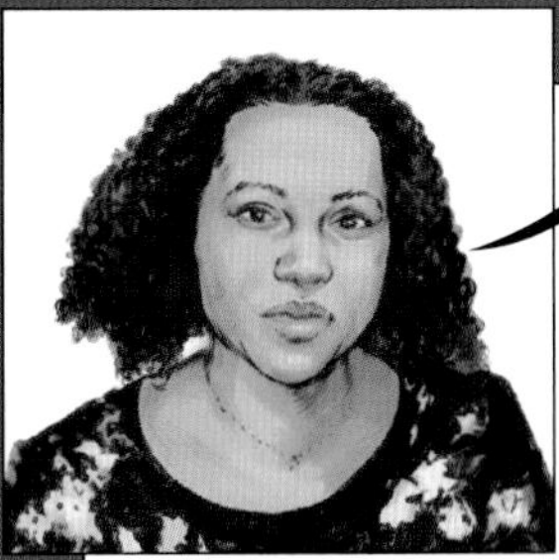

DID YOU KNOW

The Lynching of Gilbert Harris

Lynchings were a tool that was used by White supremacy groups (like the KKK and angry White mobs) to gain control over communities after the Civil War. Black men and Black boys were the frequent targets of these brutal killings. Sadly, there are also historical lynchings of others that were killed because of their identities: women, Latinx people, Indigenous people, Italian Americans, Asian Americans, and some White Americans. The lynchings, understandably, would instill fear in people, which helped to maintain White power. In fact, just nine years before Gilbert Harris was killed, there was a lynching of a man named Will Norman in Hot Springs, Arkansas, by an estimated 4,000 White men.

Hearing about the lynching of Gilbert Harris was a pivotal moment in Mamie's life. Although Mamie did not witness it directly, Harris's murder opened her eyes to injustice, discrimination, and unfair treatment of people in her community. This event became a catalyst for her work supporting and advocating for the rights of Black and Brown youth. During an interview later in her life, Mamie mentioned that Hot Springs residents were outraged by the lynching and spoke out about it. Mamie talked about how this lynching impacted the entire town, both Black and White people. She explained:

> *There were many people in the town who were White who didn't like it [the lynching] either. And they expressed themselves...They were quite outraged. Everybody was outraged. Everybody talked*

about it. You know, people went to people's houses,
and back and forth, within the neighborhood, to
really express [themselves]. Everybody was help-
less, really. But they could express outrage, which
is what they did.

Although people felt helpless, they still used their voice to express their concerns. This collective expression made a difference, as fortunately, there were no more lynchings in Hot Springs after Gilbert Harris.

The struggle for power and control continued, but often in more subtle ways. Even though there was never a lynching again in Hot Springs, on June 2, 1934, the United Daughters of the Confederacy built the Hot Springs Confederate Monument on the exact spot where both Mr. Harris and Mr. Norman were murdered. The location was selected deliberately to send a message. The large, marble statue acted as a reminder to the community that White people were once in control and signaled a refusal to let go of power or change racist or segregationist thoughts and behaviors. These fights continue today in the United States with both overt and subtle modern-day power struggles. There have been unjust police killings of Black men, such as the murder of George Floyd on May 25, 2020, that sparked international protests. There are also the more subtle tactics like some politicians pushing to ban books dealing with race or gender identity. Sometimes there are other acts like prohibiting certain hair styles or clothing worn by Black kids at school. Just as there were Black and White activists in Mamie's town who prevented further lynchings, adults and children continue to be activists against White supremacy by removing confederate monuments or speaking out against policies that erase other people and their identities.

TRY THIS

Use Your Voice, Create a Protest Sign

Mamie's story shows the strength of voice and expression and the power of community coming together for a common good. In today's society, young people share their viewpoints collectively through like-minded organizations, such as the Youth Activism Project, Amnesty International, and DoSomething. Protests and protest signs are other ways that people demonstrate collective voice. Now it's your turn to try using collective voice!

Think of a topic that you are passionate about. It could be anything from social injustice to climate change to school policies to gun control. Make sure you do some background research (and use your media literacy skills) to have all the supports behind your argument. Then take some poster board and markers and make a catchy slogan that supports your viewpoint. You can hang the poster sign somewhere others can see it, such as in a window or hallway. Use this as an opportunity to be brave and talk about your views, as the voice of youth holds much power. Here are some youth signs for inspiration.

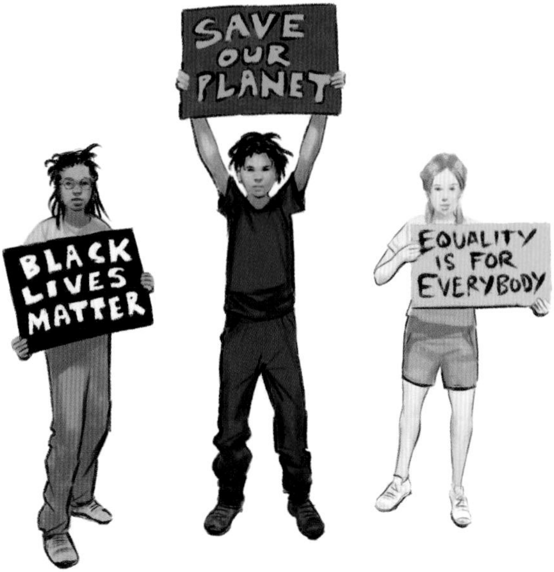
SAVE OUR PLANET
BLACK LIVES MATTER
EQUALITY IS FOR EVERYBODY

CHAPTER 2

From a One-Room School House to Howard University

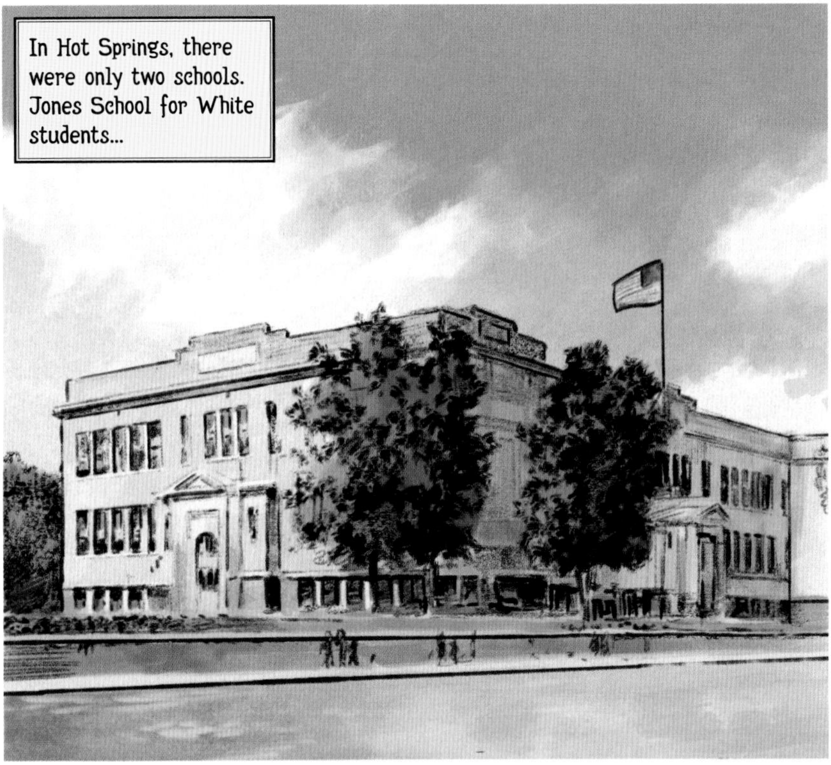
In Hot Springs, there were only two schools. Jones School for White students...

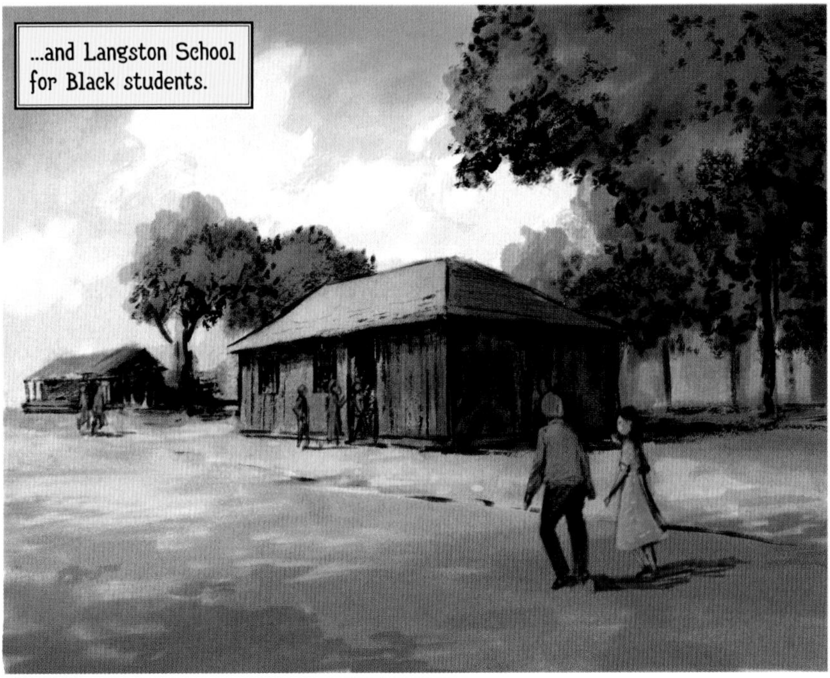
...and Langston School for Black students.

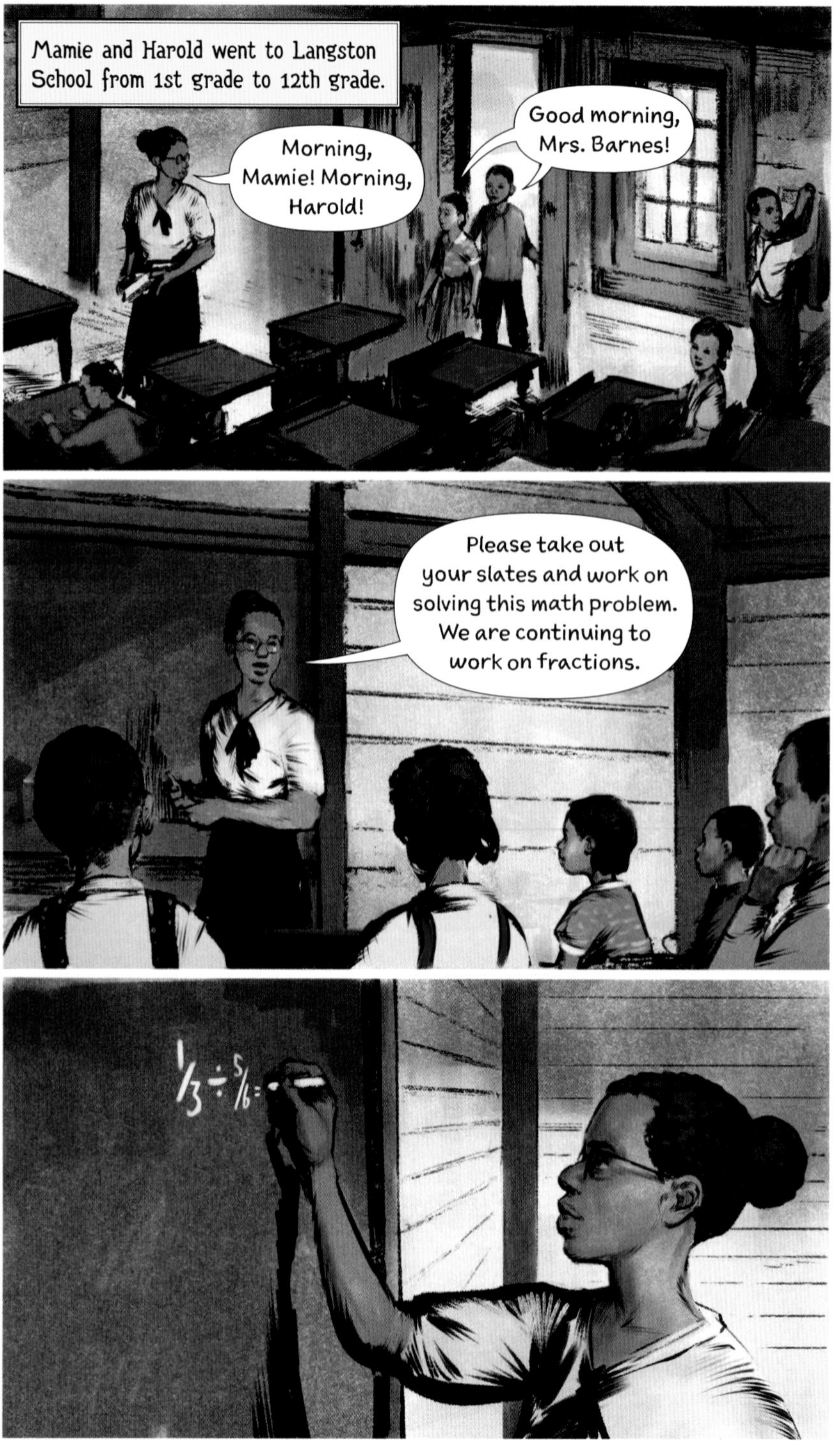
Mamie and Harold went to Langston School from 1st grade to 12th grade.
Morning, Mamie! Morning, Harold!
Good morning, Mrs. Barnes!
Please take out your slates and work on solving this math problem. We are continuing to work on fractions.
1/3 ÷ 5/6 =

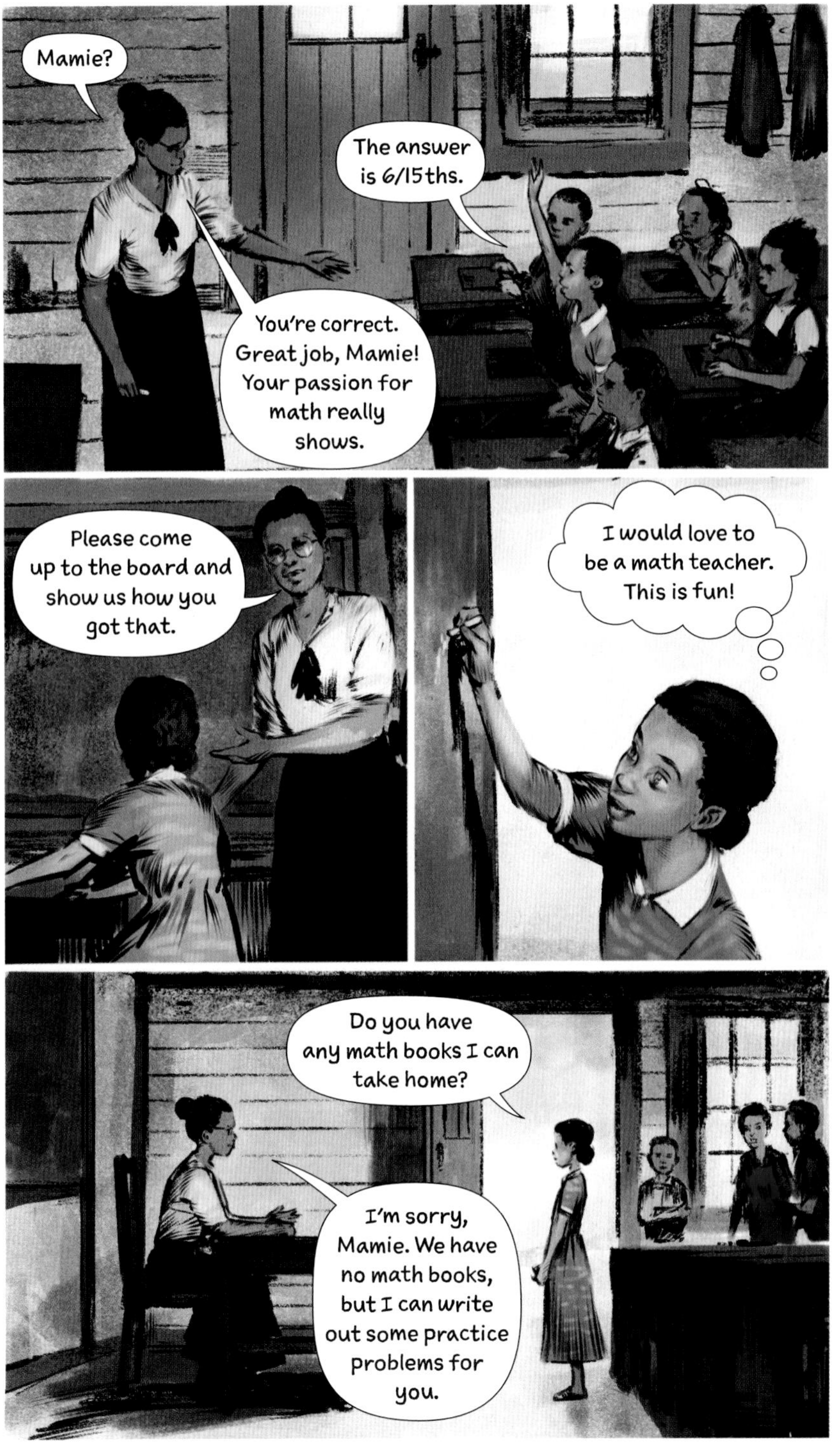
Mamie?
The answer is 6/15ths.
You're correct. Great job, Mamie! Your passion for math really shows.
Please come up to the board and show us how you got that.
I would love to be a math teacher. This is fun!
Do you have any math books I can take home?
I'm sorry, Mamie. We have no math books, but I can write out some practice problems for you.

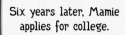
Six years later, Mamie applies for college.

I think you should structure this sentence a bit differently and then say why you want to be a math teacher and study at Howard University.

I completely see what you mean.

Oh, this is good. Much better. Really shows your genuine self and strong character and your purpose for applying.

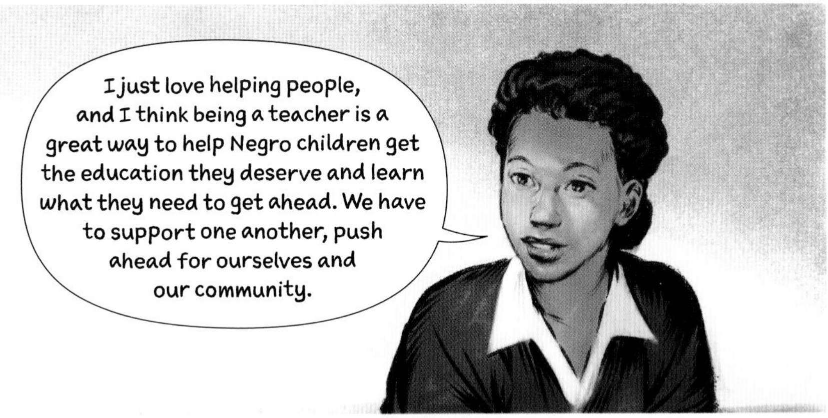
I just love helping people, and I think being a teacher is a great way to help Negro children get the education they deserve and learn what they need to get ahead. We have to support one another, push ahead for ourselves and our community.

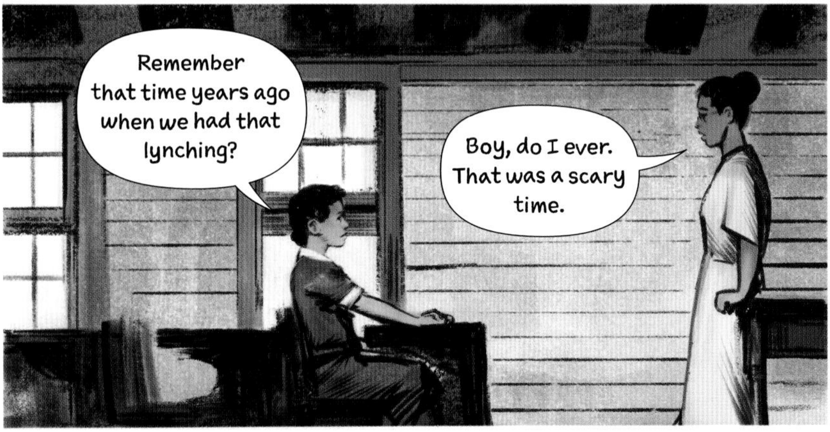
Remember that time years ago when we had that lynching?
Boy, do I ever. That was a scary time.

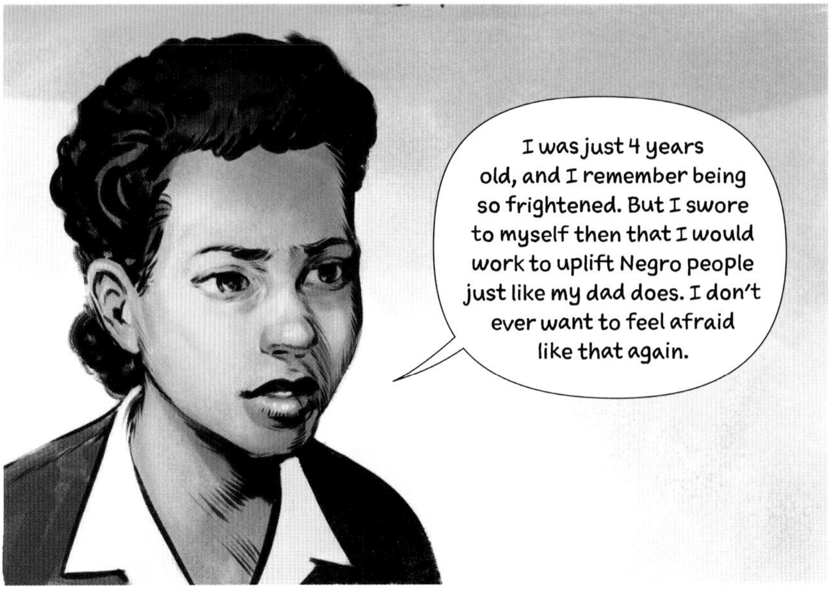
I was just 4 years old, and I remember being so frightened. But I swore to myself then that I would work to uplift Negro people just like my dad does. I don't ever want to feel afraid like that again.

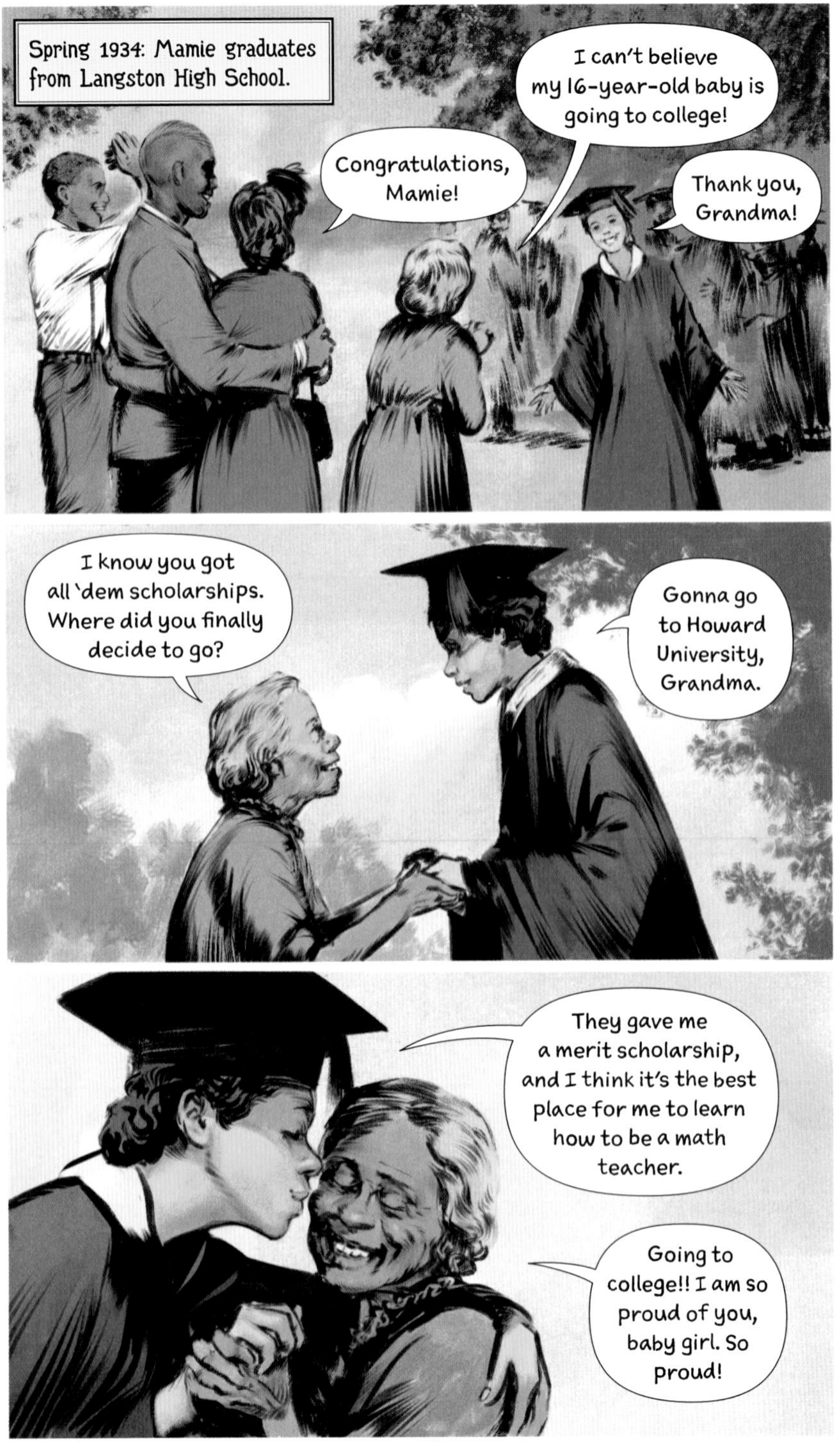

Spring 1934: Mamie graduates from Langston High School.
Congratulations, Mamie!
I can't believe my 16-year-old baby is going to college!
Thank you, Grandma!
I know you got all 'dem scholarships. Where did you finally decide to go?
Gonna go to Howard University, Grandma.
They gave me a merit scholarship, and I think it's the best place for me to learn how to be a math teacher.
Going to college!! I am so proud of you, baby girl. So proud!

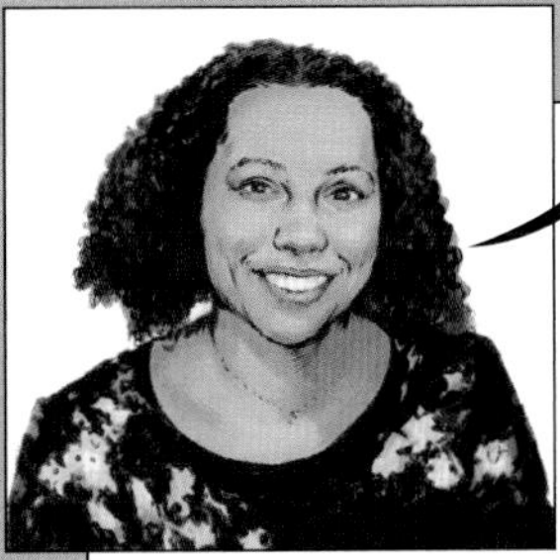

DID YOU KNOW

There Used to Be Many Black Teachers

Mamie wanted to be a math teacher, as she always wanted to work with youth, just like Mrs. Barnes. Teaching was a very lucrative career for Black people before 1954 (*Brown v. Board of Education* case, see Chapter 4). Prior to 1954, Black teachers and principals made up over half of the teaching population in the United States. Unfortunately, Black teachers only make up 7% of the teaching population today. So, what happened?

Prior to 1954, schools were segregated. That means White students and White teachers were in one school, and Black students and Black teachers were in another school. Since Black students were taught exclusively by Black teachers, there was a larger population of Black teachers. When the schools were desegregated, White teachers were teaching Black students. But most White students, parents, and administrators did not want their children to be taught by Black teachers. Thus, most of the Black teachers and administrators lost their jobs after the *Brown v. Board of Education* case. This job loss was an unintended consequence of the desegregration case.

After 1954, the National Association for the Advancement of Colored People (NAACP) did spend time in court supporting displaced Black teachers and administrators. Although they did win back pay, most of these teachers never got their jobs back. The large displacement of Black teachers has never recovered in the United States. Yet educators, scholars,

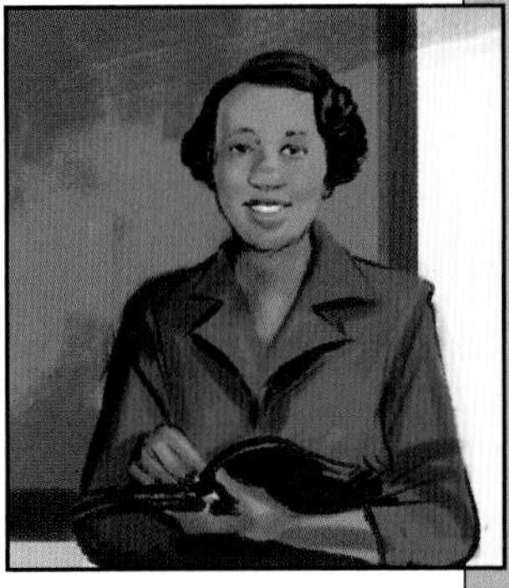

and activists are still working hard to figure out how to get more Black teachers certified and into the profession.

Today, the largest certifiers of Black teachers are Historically Black Colleges and Universities (HBCUs) like Howard University. HBCUs were established, some prior to the emancipation of slavery, to educate Black students. The schools often adopt the phrase "life as we climb," which shows their commitment to Black people supporting each other in these spaces. Lincoln University, which was founded in 1854 in Pennsylvania, was the first HBCU to start granting degrees. There are currently 101 HBCUs that exist in the United States, and they are spread across the Northern and Southern states.

Howard University opened in 1867, just after the abolishment of American slavery. The school initially focused on educating African Americans as teachers, ministers, lawyers, and doctors. Even though she had scholarships to other HBCUs, Howard University had a long history with training teachers, and that appealed to Mamie. Howard University continues to play an important role in Black education and is considered one of the most prestigious HBCUs today. The United States' first Black and female vice president, Kamala Harris, also went to Howard University.

TRY THIS

School History Fact-Find

Whether you live in a small town, a rural countryside, or a big city, all school buildings have a rich history to them. Some school buildings might have been around when schools were racially segregated. Some school buildings might be brand new, but all school buildings and structures have a history.

Go on a fact-finding mission to learn about the schools in your area. When was the school built? Who was the school built for? Did the school exist when there were racially segregated schools? Did the school have different names over the years? Does the school happen to be named after someone? If so, what was that person's role in history?

A fun place to start your historical fact-find can be if your city or town has a local historical society or museum. Also, the local library may have old photos and historical records about the school. Interview an adult that went to the school. What was the school like when they attended? How is the school different and/or the same today compared to when they were in school? Ask the current principal if they know about the history of the school. Have fun playing detective and figuring out the history behind a school building you may never have thought twice about until now.

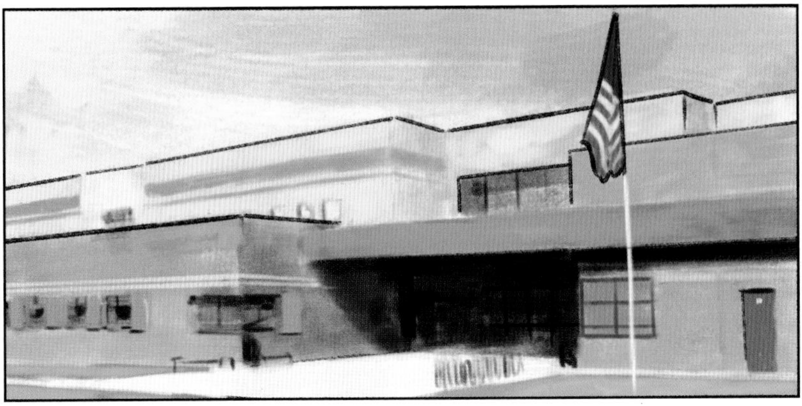

CHAPTER 3

Early Research at Howard University

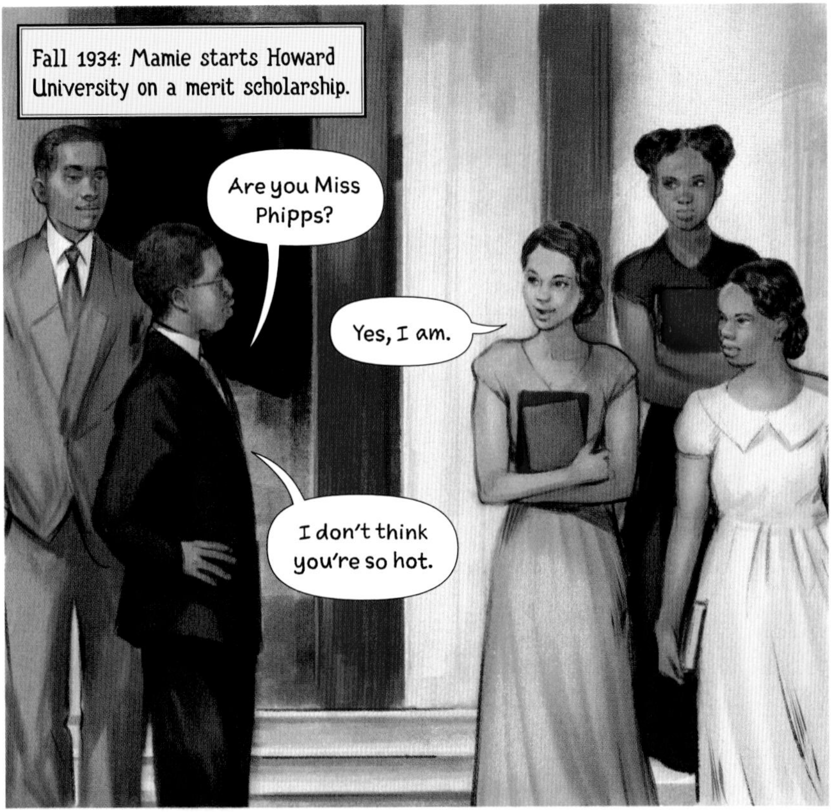
Fall 1934: Mamie starts Howard University on a merit scholarship.
Are you Miss Phipps?
Yes, I am.
I don't think you're so hot.

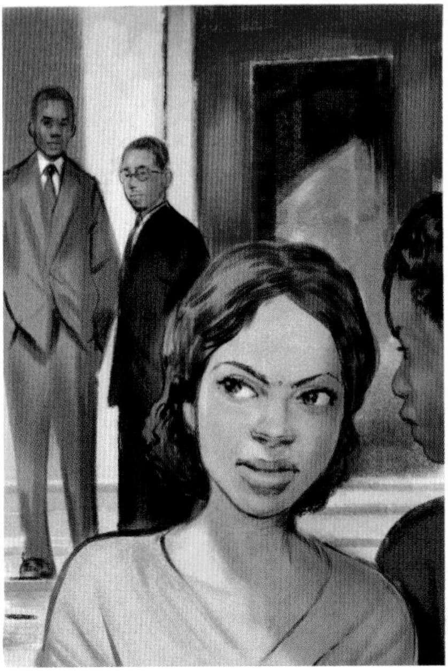

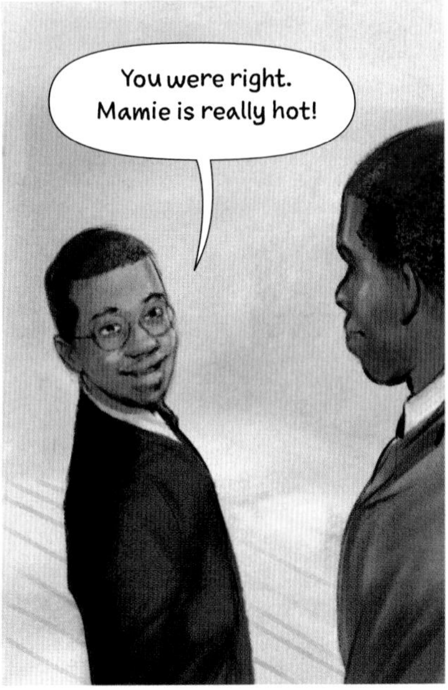
You were right. Mamie is really hot!

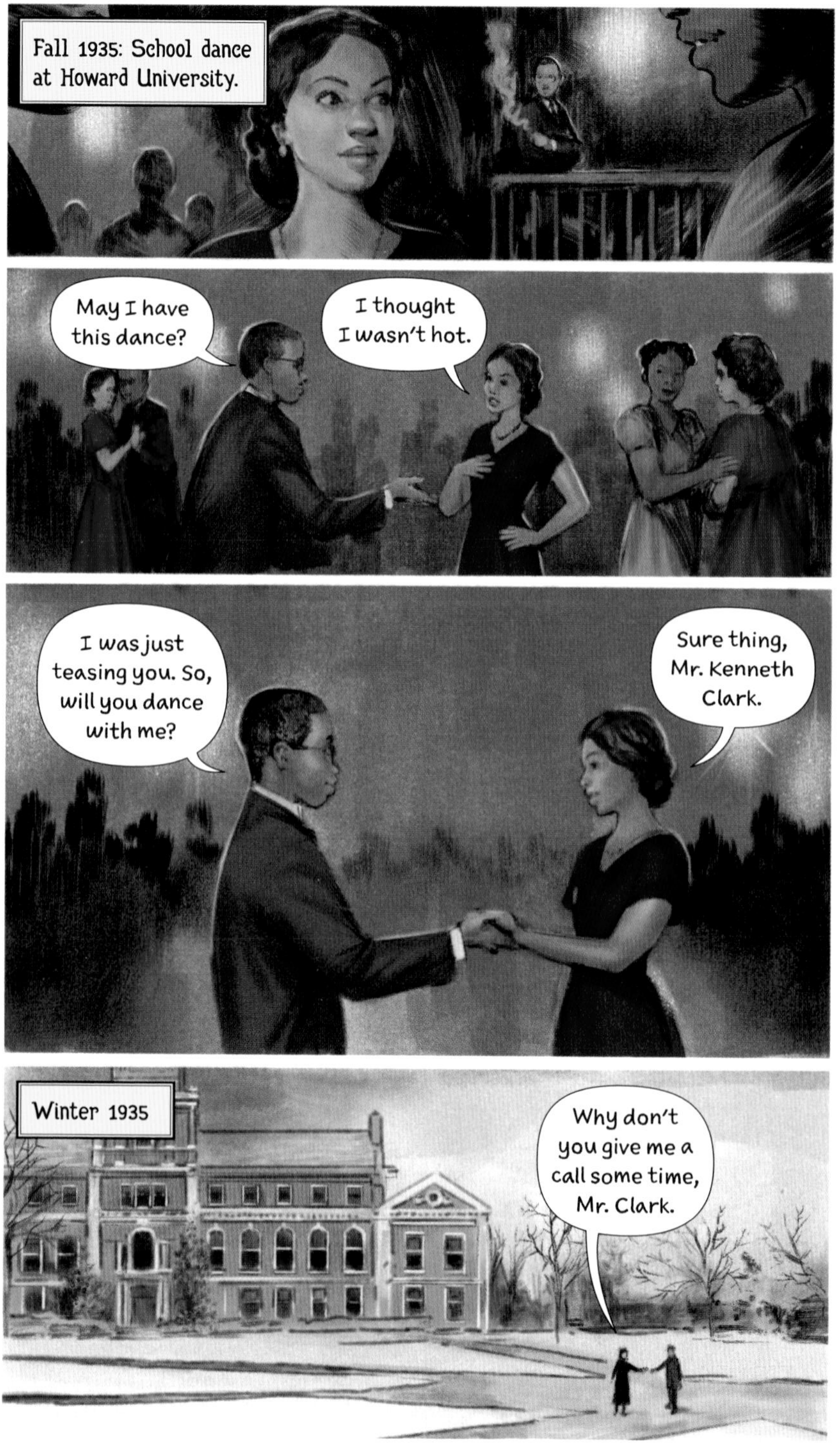
Fall 1935: School dance at Howard University.
May I have this dance?
I thought I wasn't hot.
I was just teasing you. So, will you dance with me?
Sure thing, Mr. Kenneth Clark.
Winter 1935
Why don't you give me a call some time, Mr. Clark.

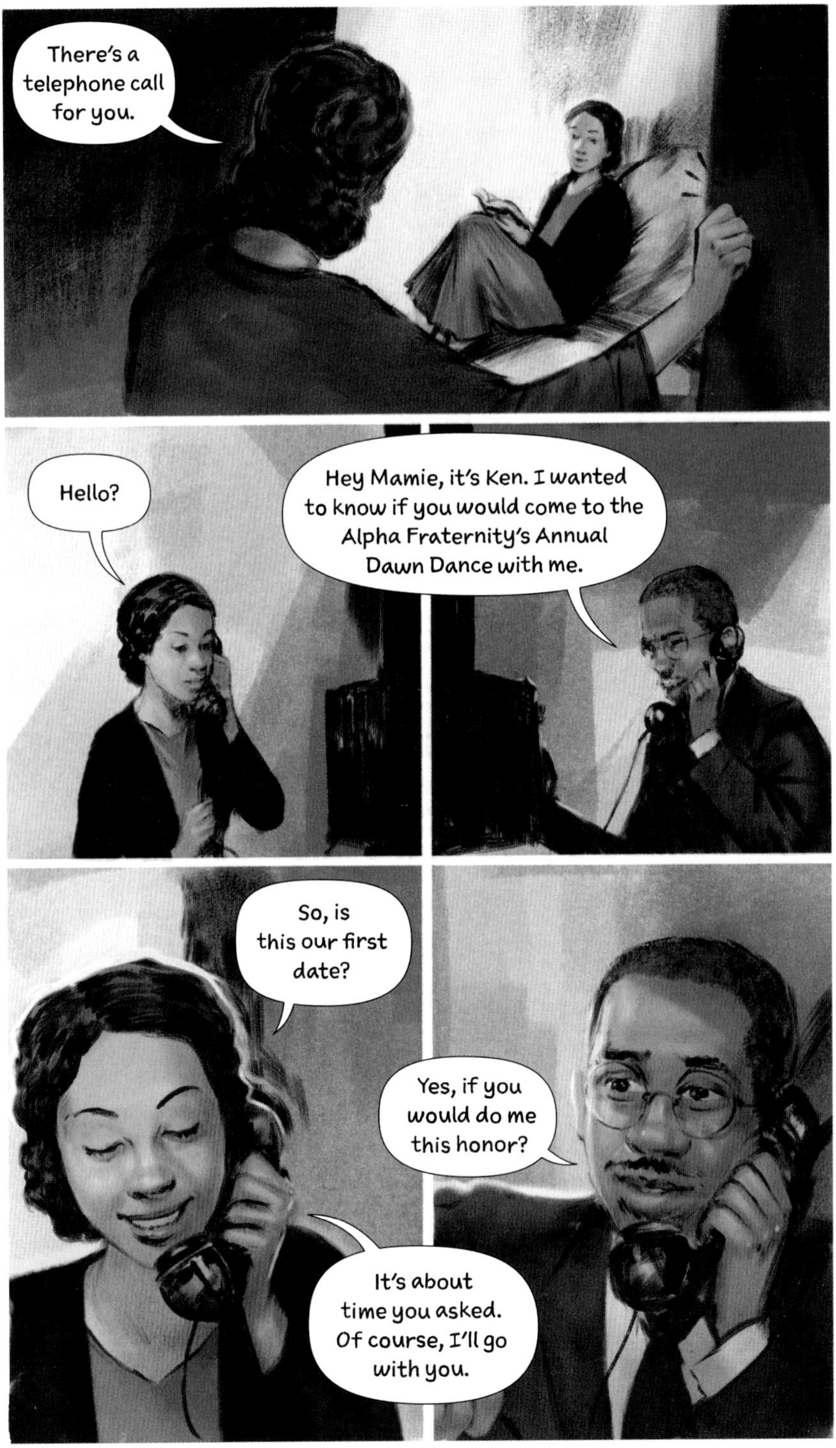
There's a telephone call for you.
Hello?
Hey Mamie, it's Ken. I wanted to know if you would come to the Alpha Fraternity's Annual Dawn Dance with me.
So, is this our first date?
Yes, if you would do me this honor?
It's about time you asked. Of course, I'll go with you.

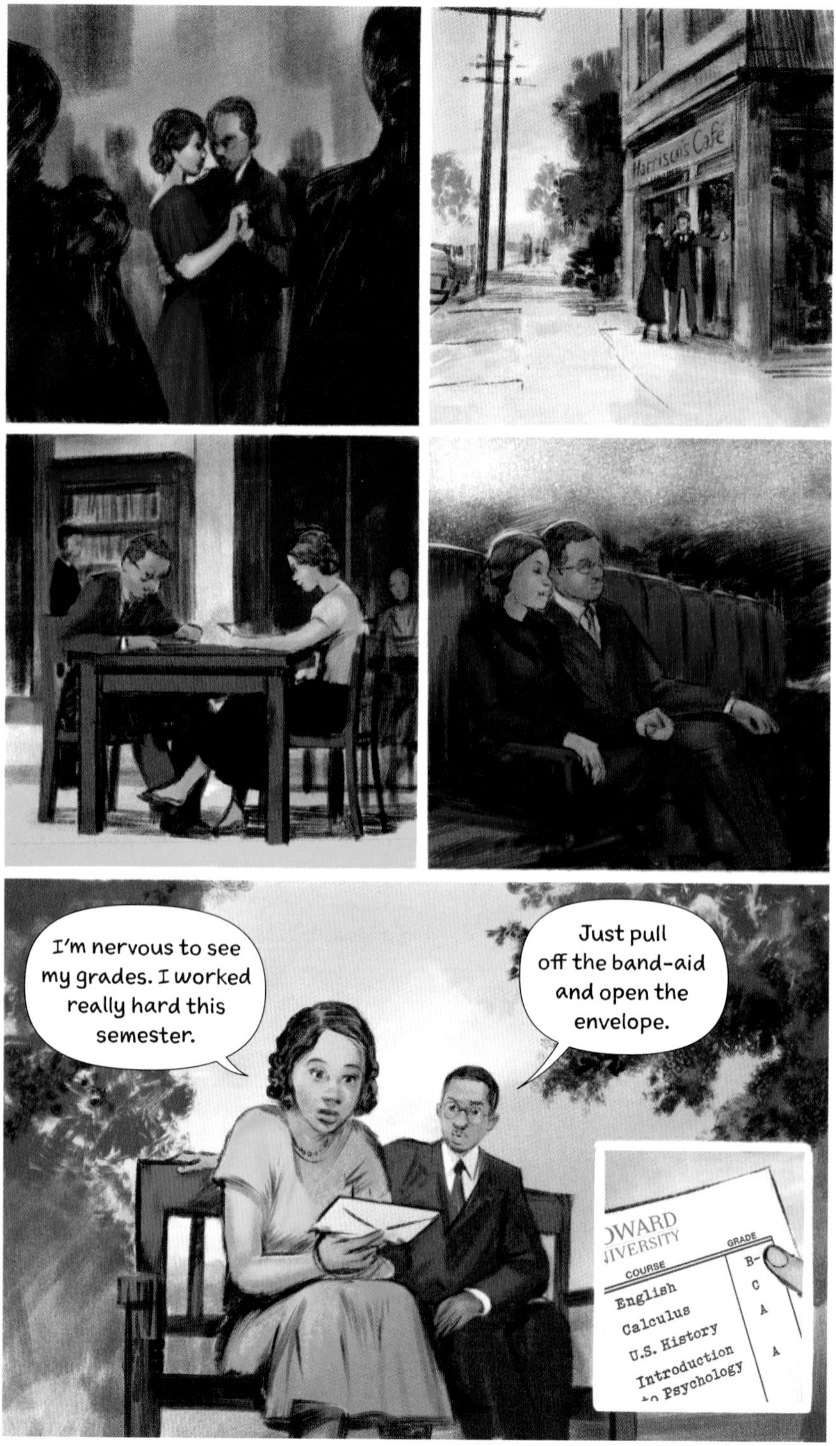
Harrison's Café
I'm nervous to see my grades. I worked really hard this semester.
Just pull off the band-aid and open the envelope.
OWARD
IVERSITY
COURSE
GRADE
English
B-
Calculus
C
U.S. History
A
Introduction
to Psychology
A

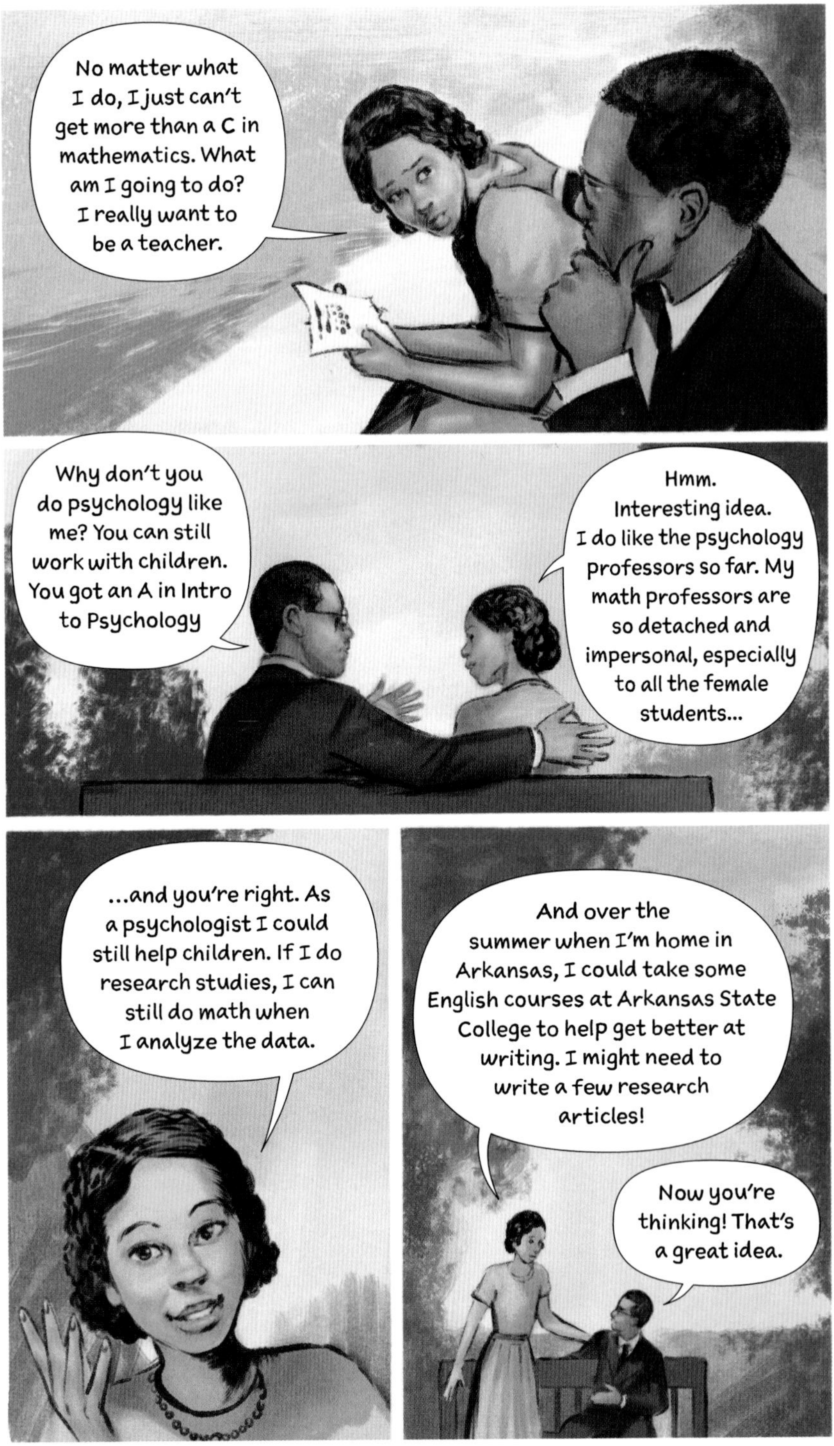
No matter what I do, I just can't get more than a C in mathematics. What am I going to do? I really want to be a teacher.
Why don't you do psychology like me? You can still work with children. You got an A in Intro to Psychology
Hmm. Interesting idea. I do like the psychology professors so far. My math professors are so detached and impersonal, especially to all the female students...
...and you're right. As a psychologist I could still help children. If I do research studies, I can still do math when I analyze the data.
And over the summer when I'm home in Arkansas, I could take some English courses at Arkansas State College to help get better at writing. I might need to write a few research articles!
Now you're thinking! That's a great idea.

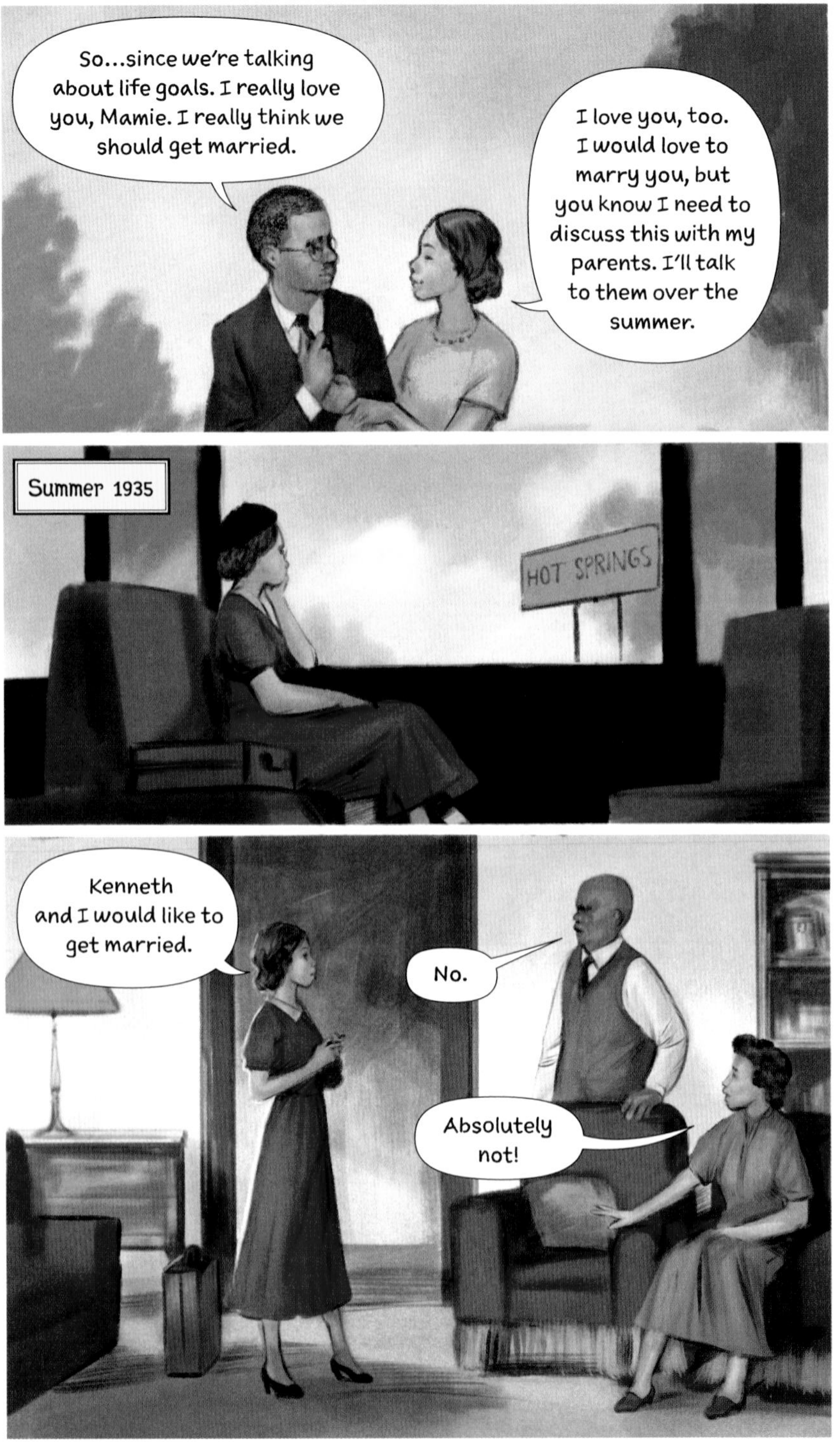
So...since we're talking about life goals. I really love you, Mamie. I really think we should get married.
I love you, too. I would love to marry you, but you know I need to discuss this with my parents. I'll talk to them over the summer.
Summer 1935
HOT SPRINGS
Kenneth and I would like to get married.
No.
Absolutely not!

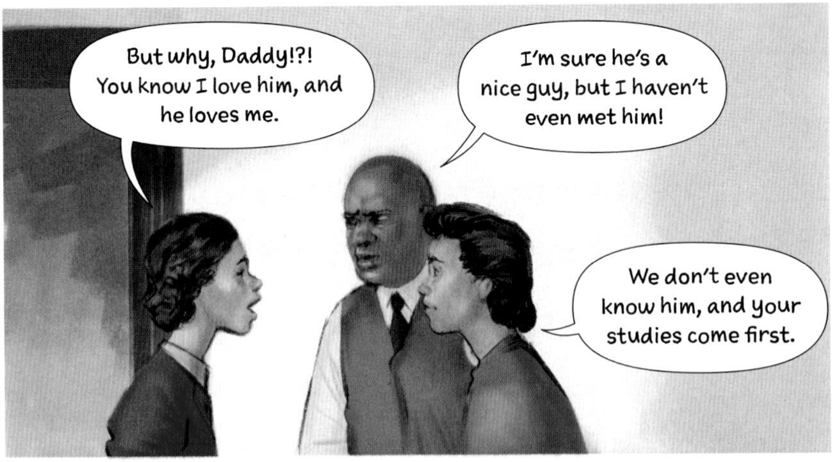
But why, Daddy!?! You know I love him, and he loves me.
I'm sure he's a nice guy, but I haven't even met him!
We don't even know him, and your studies come first.

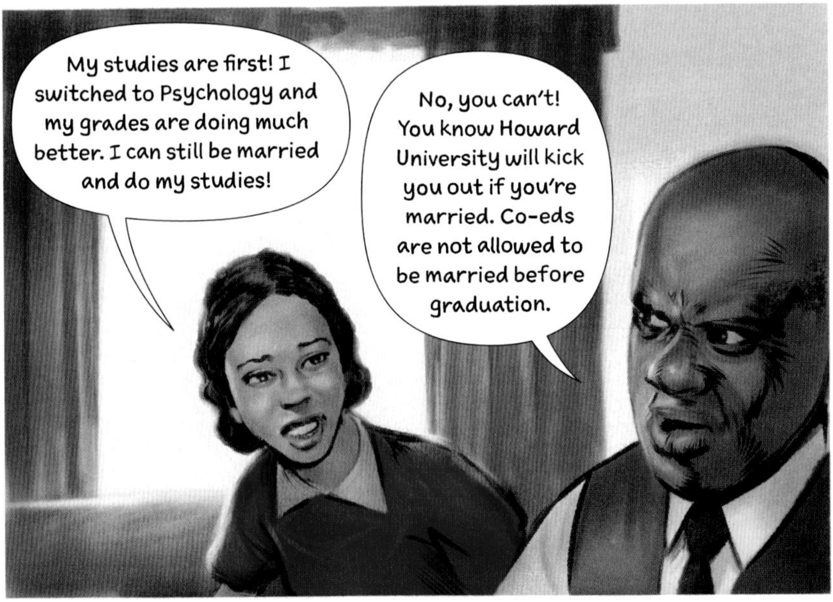
My studies are first! I switched to Psychology and my grades are doing much better. I can still be married and do my studies!
No, you can't! You know Howard University will kick you out if you're married. Co-eds are not allowed to be married before graduation.

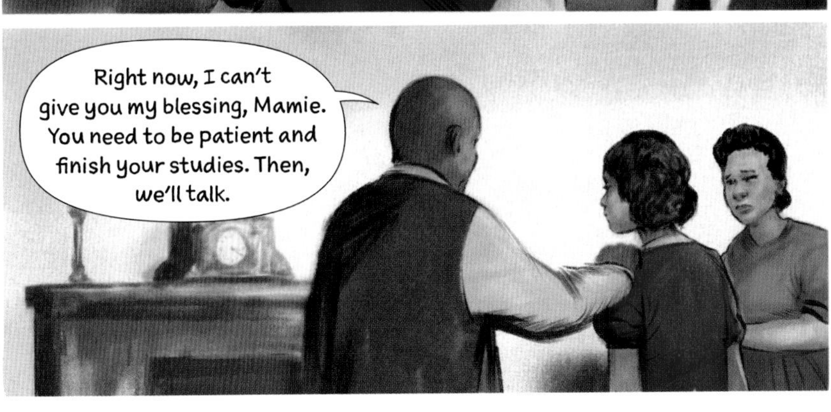
Right now, I can't give you my blessing, Mamie. You need to be patient and finish your studies. Then, we'll talk.

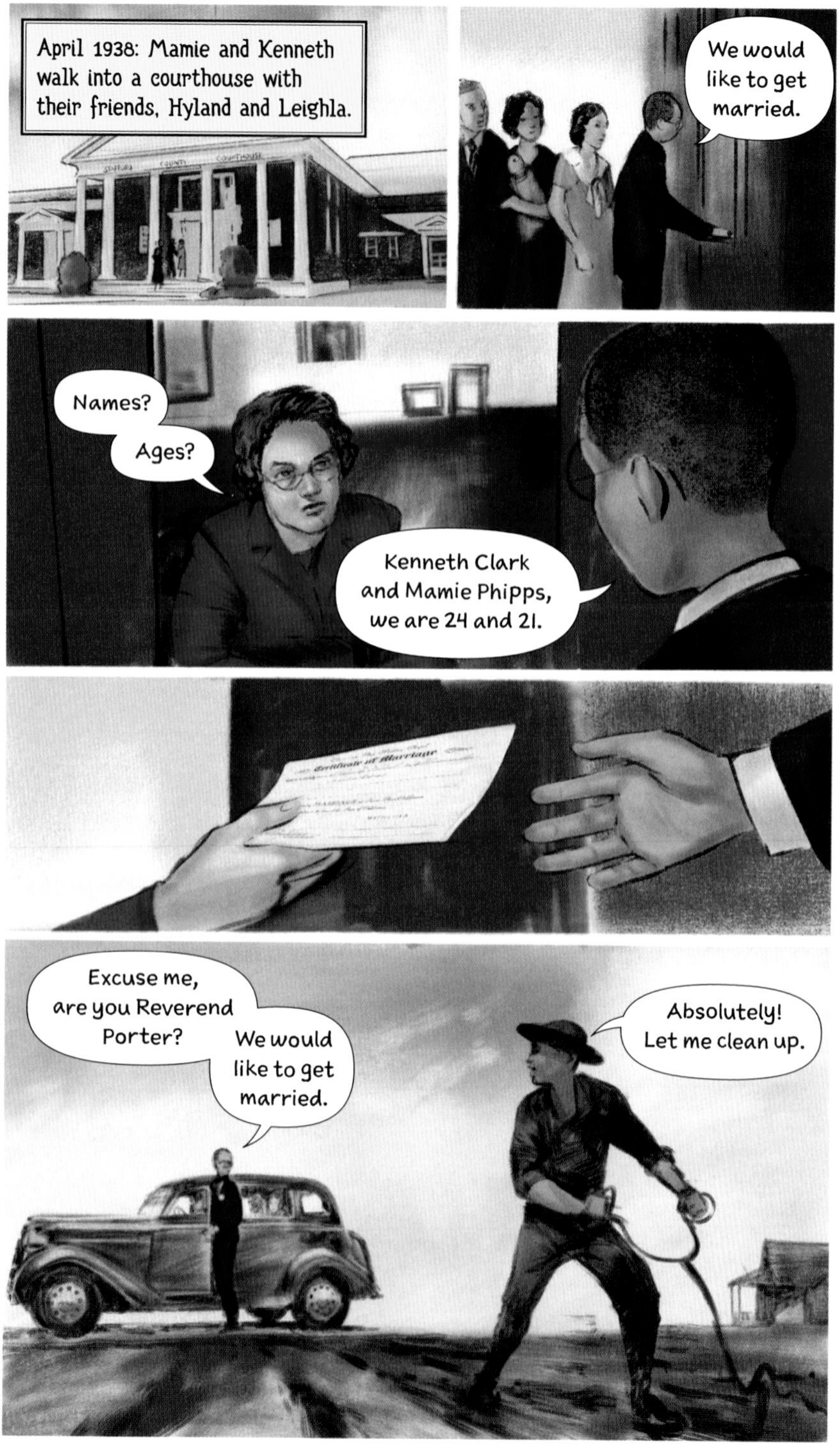

April 1938: Mamie and Kenneth walk into a courthouse with their friends, Hyland and Leighla.
We would like to get married.
Names?
Ages?
Kenneth Clark and Mamie Phipps, we are 24 and 21.
Excuse me, are you Reverend Porter?
We would like to get married.
Absolutely! Let me clean up.

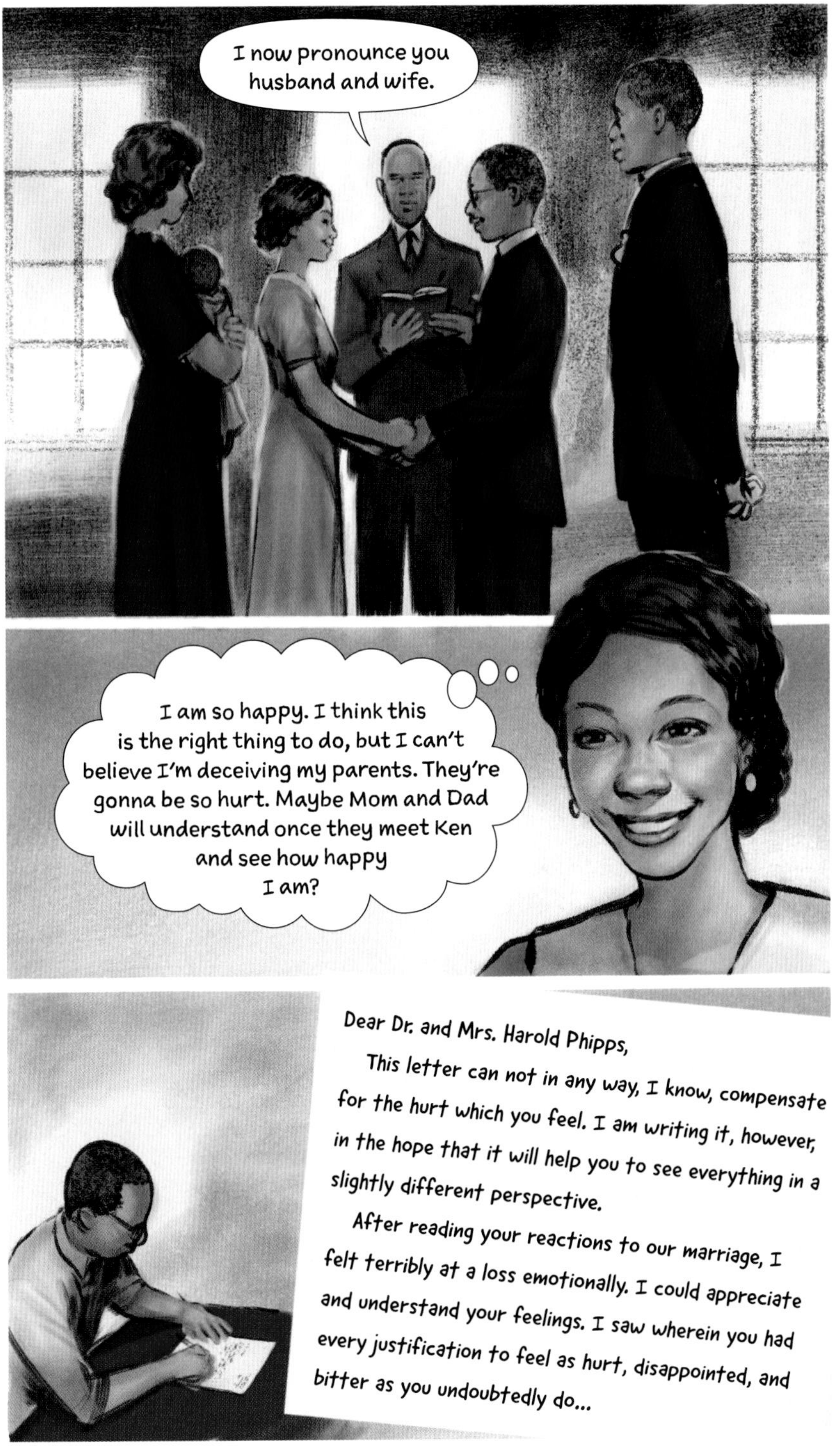
I now pronounce you husband and wife.
I am so happy. I think this is the right thing to do, but I can't believe I'm deceiving my parents. They're gonna be so hurt. Maybe Mom and Dad will understand once they meet Ken and see how happy I am?
Dear Dr. and Mrs. Harold Phipps,
This letter can not in any way, I know, compensate for the hurt which you feel. I am writing it, however, in the hope that it will help you to see everything in a slightly different perspective.
After reading your reactions to our marriage, I felt terribly at a loss emotionally. I could appreciate and understand your feelings. I saw wherein you had every justification to feel as hurt, disappointed, and bitter as you undoubtedly do...

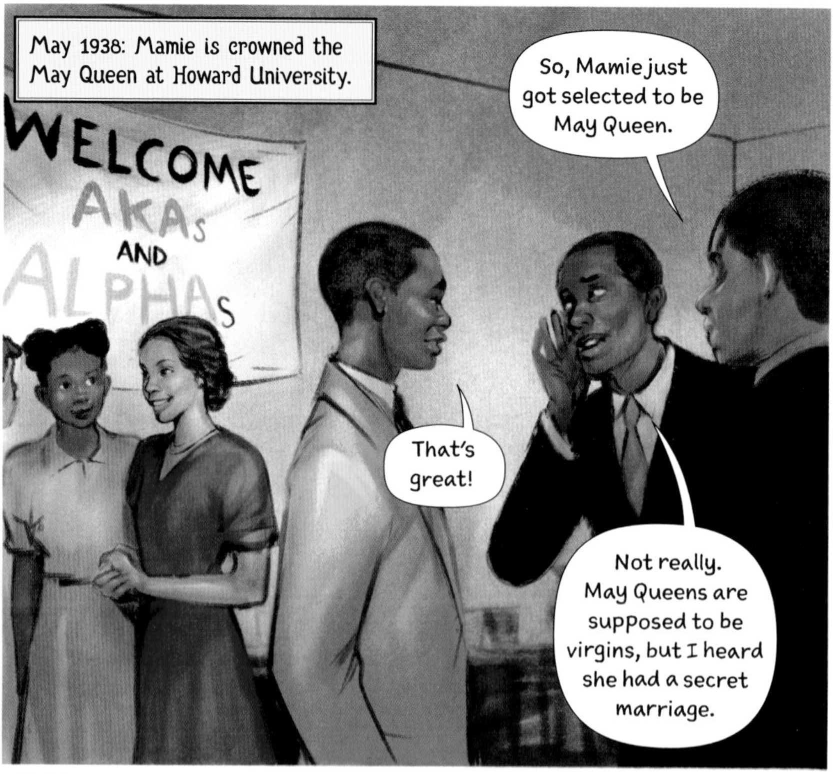
May 1938: Mamie is crowned the May Queen at Howard University.
WELCOME AKAs AND ALPHAs
So, Mamie just got selected to be May Queen.
That's great!
Not really. May Queens are supposed to be virgins, but I heard she had a secret marriage.

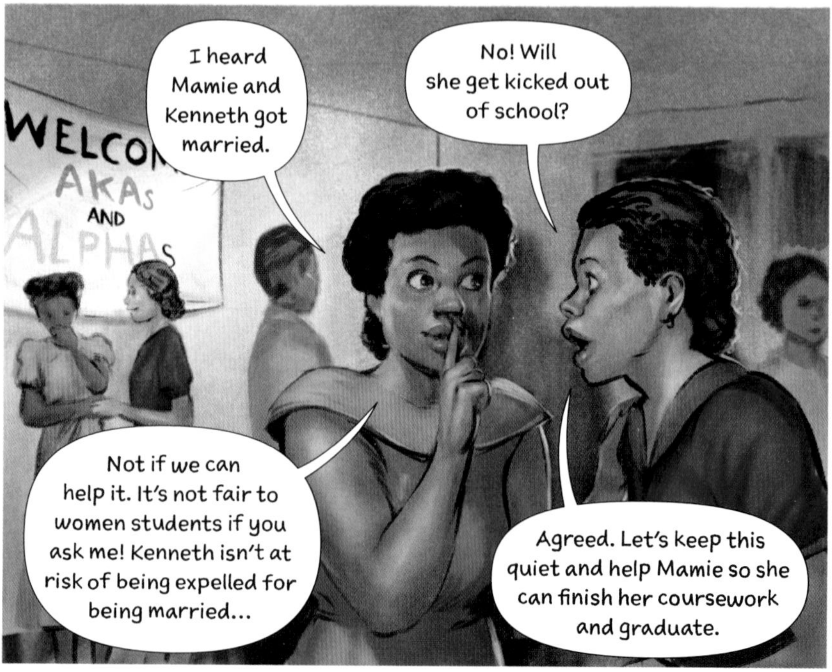
WELCOM AKAs AND ALPHAs
I heard Mamie and Kenneth got married.
No! Will she get kicked out of school?
Not if we can help it. It's not fair to women students if you ask me! Kenneth isn't at risk of being expelled for being married...
Agreed. Let's keep this quiet and help Mamie so she can finish her coursework and graduate.

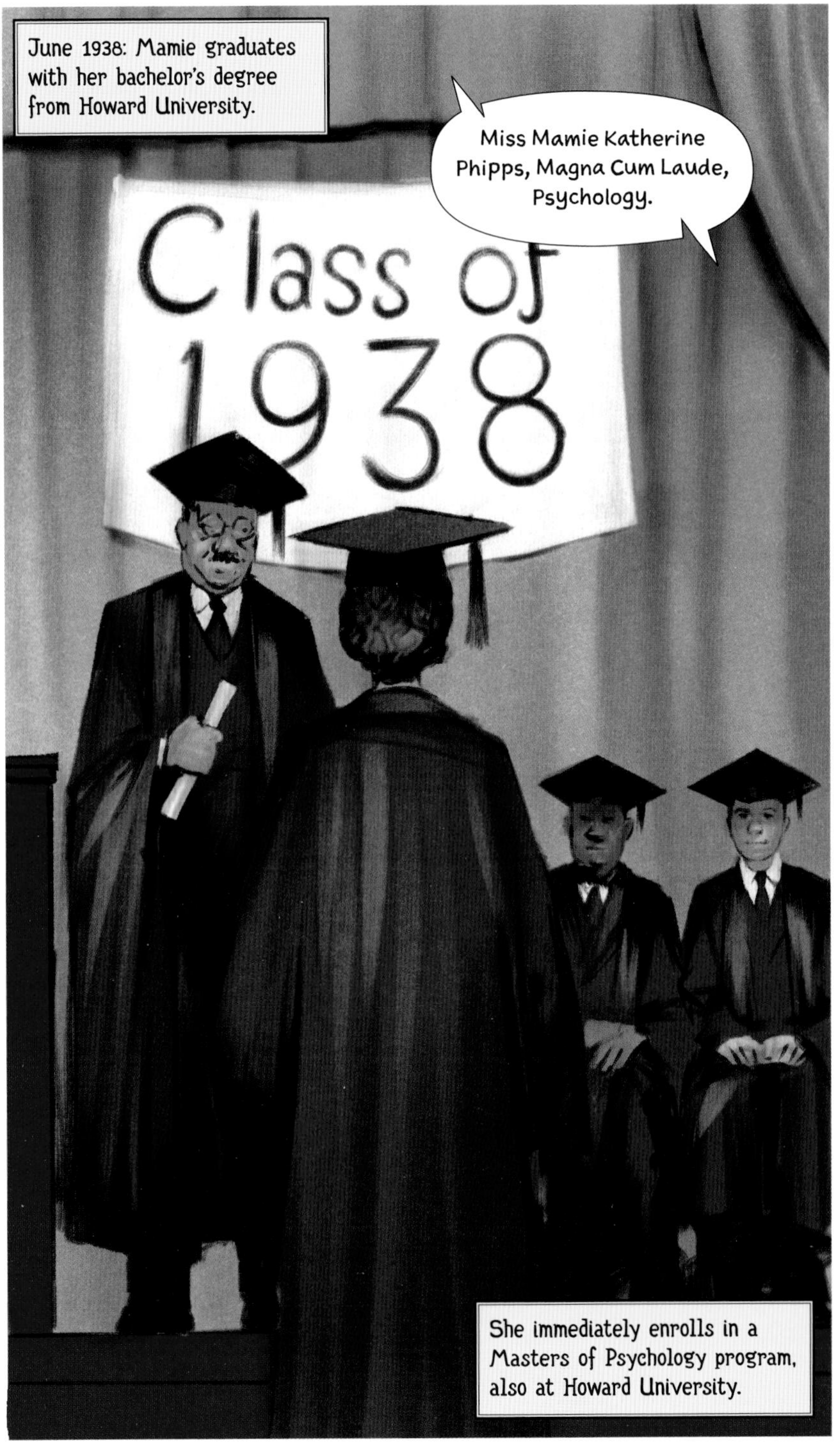
June 1938: Mamie graduates with her bachelor's degree from Howard University.
Miss Mamie Katherine Phipps, Magna Cum Laude, Psychology.
Class of 1938
She immediately enrolls in a Masters of Psychology program, also at Howard University.

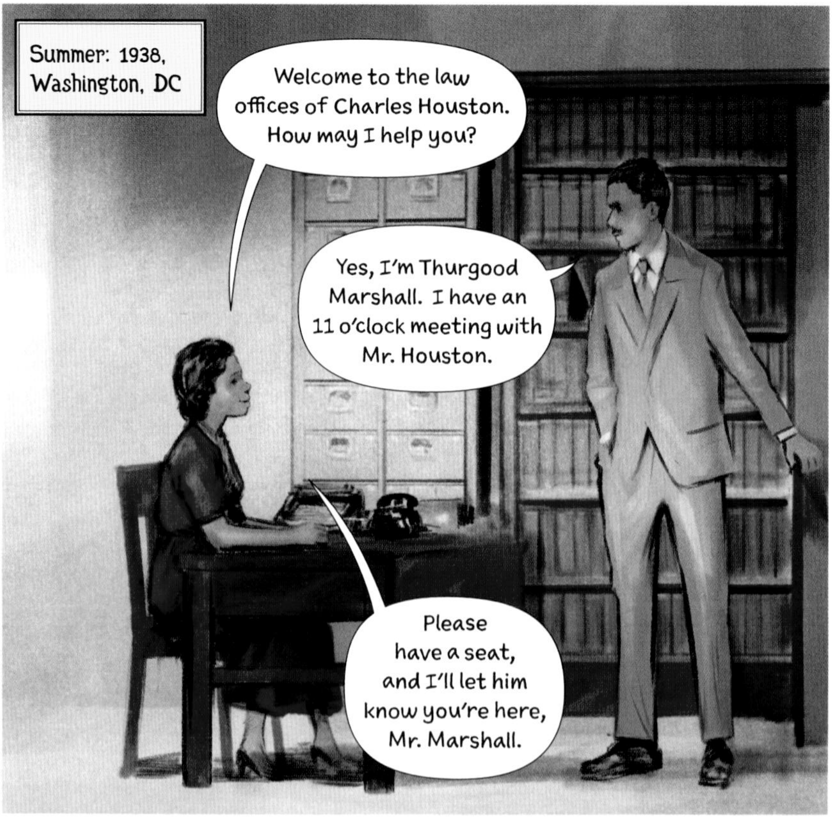
Summer: 1938, Washington, DC
Welcome to the law offices of Charles Houston. How may I help you?
Yes, I'm Thurgood Marshall. I have an 11 o'clock meeting with Mr. Houston.
Please have a seat, and I'll let him know you're here, Mr. Marshall.

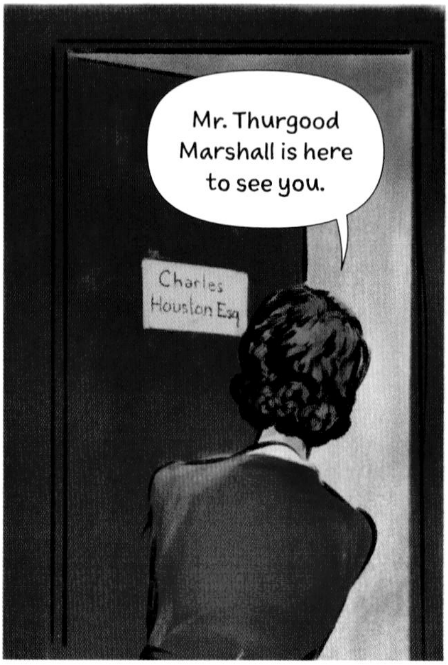
Mr. Thurgood Marshall is here to see you.
Charles Houston Esq

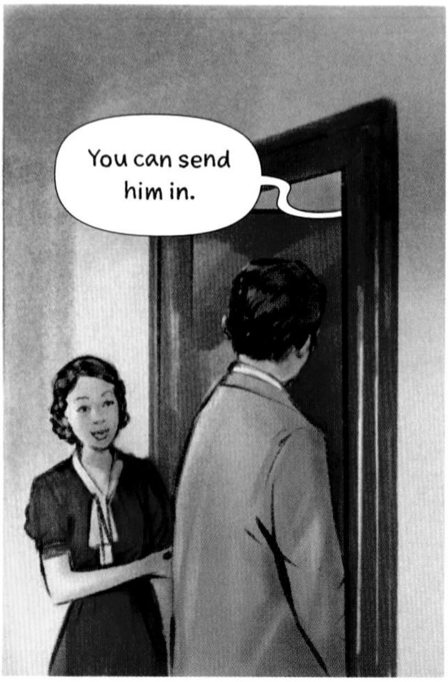
You can send him in.

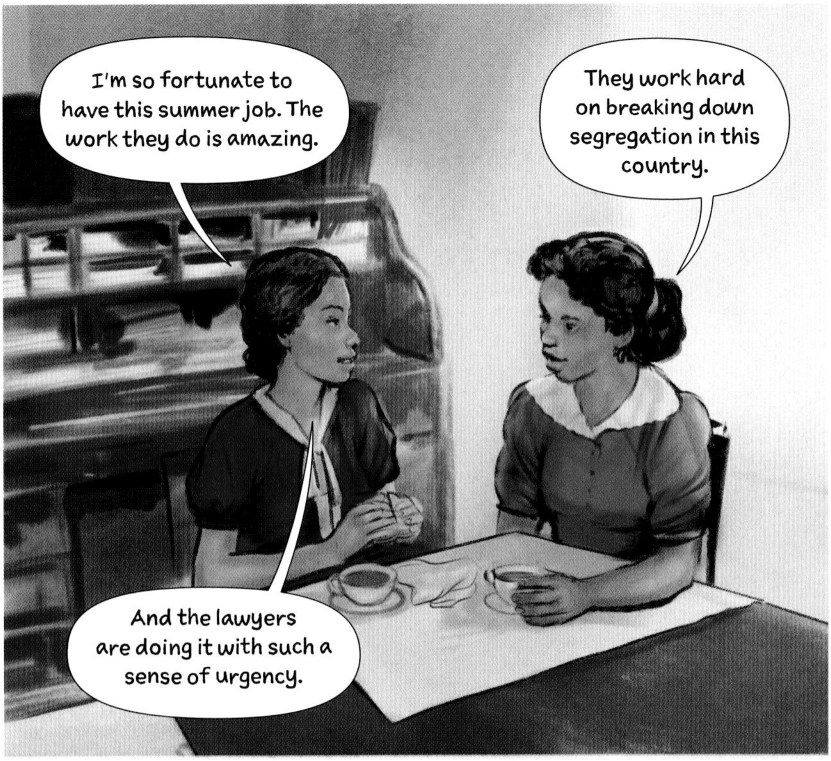
I'm so fortunate to have this summer job. The work they do is amazing.
They work hard on breaking down segregation in this country.
And the lawyers are doing it with such a sense of urgency.

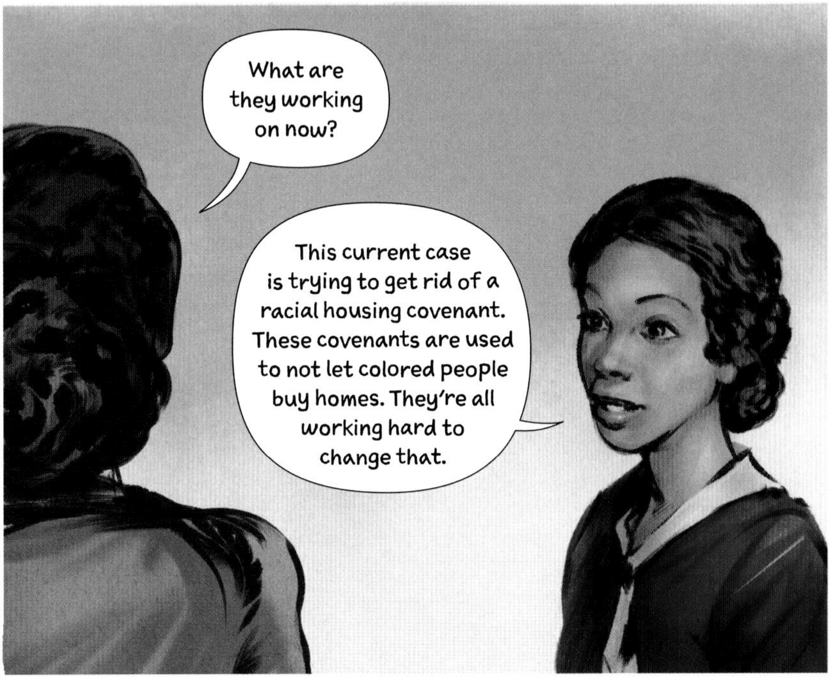
What are they working on now?
This current case is trying to get rid of a racial housing covenant. These covenants are used to not let colored people buy homes. They're all working hard to change that.

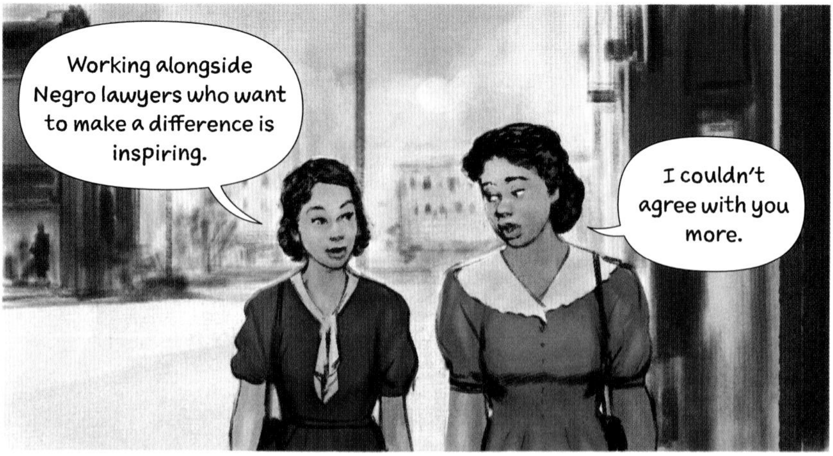
Working alongside Negro lawyers who want to make a difference is inspiring.
I couldn't agree with you more.

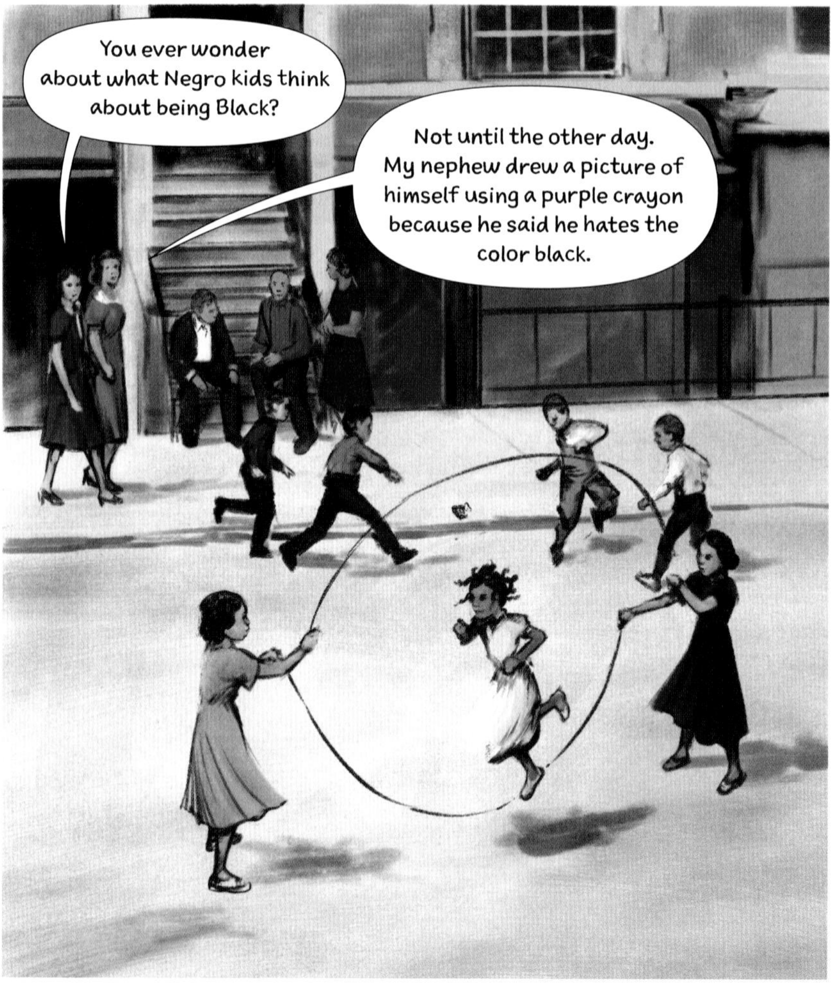
You ever wonder about what Negro kids think about being Black?
Not until the other day. My nephew drew a picture of himself using a purple crayon because he said he hates the color black.

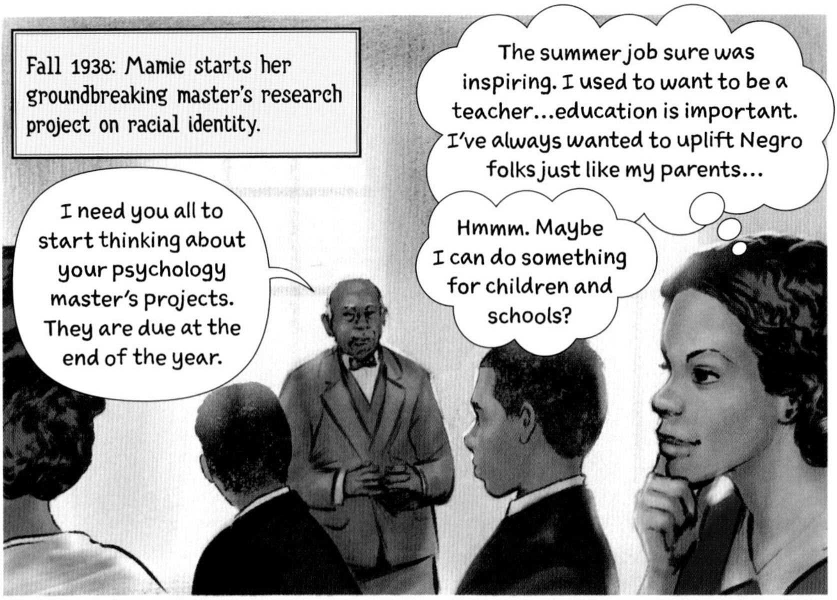
Fall 1938: Mamie starts her groundbreaking master's research project on racial identity.
The summer job sure was inspiring. I used to want to be a teacher...education is important. I've always wanted to uplift Negro folks just like my parents...
I need you all to start thinking about your psychology master's projects. They are due at the end of the year.
Hmmm. Maybe I can do something for children and schools?

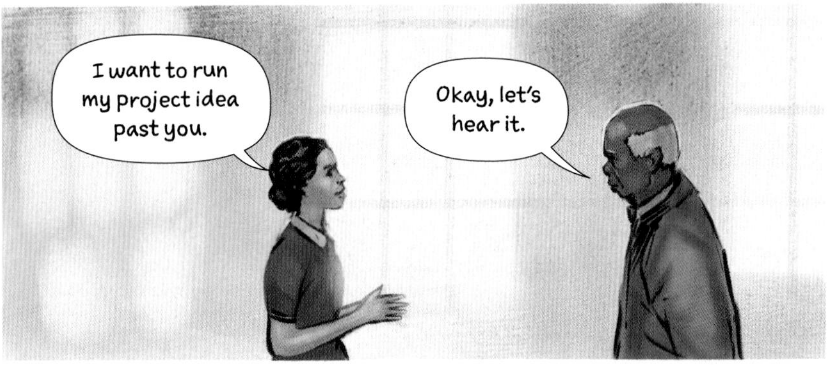
I want to run my project idea past you.
Okay, let's hear it.

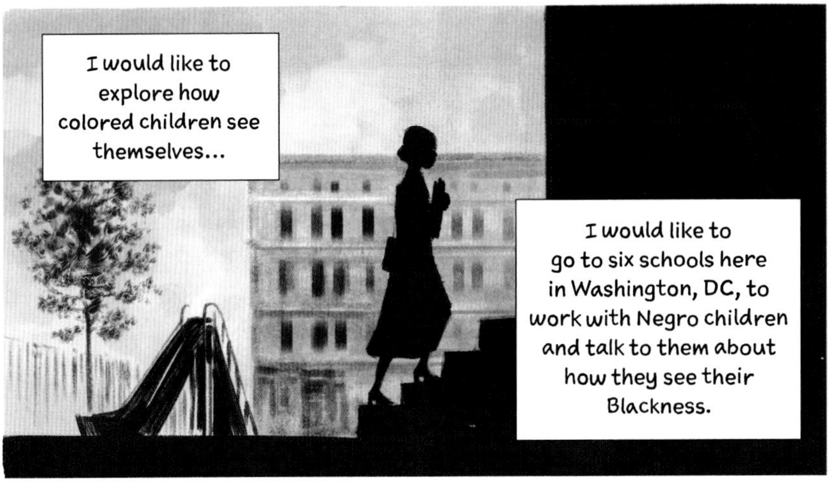
I would like to explore how colored children see themselves...
I would like to go to six schools here in Washington, DC, to work with Negro children and talk to them about how they see their Blackness.

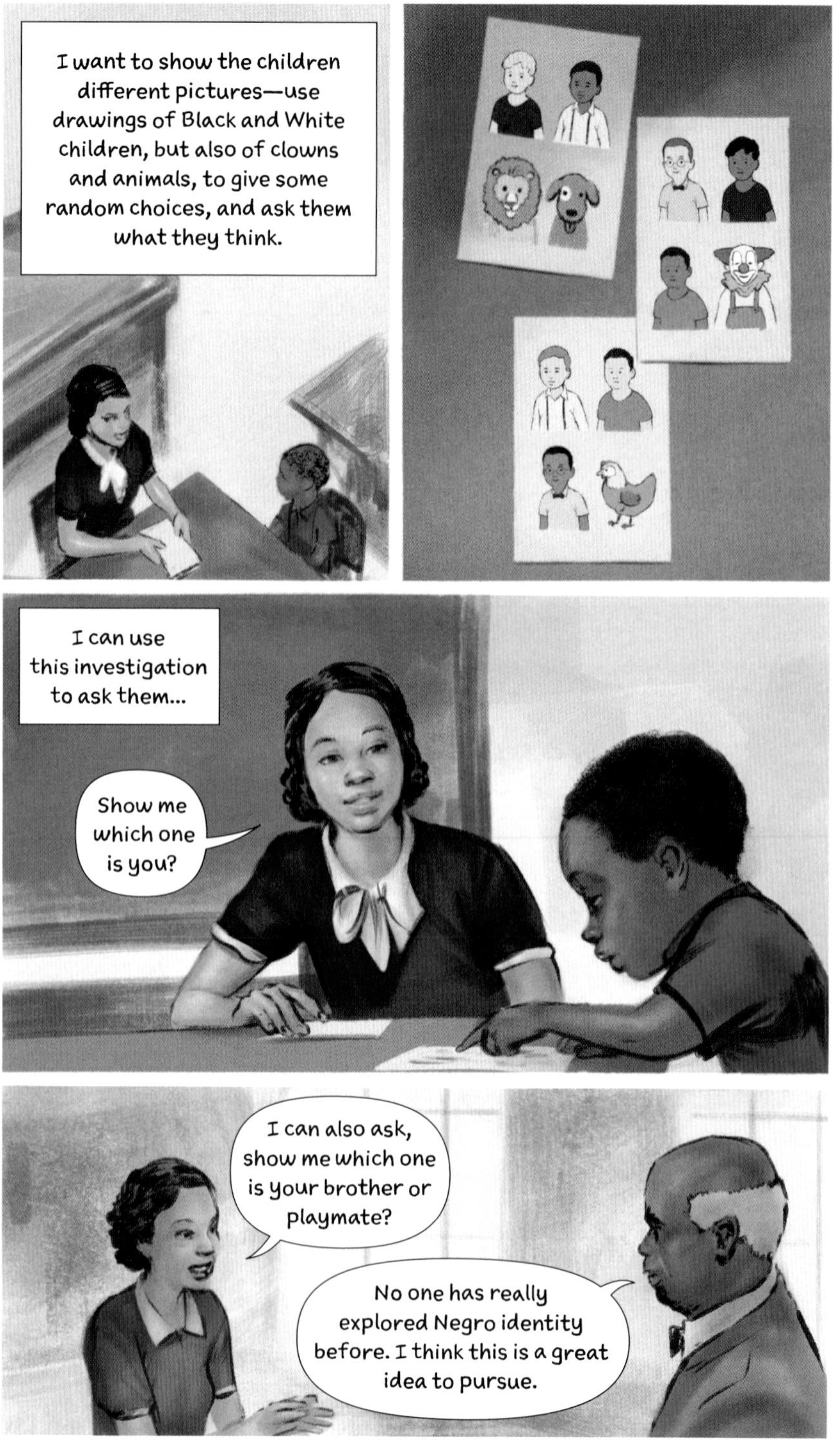

I want to show the children different pictures—use drawings of Black and White children, but also of clowns and animals, to give some random choices, and ask them what they think.
I can use this investigation to ask them...
Show me which one is you?
I can also ask, show me which one is your brother or playmate?
No one has really explored Negro identity before. I think this is a great idea to pursue.

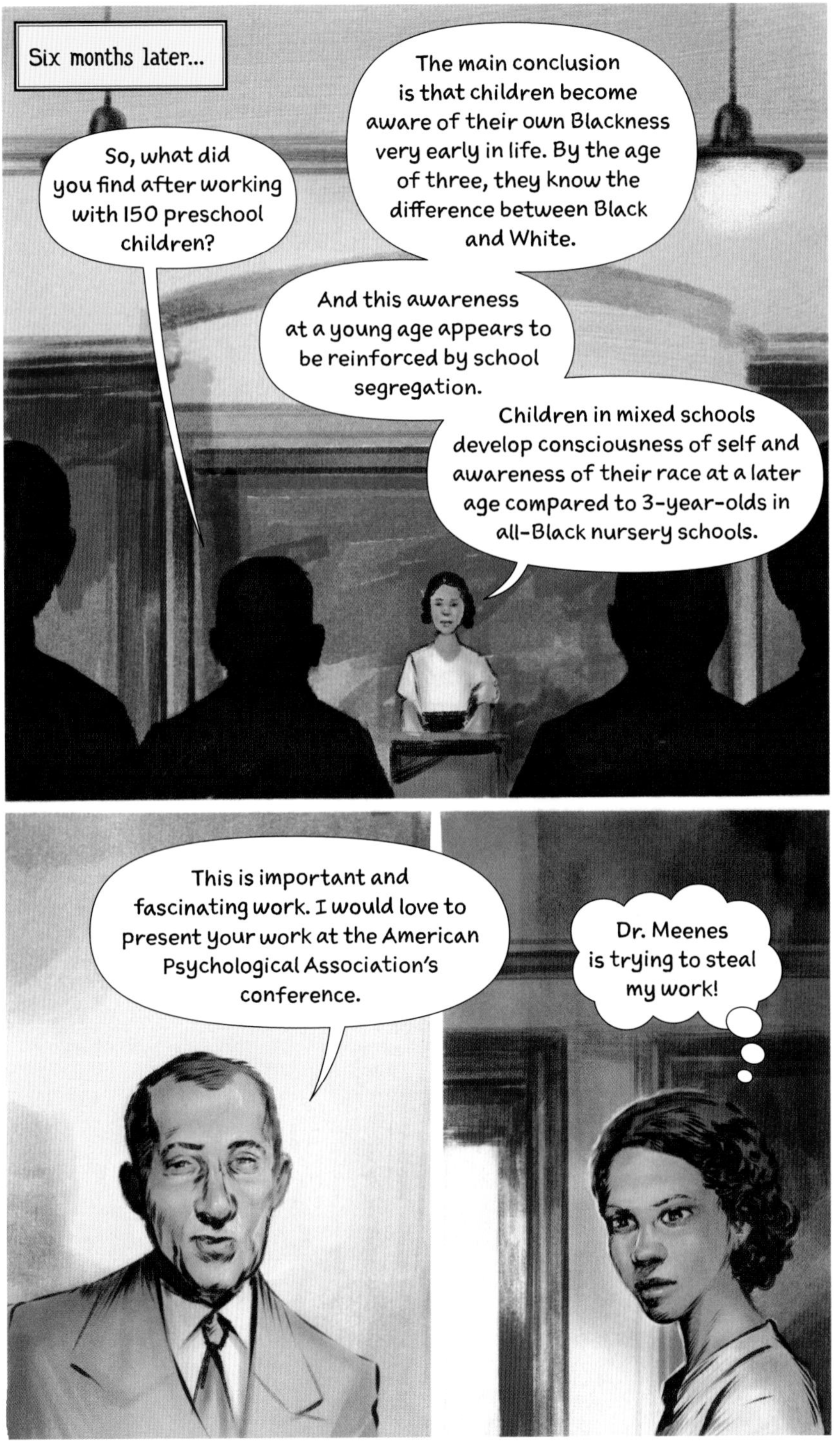
Six months later...
So, what did you find after working with 150 preschool children?
The main conclusion is that children become aware of their own Blackness very early in life. By the age of three, they know the difference between Black and White.
And this awareness at a young age appears to be reinforced by school segregation.
Children in mixed schools develop consciousness of self and awareness of their race at a later age compared to 3-year-olds in all-Black nursery schools.
This is important and fascinating work. I would love to present your work at the American Psychological Association's conference.
Dr. Meenes is trying to steal my work!

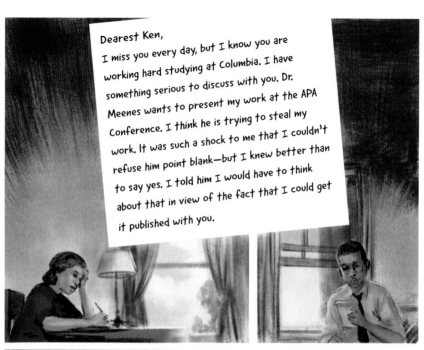

Dearest Ken,

I miss you every day, but I know you are working hard studying at Columbia. I have something serious to discuss with you. Dr. Meenes wants to present my work at the APA Conference. I think he is trying to steal my work. It was such a shock to me that I couldn't refuse him point blank—but I knew better than to say yes. I told him I would have to think about that in view of the fact that I could get it published with you.

I have to help Mamie get her work published quickly so Dr. Meenes doesn't try to steal it.

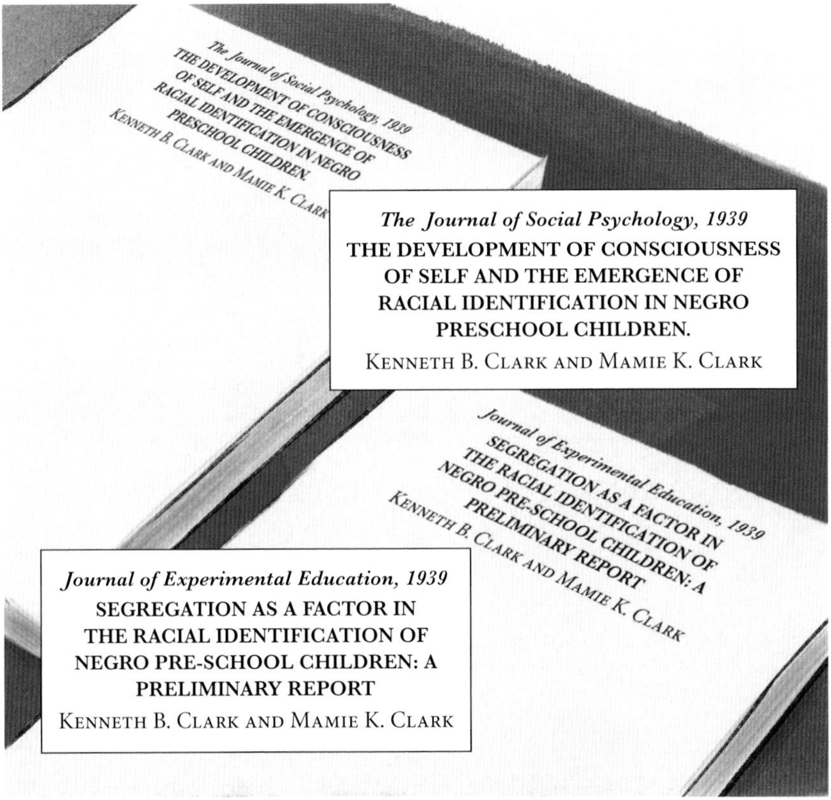
The Journal of Social Psychology, 1939
THE DEVELOPMENT OF CONSCIOUSNESS OF SELF AND THE EMERGENCE OF RACIAL IDENTIFICATION IN NEGRO PRESCHOOL CHILDREN.
Kenneth B. Clark and Mamie K. Clark
Journal of Experimental Education, 1939
SEGREGATION AS A FACTOR IN THE RACIAL IDENTIFICATION OF NEGRO PRE-SCHOOL CHILDREN: A PRELIMINARY REPORT
Kenneth B. Clark and Mamie K. Clark

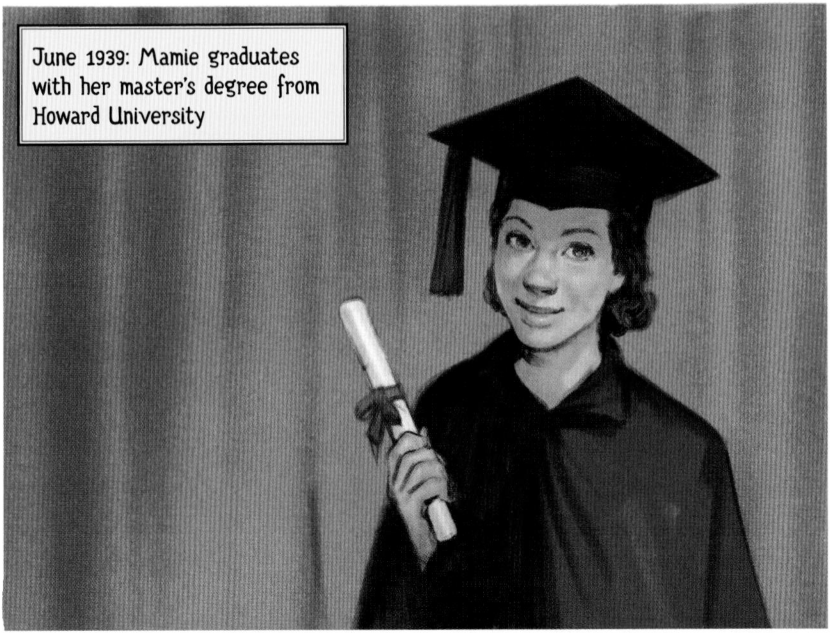
June 1939: Mamie graduates with her master's degree from Howard University

Dr. Mamie Phipps Clark's Research

Dr. Mamie Phipps Clark's lifework on racial identity development all started with her master's thesis research. For her research, she showed children a set of pictures similar to these:

Set A

Set B

Set C

After looking at this sheet, Dr. Clark would ask the following questions based on the children's gender. For boy participants, she would ask: *Show me which one is you? Which one is [insert child's name here]?* For the girl participants, she would ask: *Show me which one is [insert name of brother, boy cousin, or boy playmate]?*

This simple, yet important, study was the basis of many important findings to come. And it is a study that we can still do today. Here is a modified and modernized version below to try on your family and friends.

Experiment Directions

Show the pictures above to your family or friends. Then ask them the following questions.

1. Which child would you like to play with or like best?

2. Which child looks nice?

3. Which child looks bad?

4. Which child is a nice color?

5. Which child looks like a White child?

6. Which child looks like a Black child?

7. Which child looks like you?

Results and Findings

On a separate sheet of paper, make a grid like the one below. Record how people answered the questions. Then after doing this experiment with at least four people, look over your results.

Question Asked	Black Boy/Girl	White Boy/Girl
1		
2		
3		
4		
5		
6		
7		

Now do some comparisons. Is one category represented more than another? How do people see themselves versus how they see the opposite race? Then ask yourself, what do you think these results are telling you about how people see and think about race?

Congratulations! You have just done a psychological experiment.

CHAPTER 4

Black Doll/White Doll Experiment

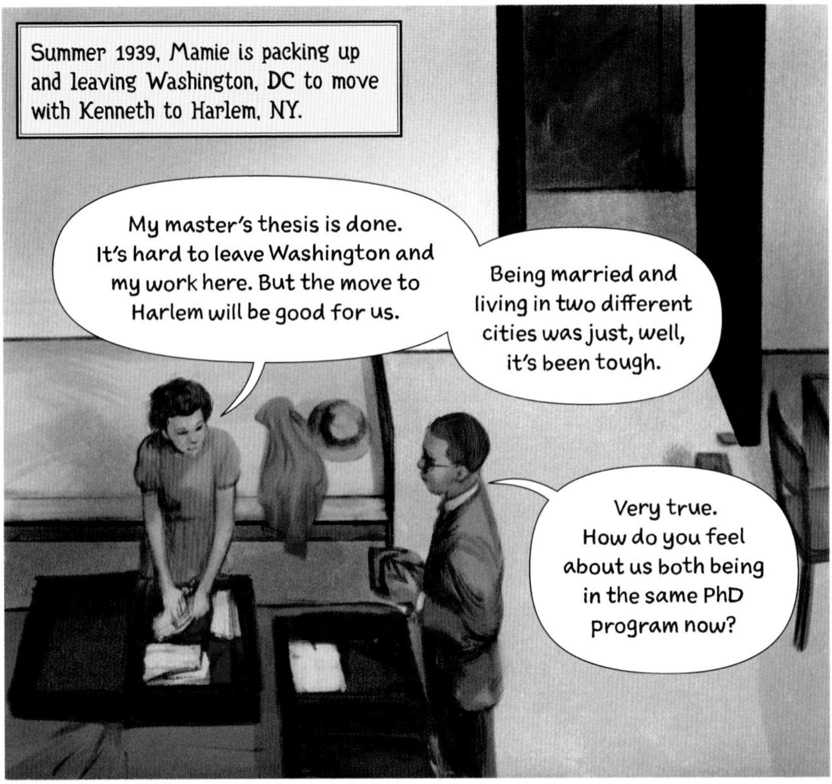
Summer 1939, Mamie is packing up and leaving Washington, DC to move with Kenneth to Harlem, NY.
My master's thesis is done. It's hard to leave Washington and my work here. But the move to Harlem will be good for us.
Being married and living in two different cities was just, well, it's been tough.
Very true. How do you feel about us both being in the same PhD program now?

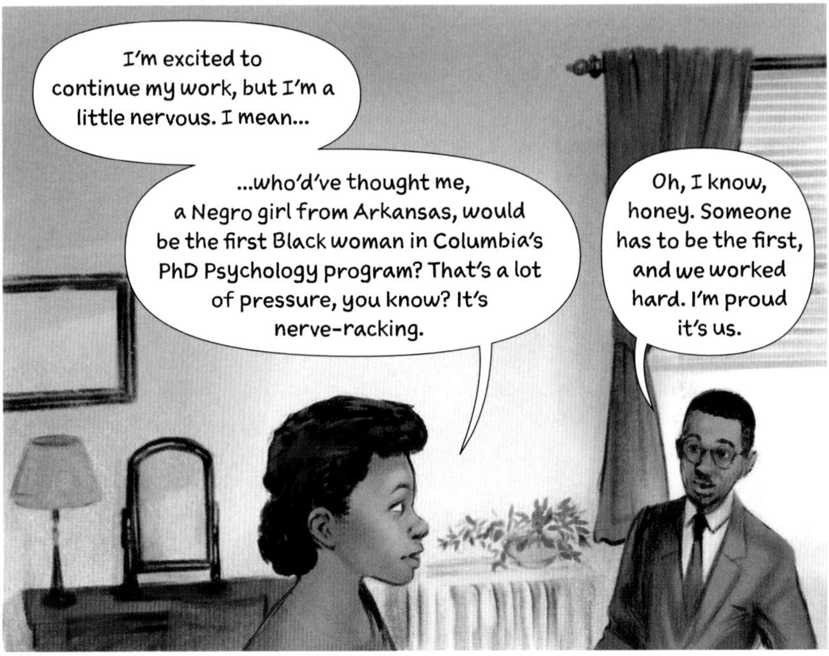
I'm excited to continue my work, but I'm a little nervous. I mean...
...who'd've thought me, a Negro girl from Arkansas, would be the first Black woman in Columbia's PhD Psychology program? That's a lot of pressure, you know? It's nerve-racking.
Oh, I know, honey. Someone has to be the first, and we worked hard. I'm proud it's us.

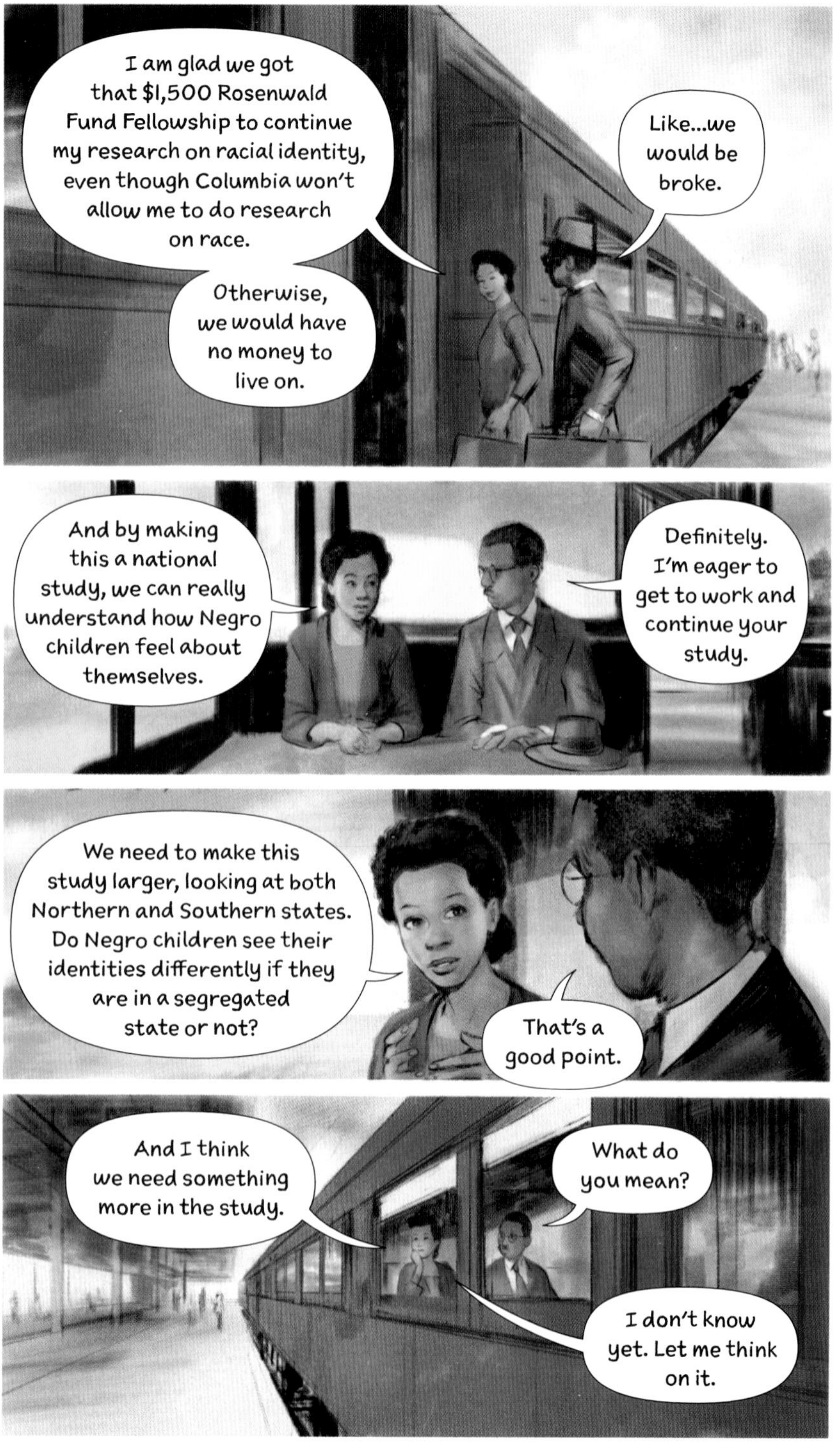
I am glad we got that $1,500 Rosenwald Fund Fellowship to continue my research on racial identity, even though Columbia won't allow me to do research on race.
Otherwise, we would have no money to live on.
Like...we would be broke.
And by making this a national study, we can really understand how Negro children feel about themselves.
Definitely. I'm eager to get to work and continue your study.
We need to make this study larger, looking at both Northern and Southern states. Do Negro children see their identities differently if they are in a segregated state or not?
That's a good point.
And I think we need something more in the study.
What do you mean?
I don't know yet. Let me think on it.

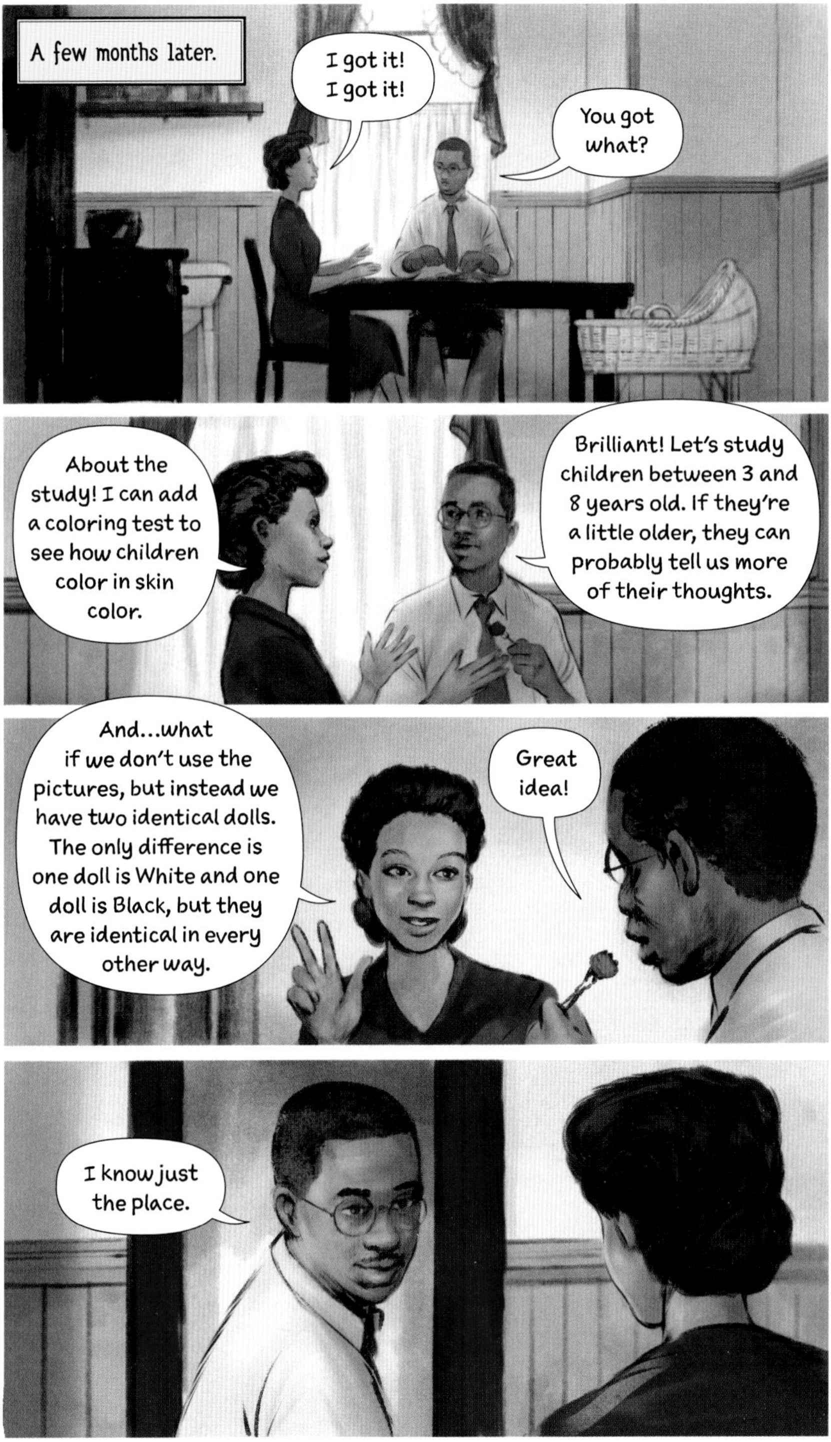
A few months later.
I got it! I got it!
You got what?
About the study! I can add a coloring test to see how children color in skin color.
Brilliant! Let's study children between 3 and 8 years old. If they're a little older, they can probably tell us more of their thoughts.
And...what if we don't use the pictures, but instead we have two identical dolls. The only difference is one doll is White and one doll is Black, but they are identical in every other way.
Great idea!
I know just the place.

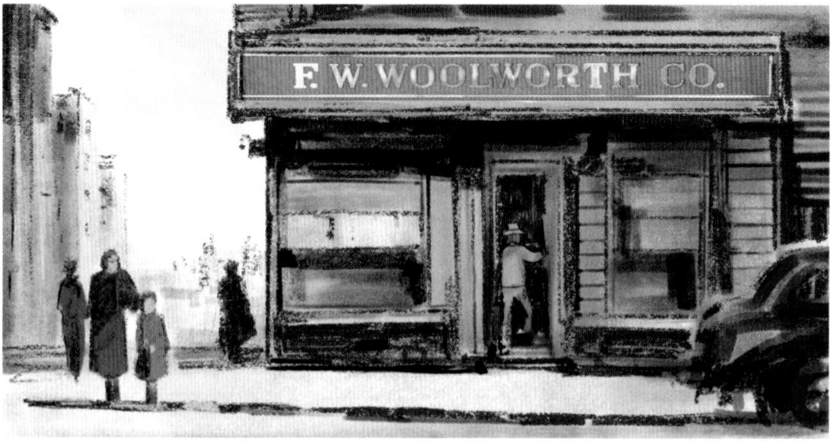
F. W. WOOLWORTH CO.

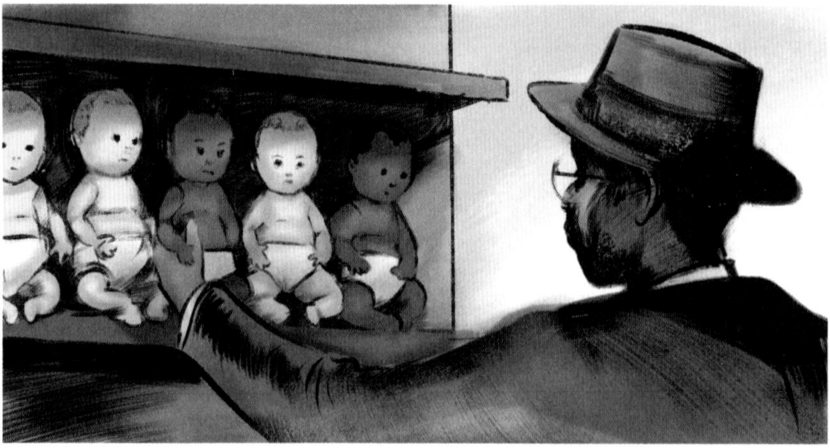

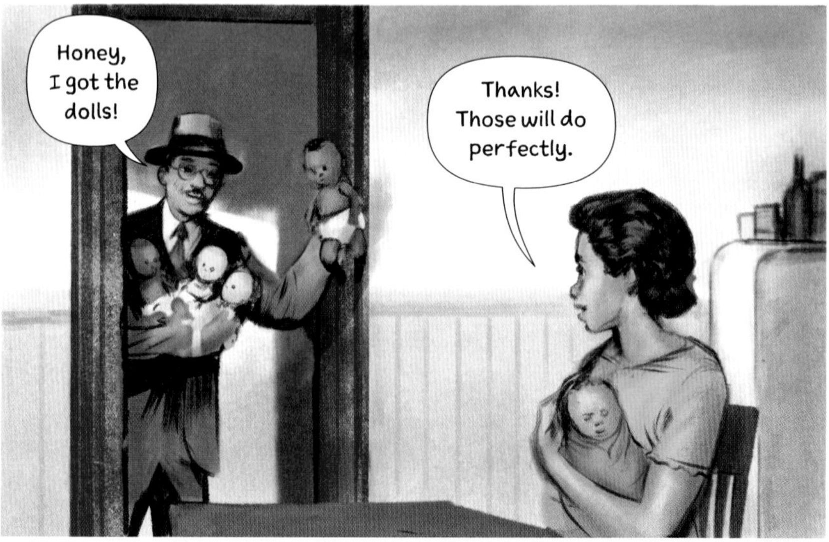
Honey, I got the dolls!
Thanks! Those will do perfectly.

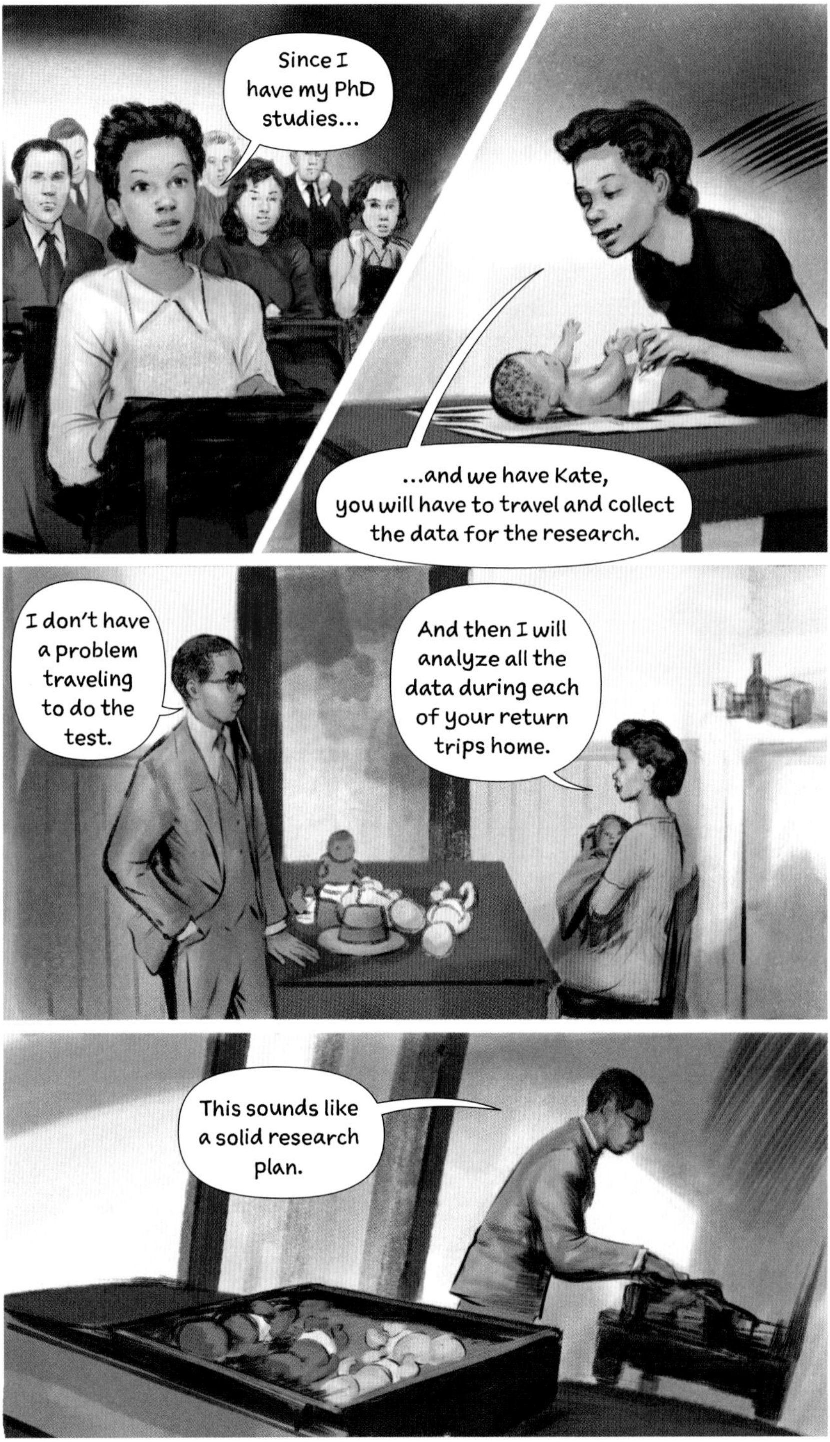
Since I have my PhD studies...
...and we have Kate, you will have to travel and collect the data for the research.
I don't have a problem traveling to do the test.
And then I will analyze all the data during each of your return trips home.
This sounds like a solid research plan.

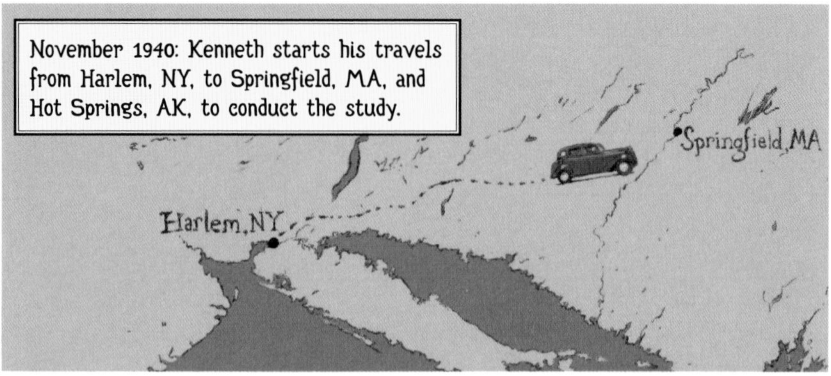
November 1940: Kenneth starts his travels from Harlem, NY, to Springfield, MA, and Hot Springs, AK, to conduct the study.
Springfield, MA
Harlem, NY

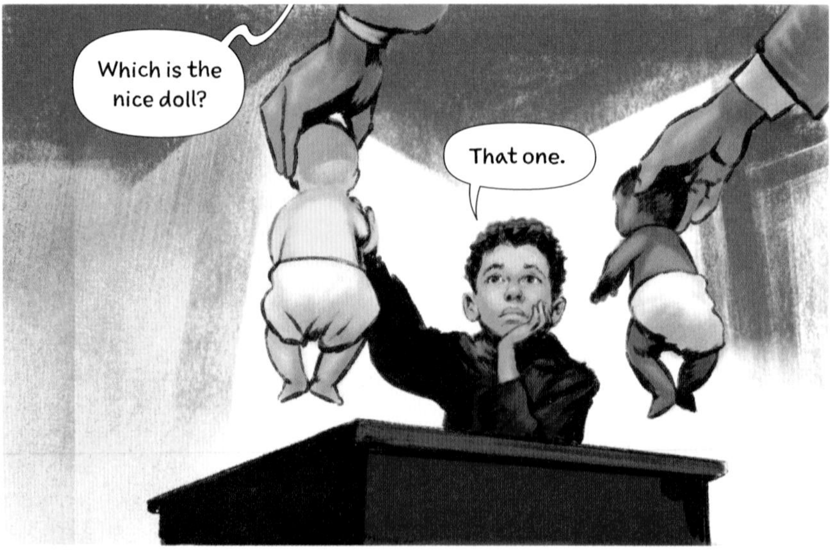
Which is the nice doll?
That one.

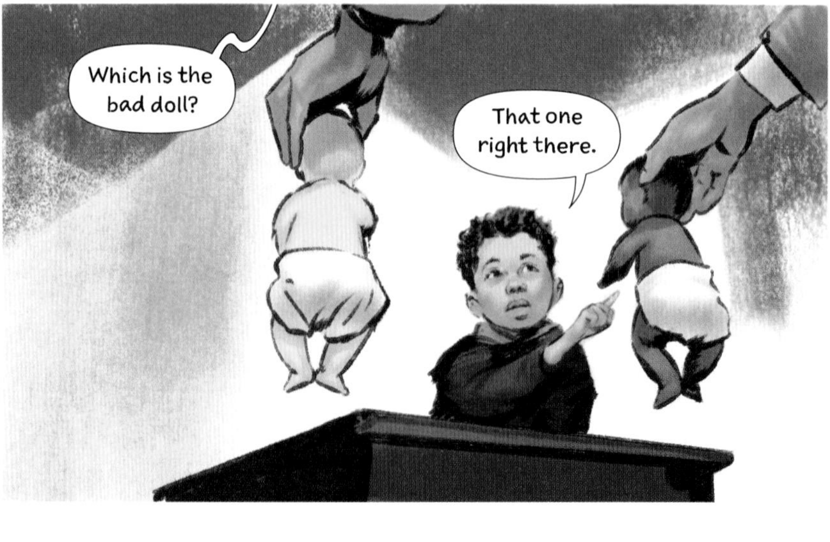
Which is the bad doll?
That one right there.

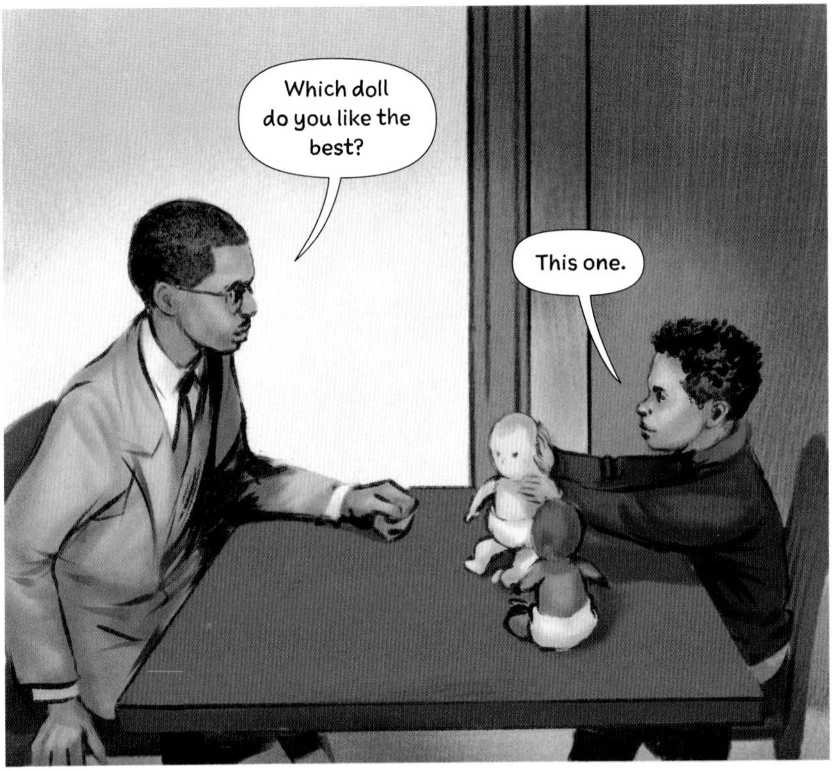
Which doll do you like the best?
This one.

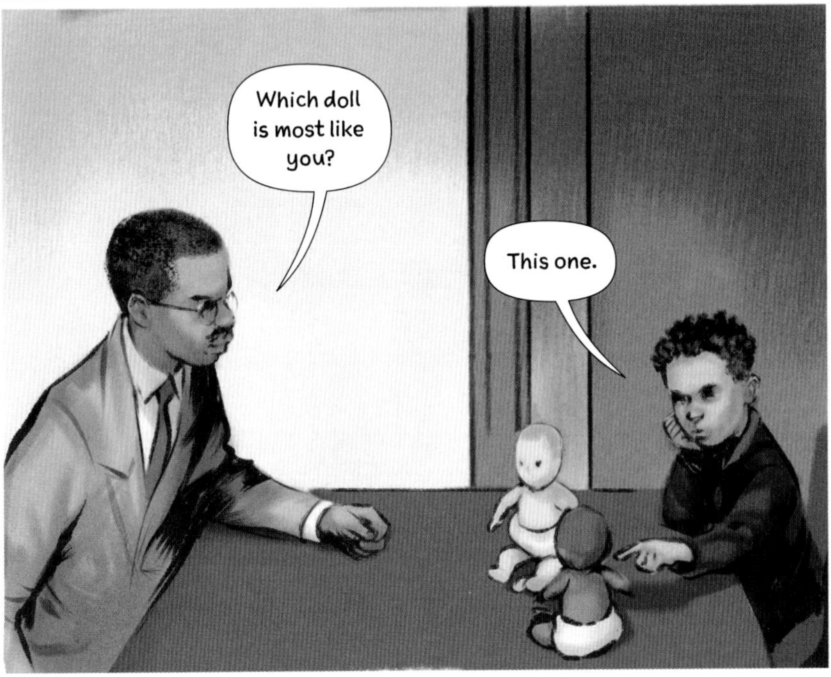
Which doll is most like you?
This one.

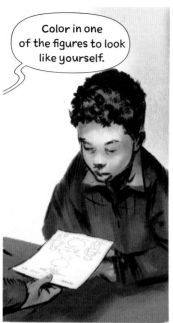

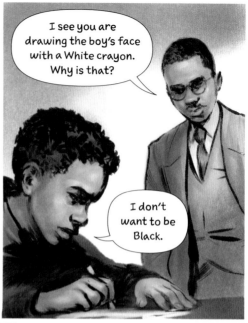

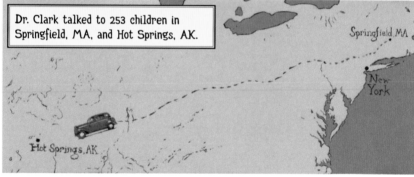

Color in one of the figures to look like yourself.
I see you are drawing the boy's face with a White crayon. Why is that?
I don't want to be Black.
Dr. Clark talked to 253 children in Springfield, MA, and Hot Springs, AK.
Springfield, MA
New York
Hot Springs, AK

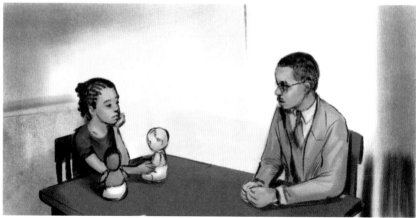

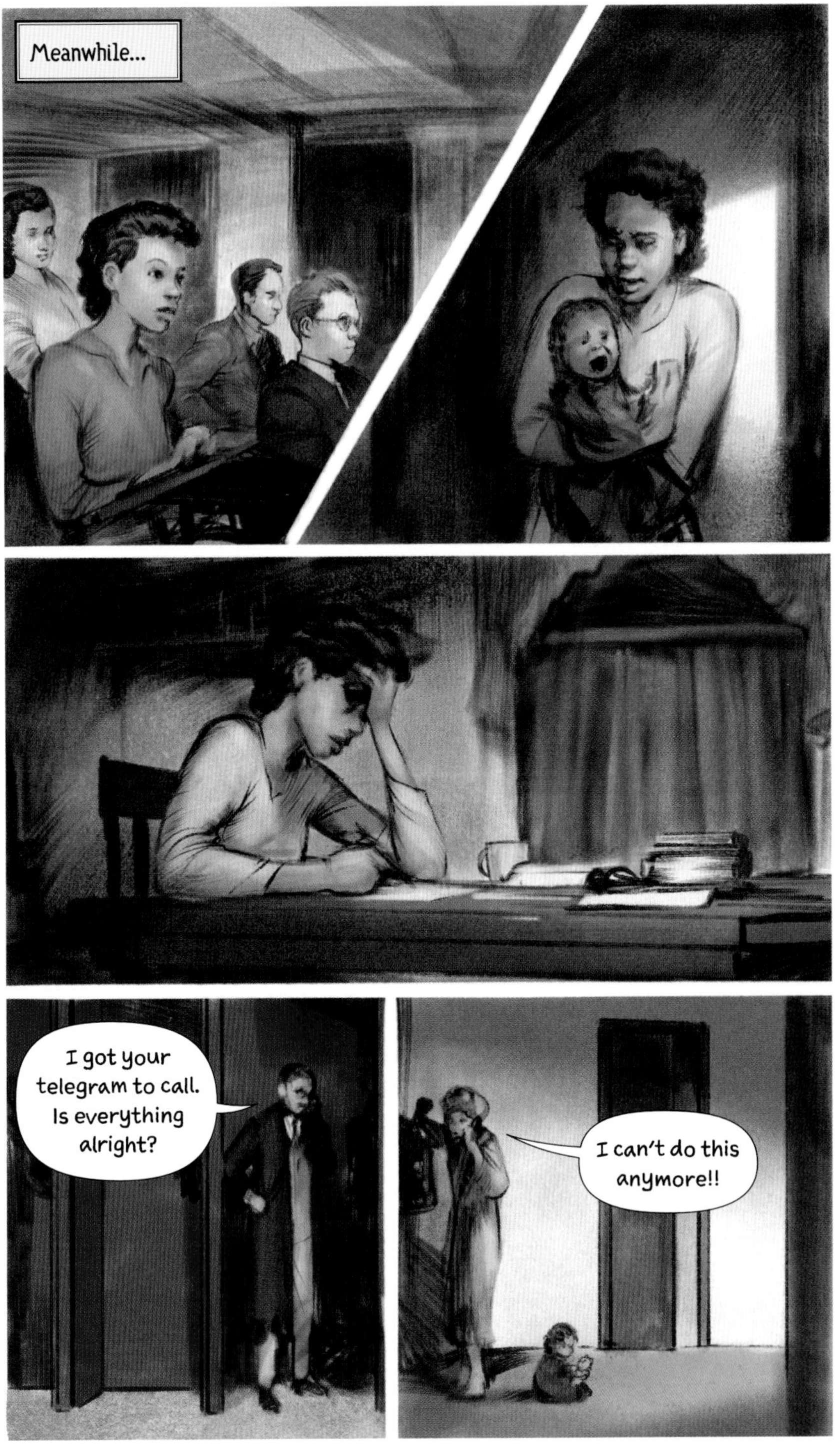
Meanwhile...
I got your telegram to call. Is everything alright?
I can't do this anymore!!

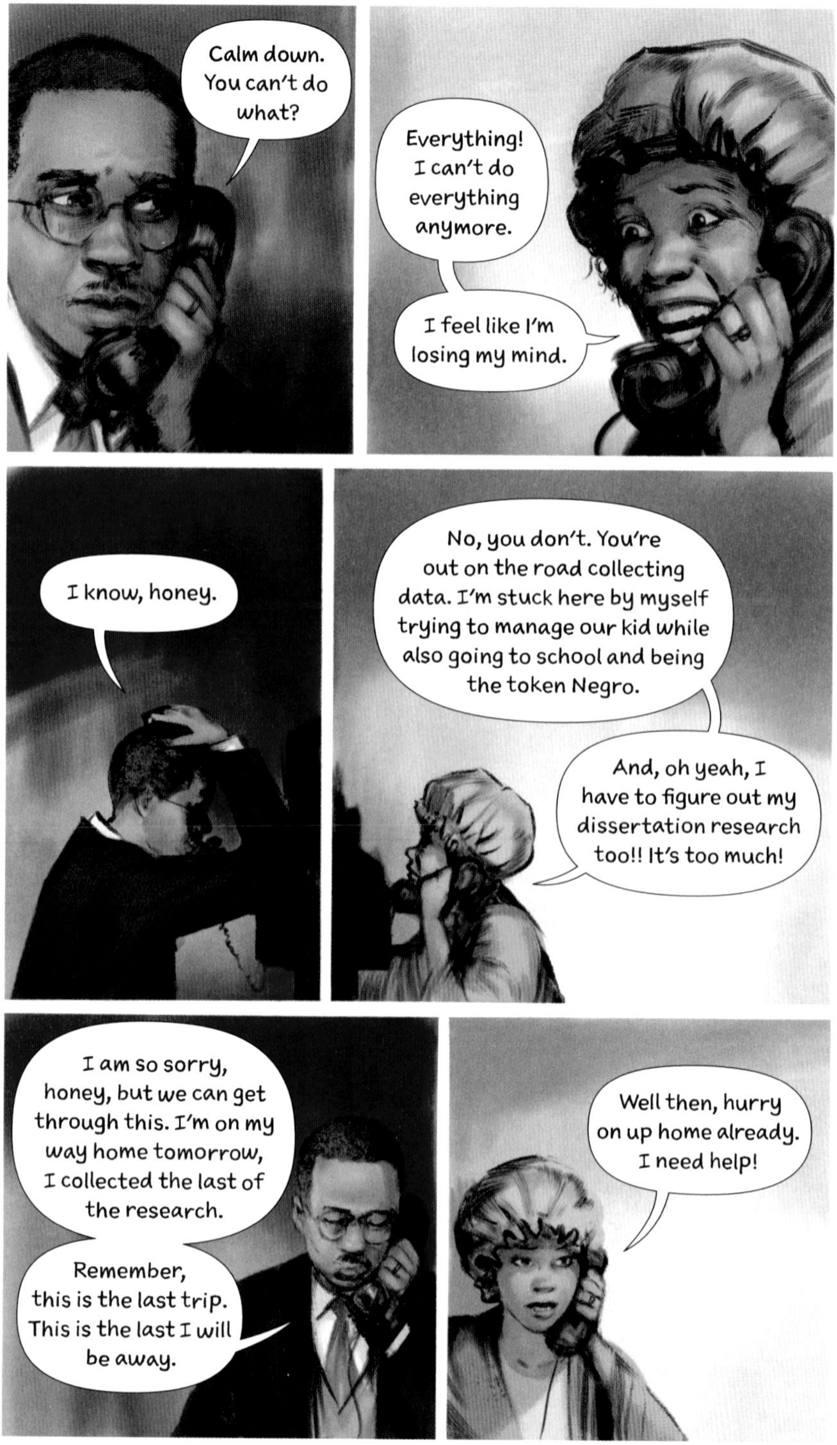
Calm down. You can't do what?
Everything! I can't do everything anymore.
I feel like I'm losing my mind.
I know, honey.
No, you don't. You're out on the road collecting data. I'm stuck here by myself trying to manage our kid while also going to school and being the token Negro.
And, oh yeah, I have to figure out my dissertation research too!! It's too much!
I am so sorry, honey, but we can get through this. I'm on my way home tomorrow, I collected the last of the research.
Remember, this is the last trip. This is the last I will be away.
Well then, hurry on up home already. I need help!

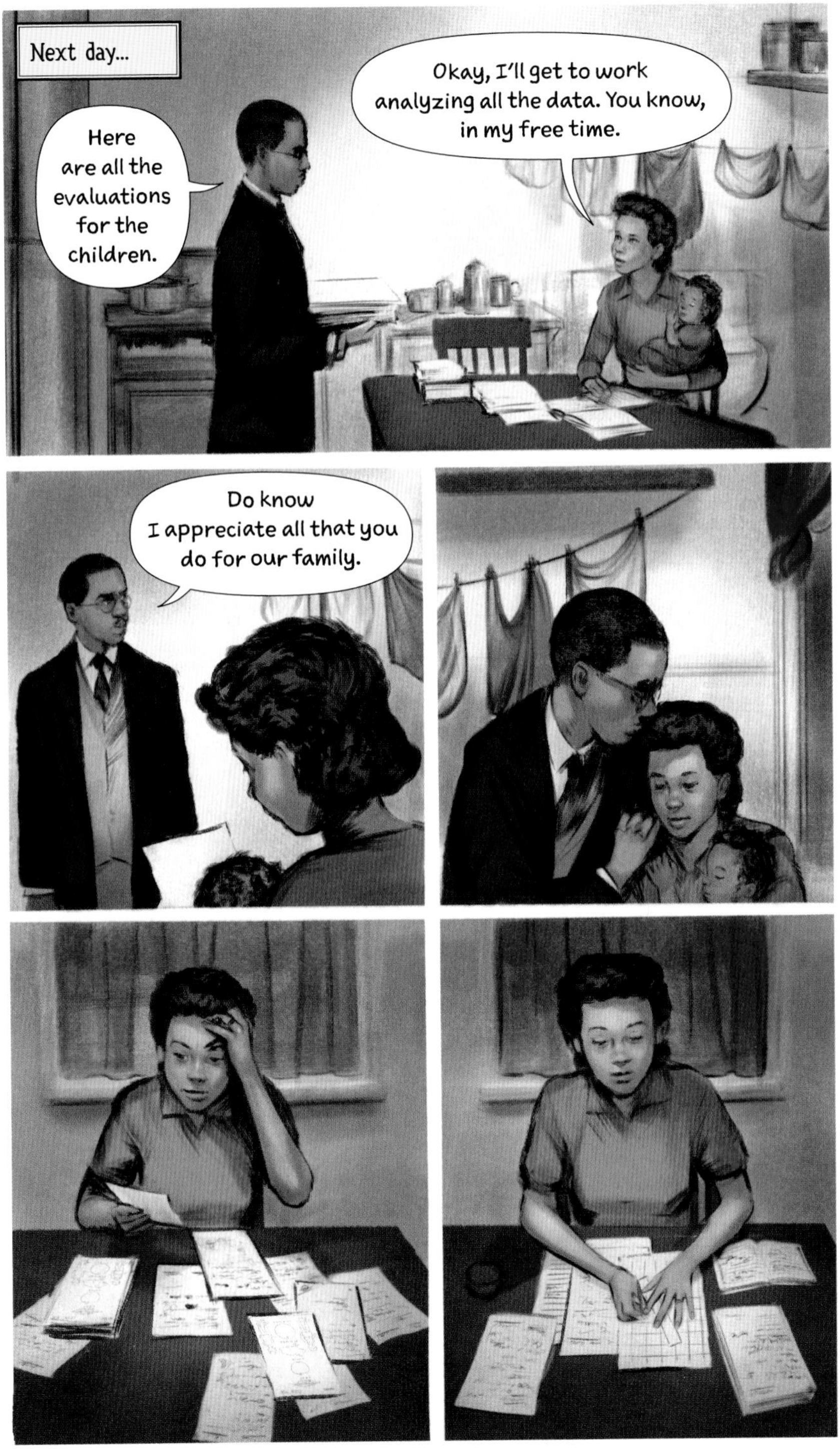

Next day...
Here are all the evaluations for the children.
Okay, I'll get to work analyzing all the data. You know, in my free time.
Do know I appreciate all that you do for our family.

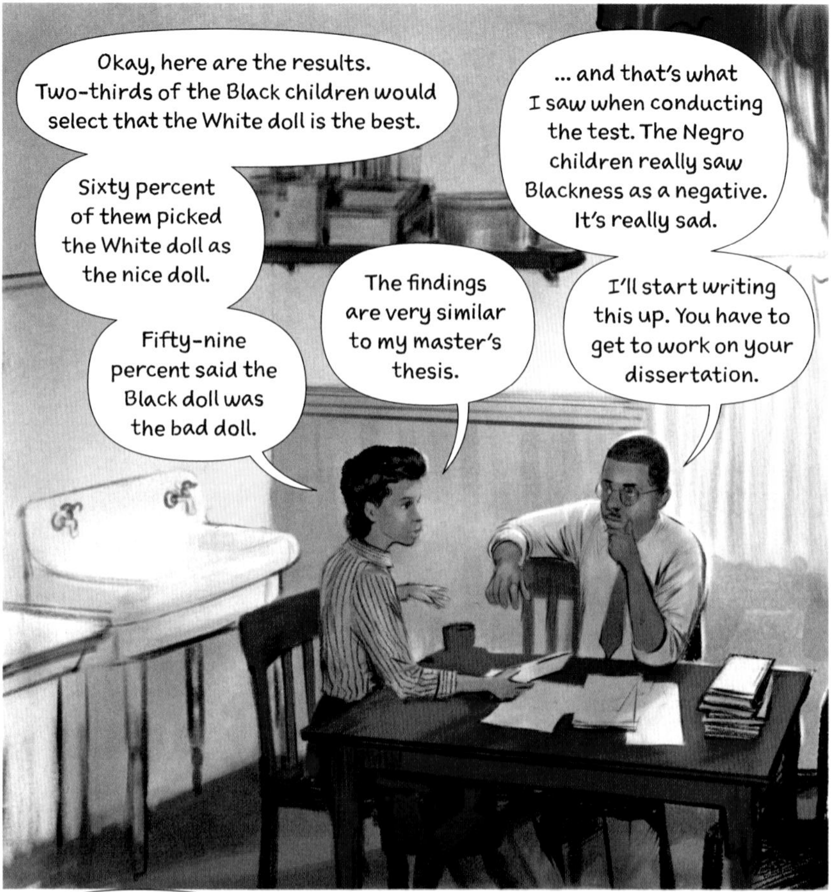
Okay, here are the results. Two-thirds of the Black children would select that the White doll is the best.
Sixty percent of them picked the White doll as the nice doll.
Fifty-nine percent said the Black doll was the bad doll.
... and that's what I saw when conducting the test. The Negro children really saw Blackness as a negative. It's really sad.
The findings are very similar to my master's thesis.
I'll start writing this up. You have to get to work on your dissertation.

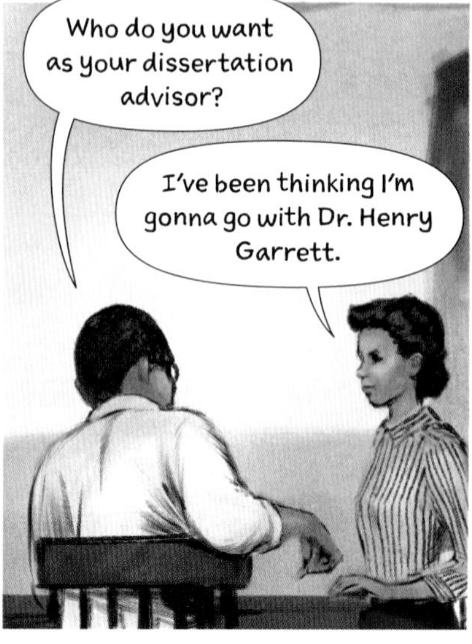
Who do you want as your dissertation advisor?
I've been thinking I'm gonna go with Dr. Henry Garrett.

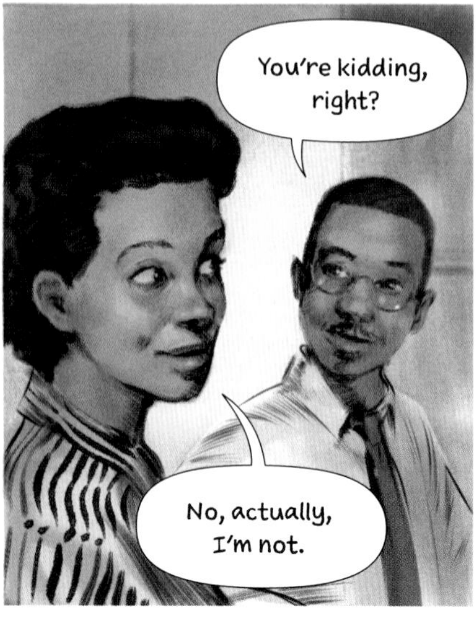
You're kidding, right?
No, actually, I'm not.

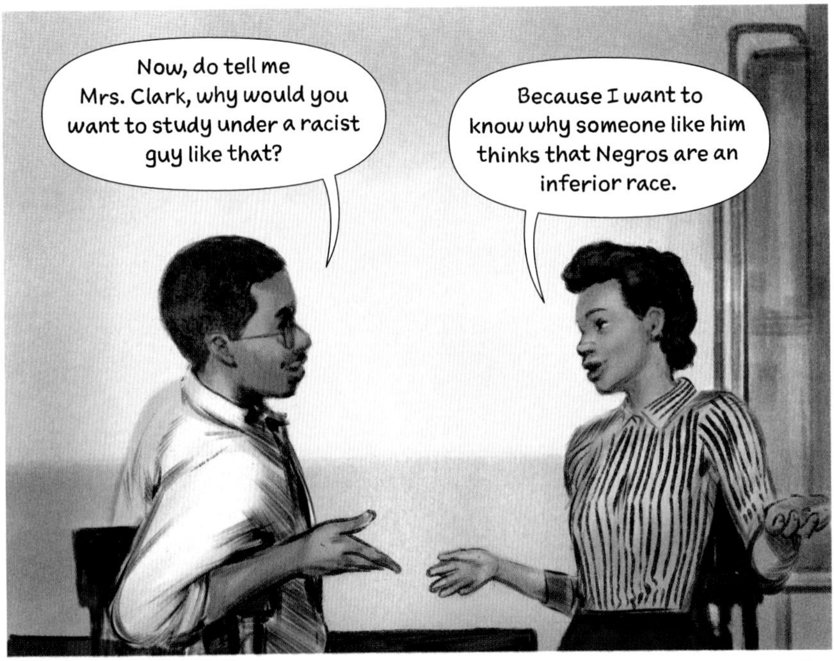
Now, do tell me Mrs. Clark, why would you want to study under a racist guy like that?
Because I want to know why someone like him thinks that Negros are an inferior race.

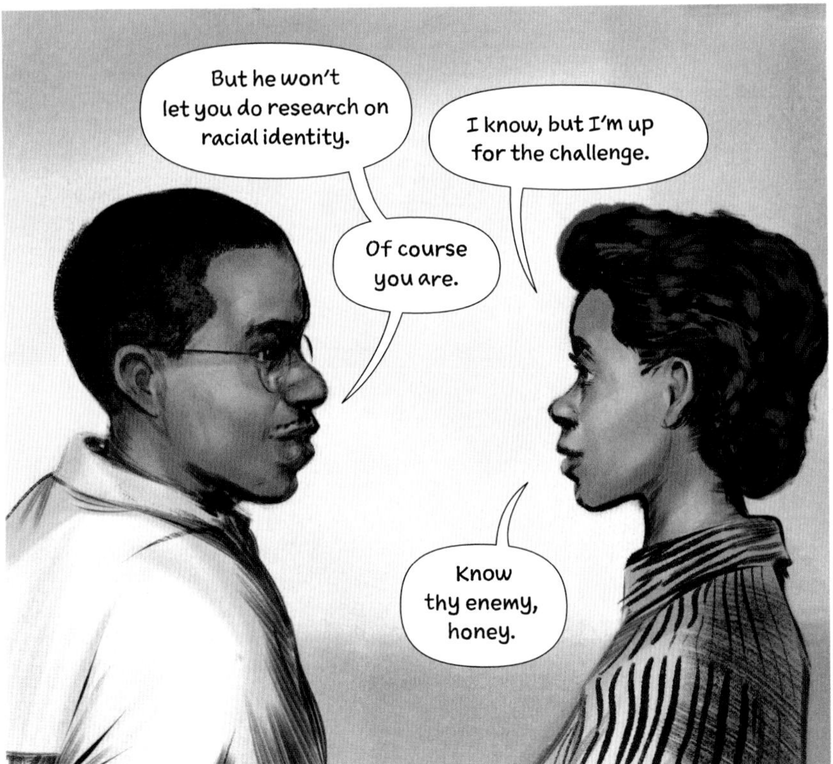
But he won't let you do research on racial identity.
I know, but I'm up for the challenge.
Of course you are.
Know thy enemy, honey.

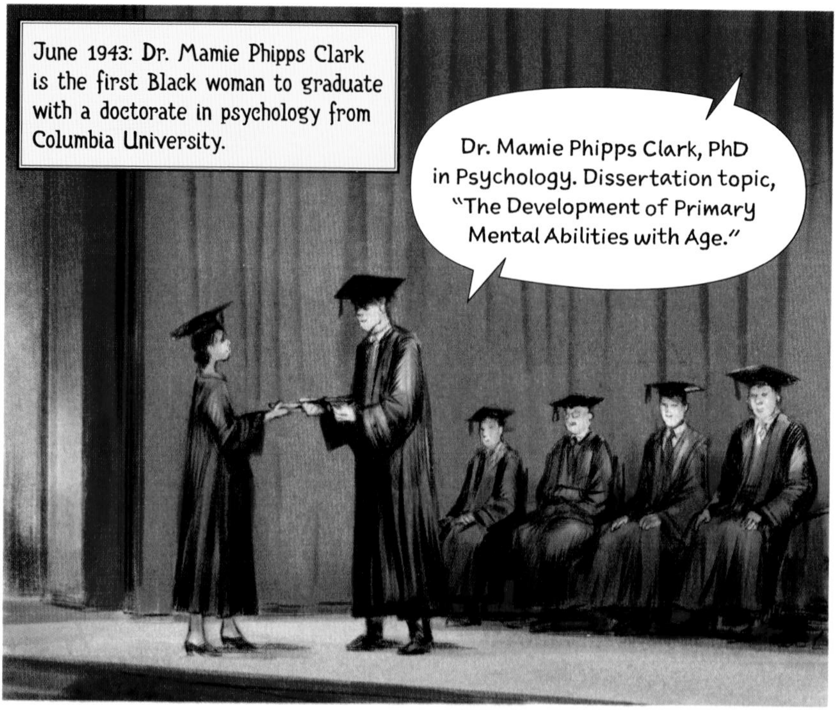
June 1943: Dr. Mamie Phipps Clark is the first Black woman to graduate with a doctorate in psychology from Columbia University.
Dr. Mamie Phipps Clark, PhD in Psychology. Dissertation topic, "The Development of Primary Mental Abilities with Age."

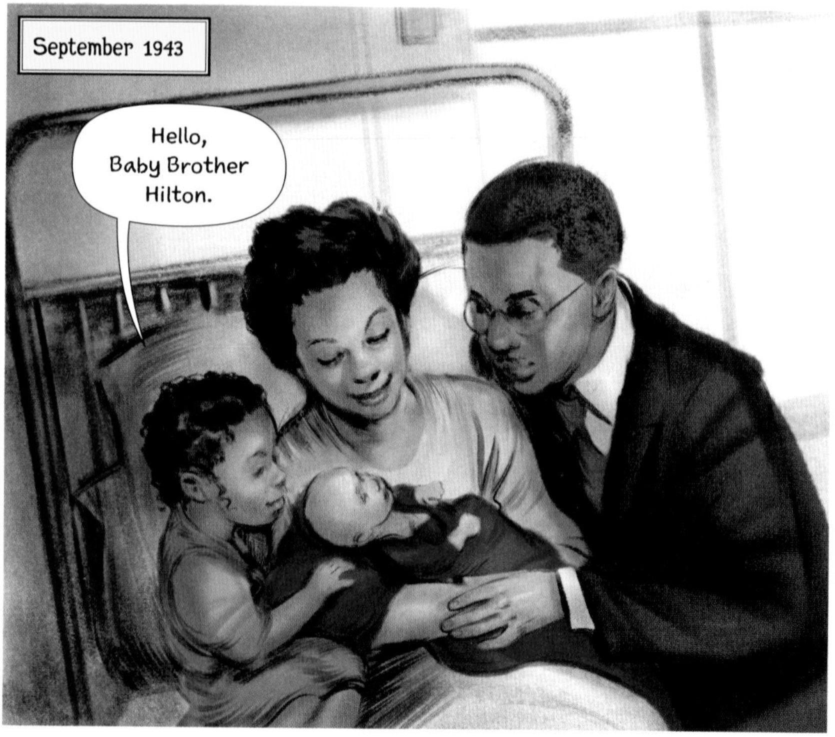
September 1943
Hello, Baby Brother Hilton.

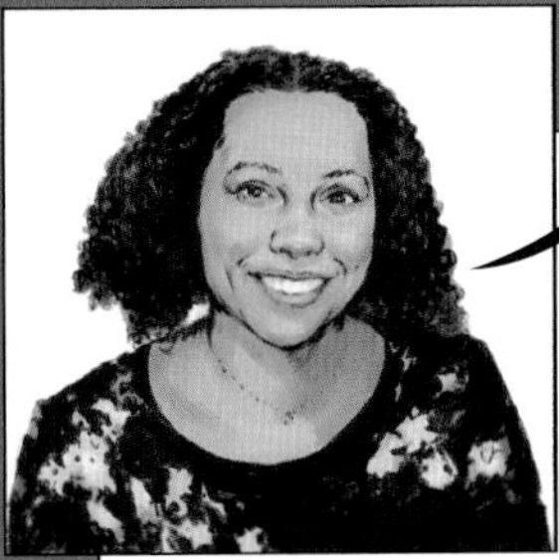

DID YOU KNOW

The Second Shift

The most common jobs for Black women in the 1940s in large cities, like where Mamie lived, were boardinghouse keepers, domestic workers, and beauticians. Those Black women that were educated in college often had jobs as secretaries or teachers. Yet for secretaries and teachers, once they were married, they were not allowed to continue their jobs. The assumption was that marriage would lead to children, and then they would be expected to stay at home.

Mamie was pushing the boundaries as a woman. First, she was the first Black women to go to Columbia University's psychology doctoral program. She was gaining access to higher levels of education that not many Black women had the opportunity to experience. Second, Mamie was also pregnant twice during her time in the program. Most women in her time would have been expected to drop out of school once they were pregnant with their first child, let alone their second. Lastly, Mamie's Rosenwald Fellowship amounted to a full-time job that awarded her a $1500 stipend to complete the Doll Study (See Chapter 4). None of this work accounts for what is often termed the "second shift."

Sociologist Arlie Hochschild was the first to coin the term "second shift," and it refers to the household chores like cooking, cleaning, or doing laundry and childcare duties people manage after working hours. The second shift can be experienced by both men and women, but generally the household and childcare duties fall onto women in the home. Mamie's life was in no way near typical for Black women in the 1940s, but her life did mirror the typical working mother in the U.S. today.

CHAPTER 5:

Research and School Desegregation

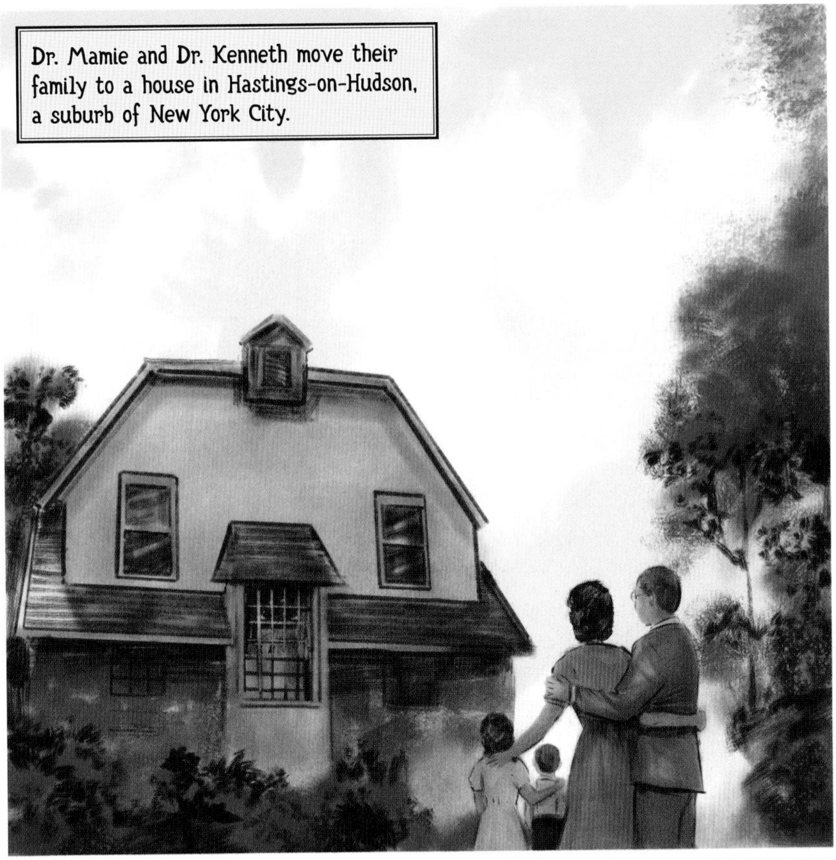
Dr. Mamie and Dr. Kenneth move their family to a house in Hastings-on-Hudson, a suburb of New York City.

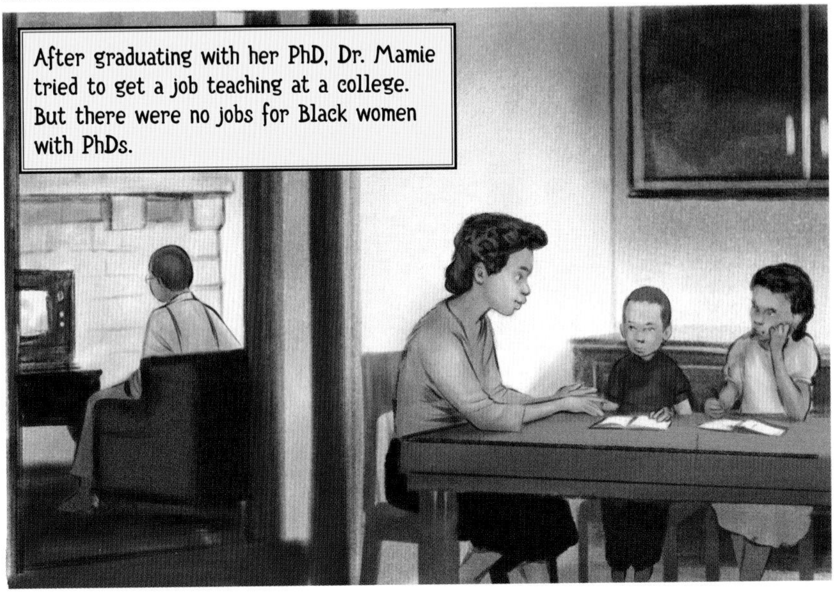
After graduating with her PhD, Dr. Mamie tried to get a job teaching at a college. But there were no jobs for Black women with PhDs.

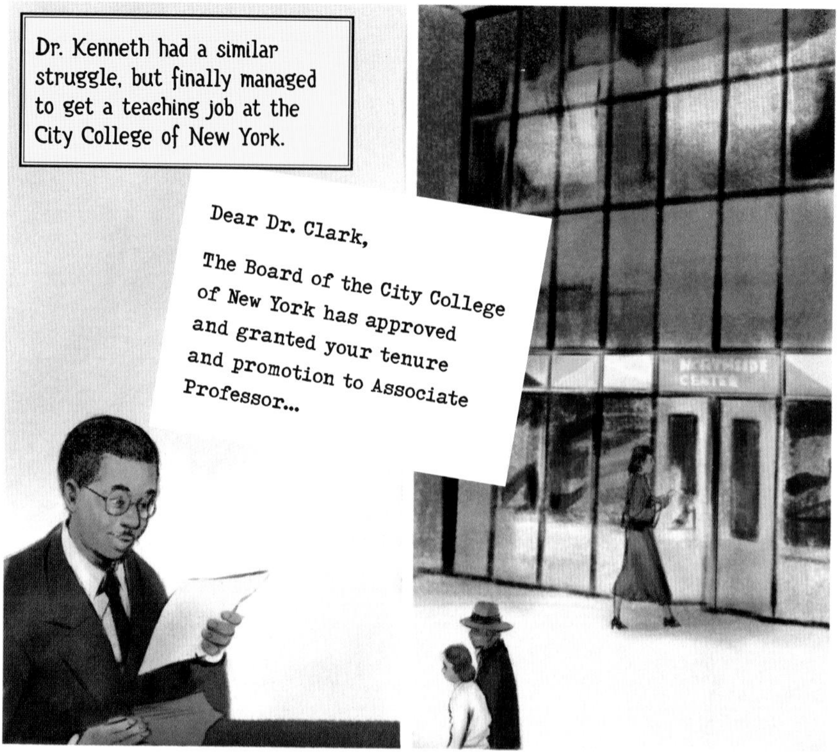
Dr. Kenneth had a similar struggle, but finally managed to get a teaching job at the City College of New York.
Dear Dr. Clark,
The Board of the City College of New York has approved and granted your tenure and promotion to Associate Professor...

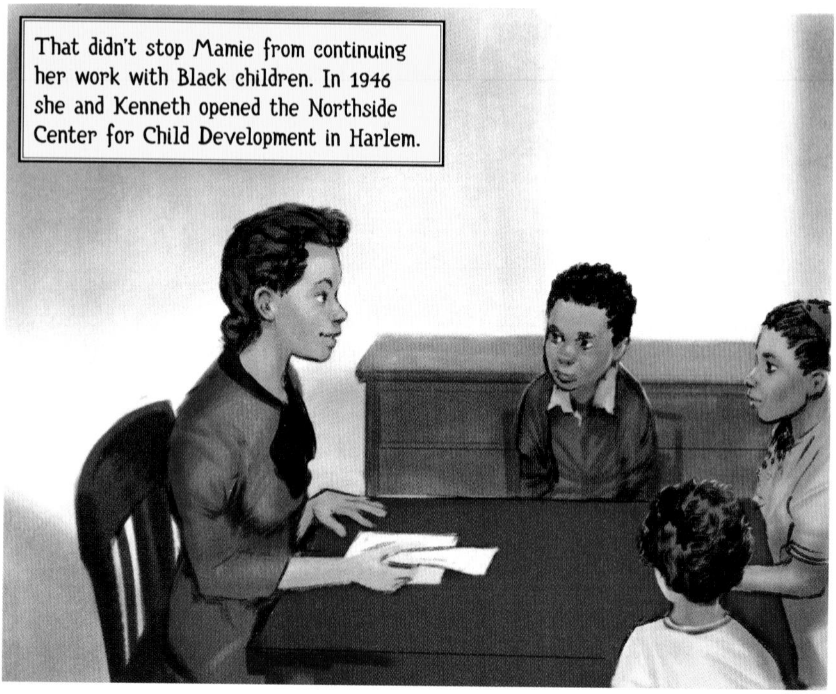
That didn't stop Mamie from continuing her work with Black children. In 1946 she and Kenneth opened the Northside Center for Child Development in Harlem.

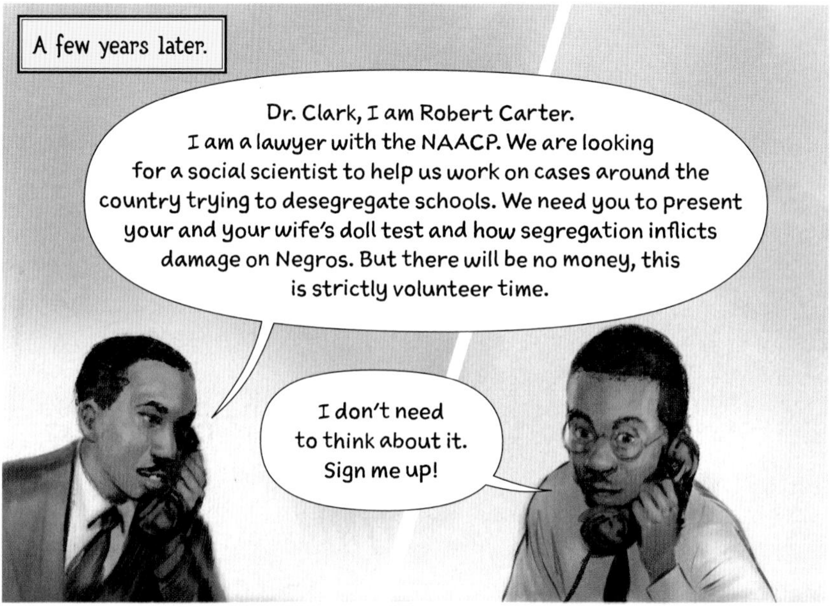
A few years later.
Dr. Clark, I am Robert Carter. I am a lawyer with the NAACP. We are looking for a social scientist to help us work on cases around the country trying to desegregate schools. We need you to present your and your wife's doll test and how segregation inflicts damage on Negros. But there will be no money, this is strictly volunteer time.
I don't need to think about it. Sign me up!

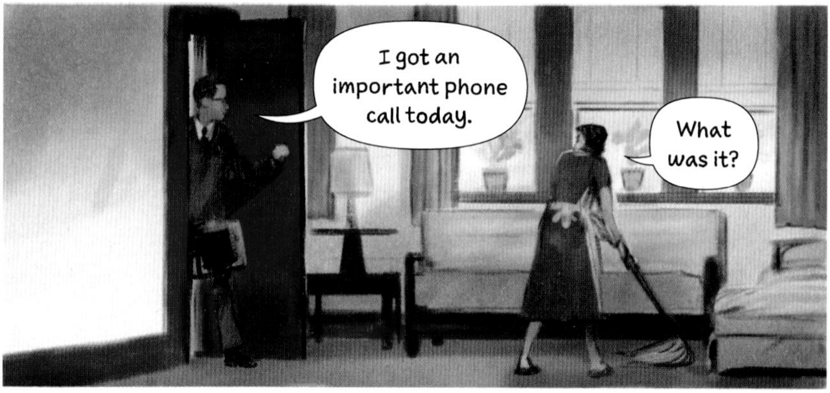
I got an important phone call today.
What was it?

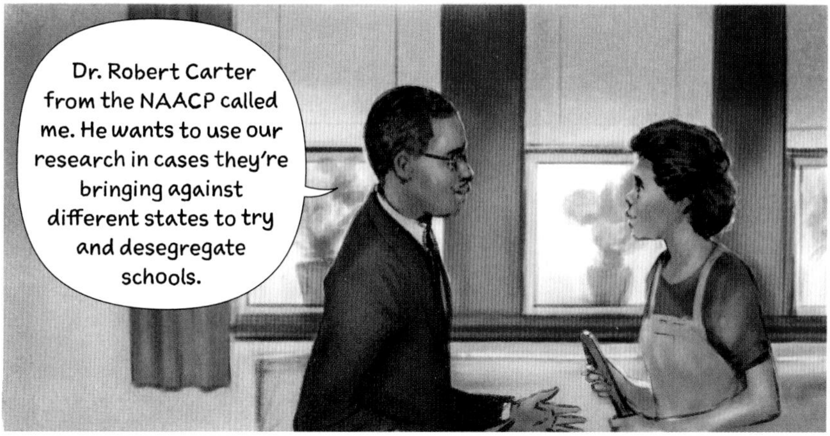
Dr. Robert Carter from the NAACP called me. He wants to use our research in cases they're bringing against different states to try and desegregate schools.

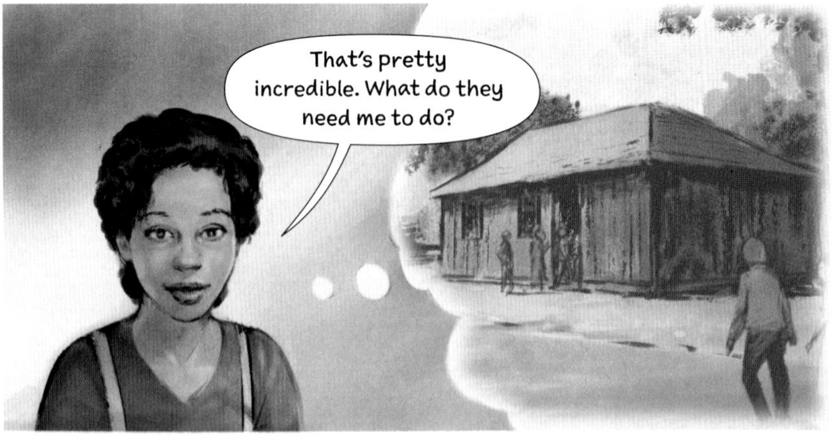
That's pretty incredible. What do they need me to do?

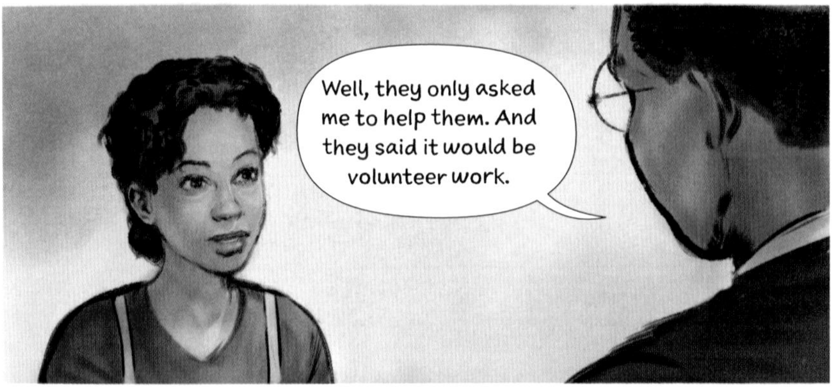
Well, they only asked me to help them. And they said it would be volunteer work.

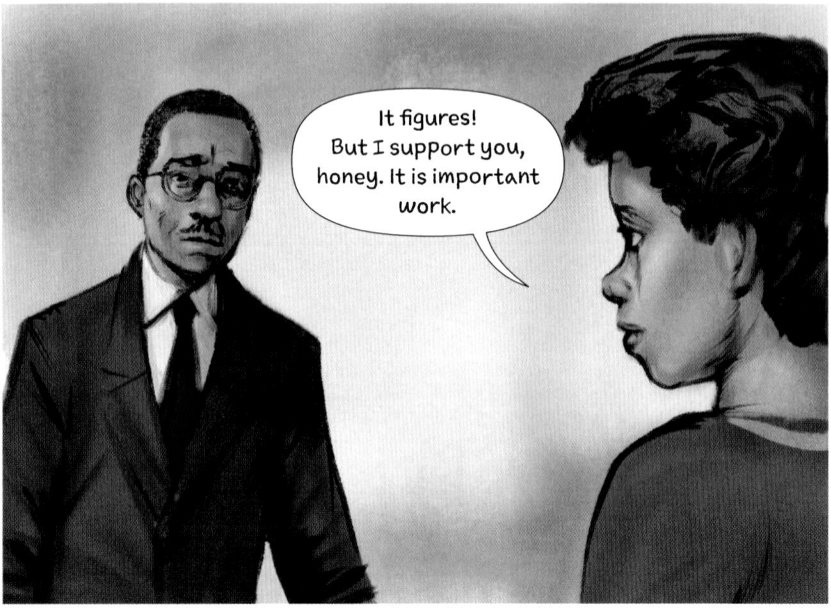
It figures! But I support you, honey. It is important work.

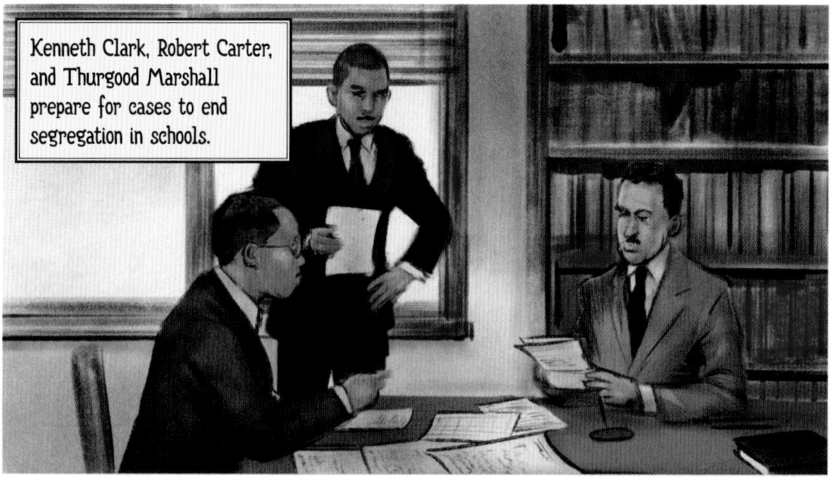
Kenneth Clark, Robert Carter, and Thurgood Marshall prepare for cases to end segregation in schools.

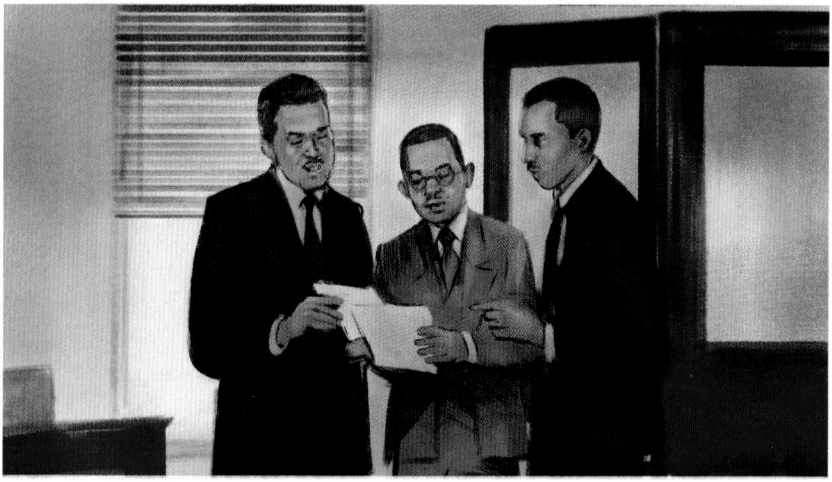

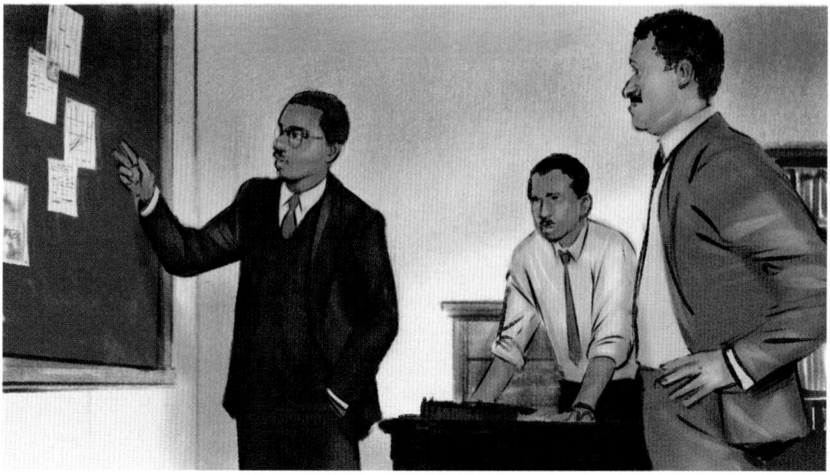

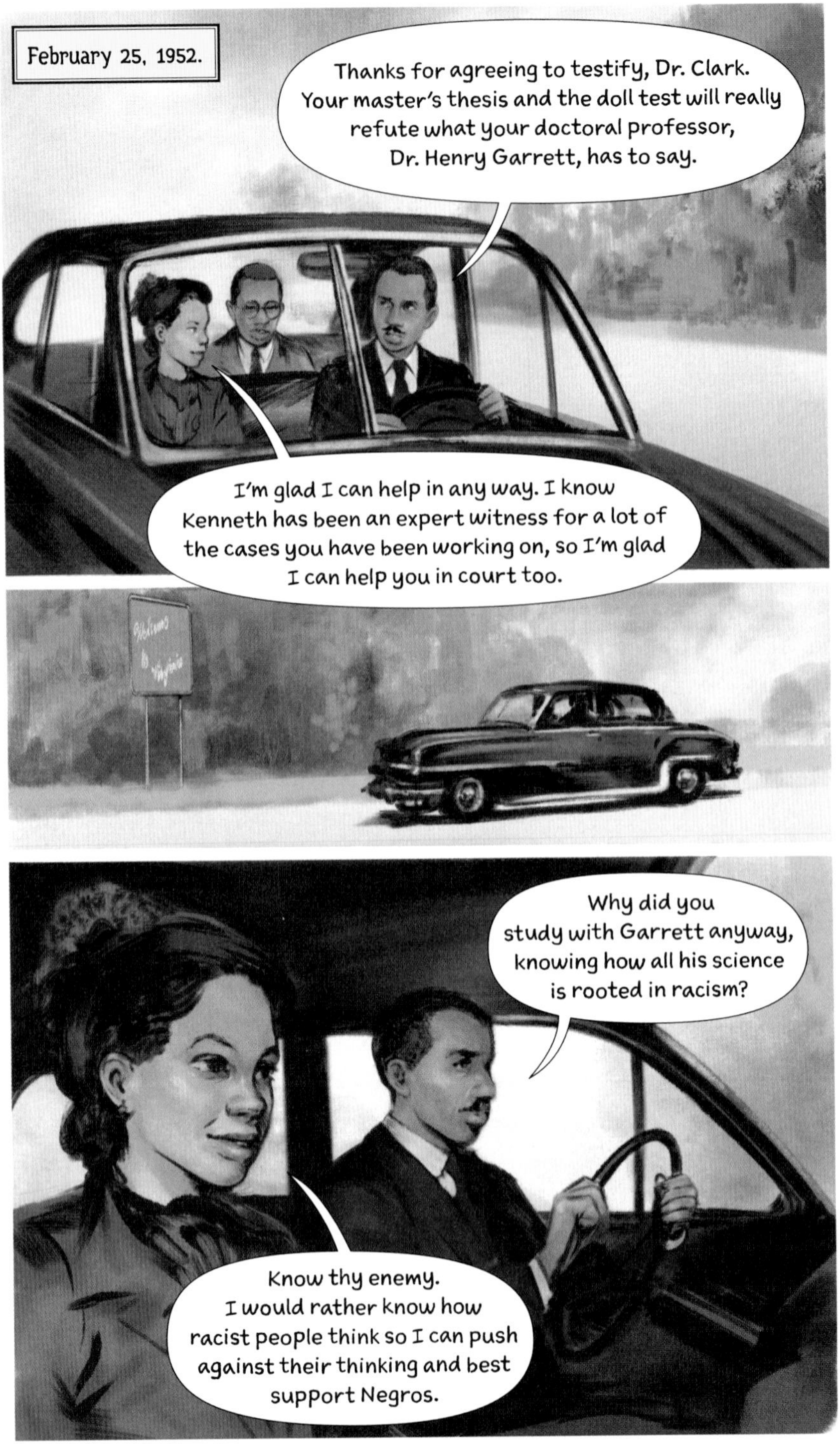
February 25, 1952.
Thanks for agreeing to testify, Dr. Clark. Your master's thesis and the doll test will really refute what your doctoral professor, Dr. Henry Garrett, has to say.
I'm glad I can help in any way. I know Kenneth has been an expert witness for a lot of the cases you have been working on, so I'm glad I can help you in court too.
Why did you study with Garrett anyway, knowing how all his science is rooted in racism?
Know thy enemy. I would rather know how racist people think so I can push against their thinking and best support Negros.

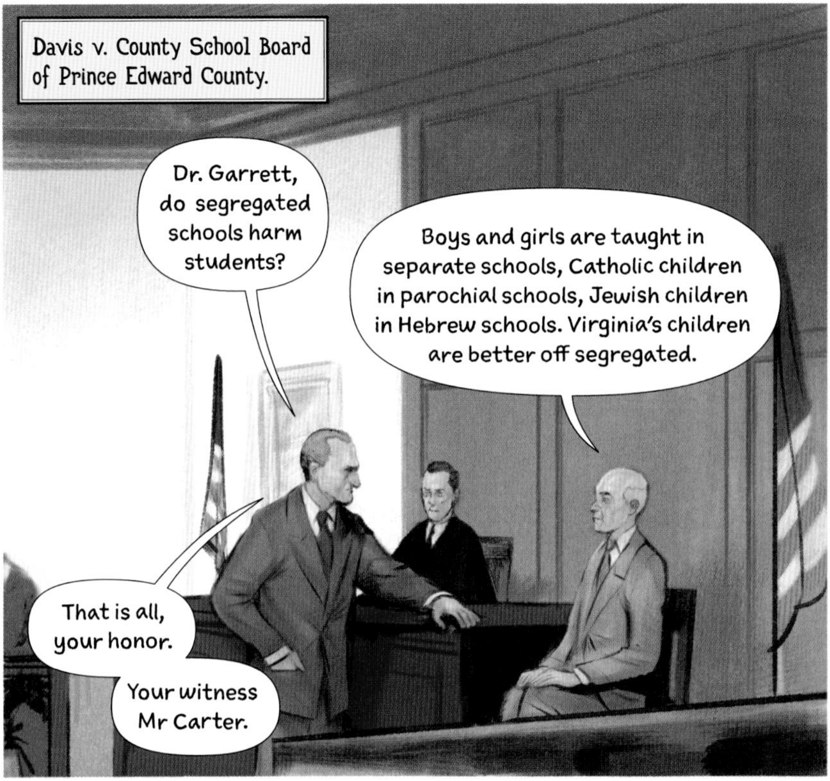
Davis v. County School Board of Prince Edward County.
Dr. Garrett, do segregated schools harm students?
Boys and girls are taught in separate schools, Catholic children in parochial schools, Jewish children in Hebrew schools. Virginia's children are better off segregated.
That is all, your honor.
Your witness Mr Carter.

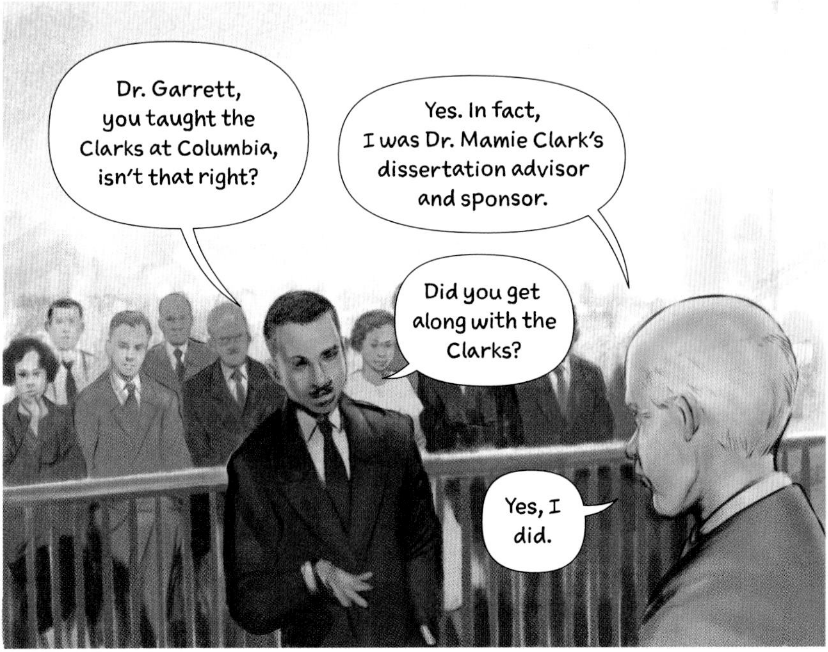
Dr. Garrett, you taught the Clarks at Columbia, isn't that right?
Yes. In fact, I was Dr. Mamie Clark's dissertation advisor and sponsor.
Did you get along with the Clarks?
Yes, I did.

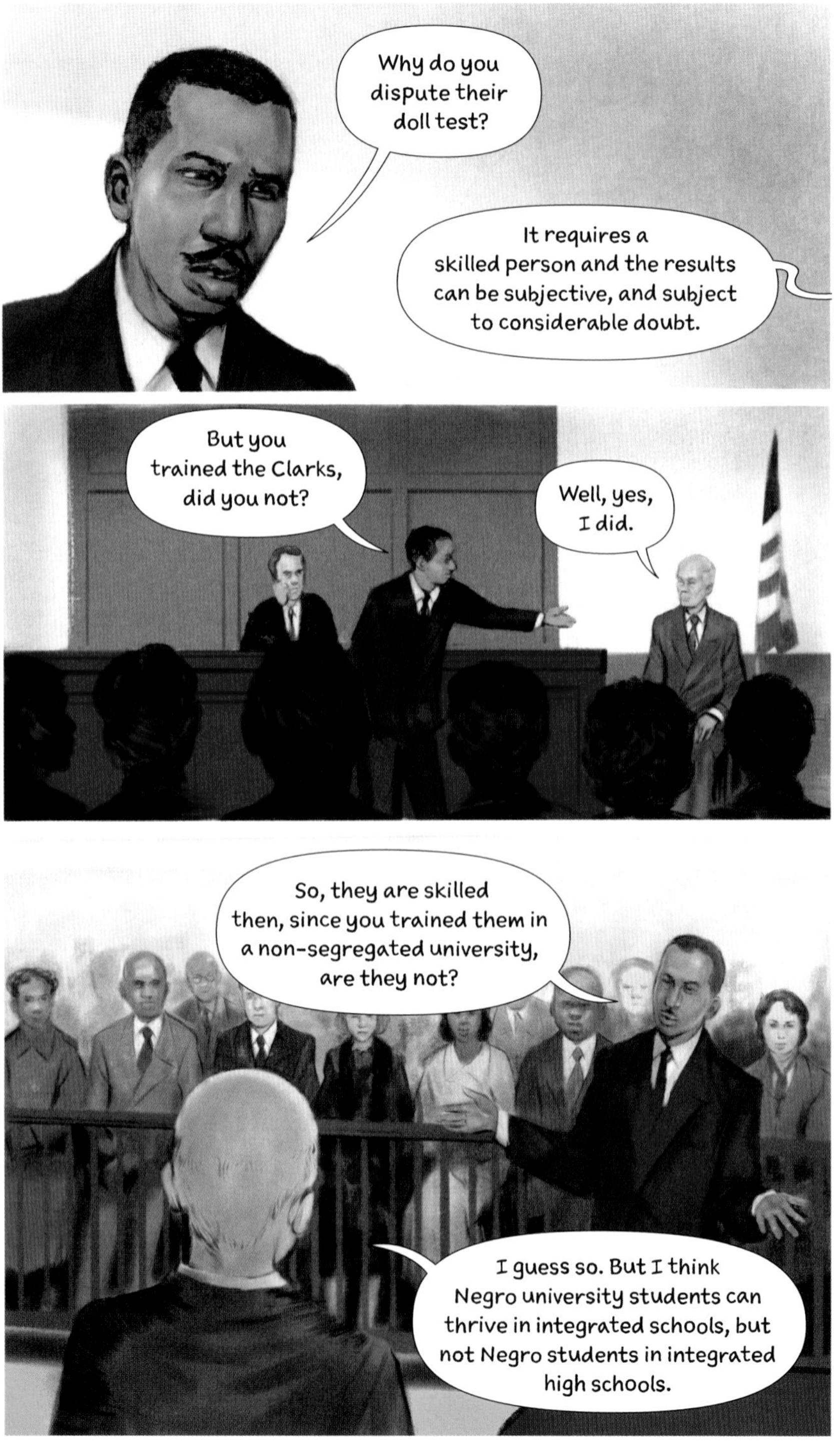
Why do you dispute their doll test?
It requires a skilled person and the results can be subjective, and subject to considerable doubt.
But you trained the Clarks, did you not?
Well, yes, I did.
So, they are skilled then, since you trained them in a non-segregated university, are they not?
I guess so. But I think Negro university students can thrive in integrated schools, but not Negro students in integrated high schools.

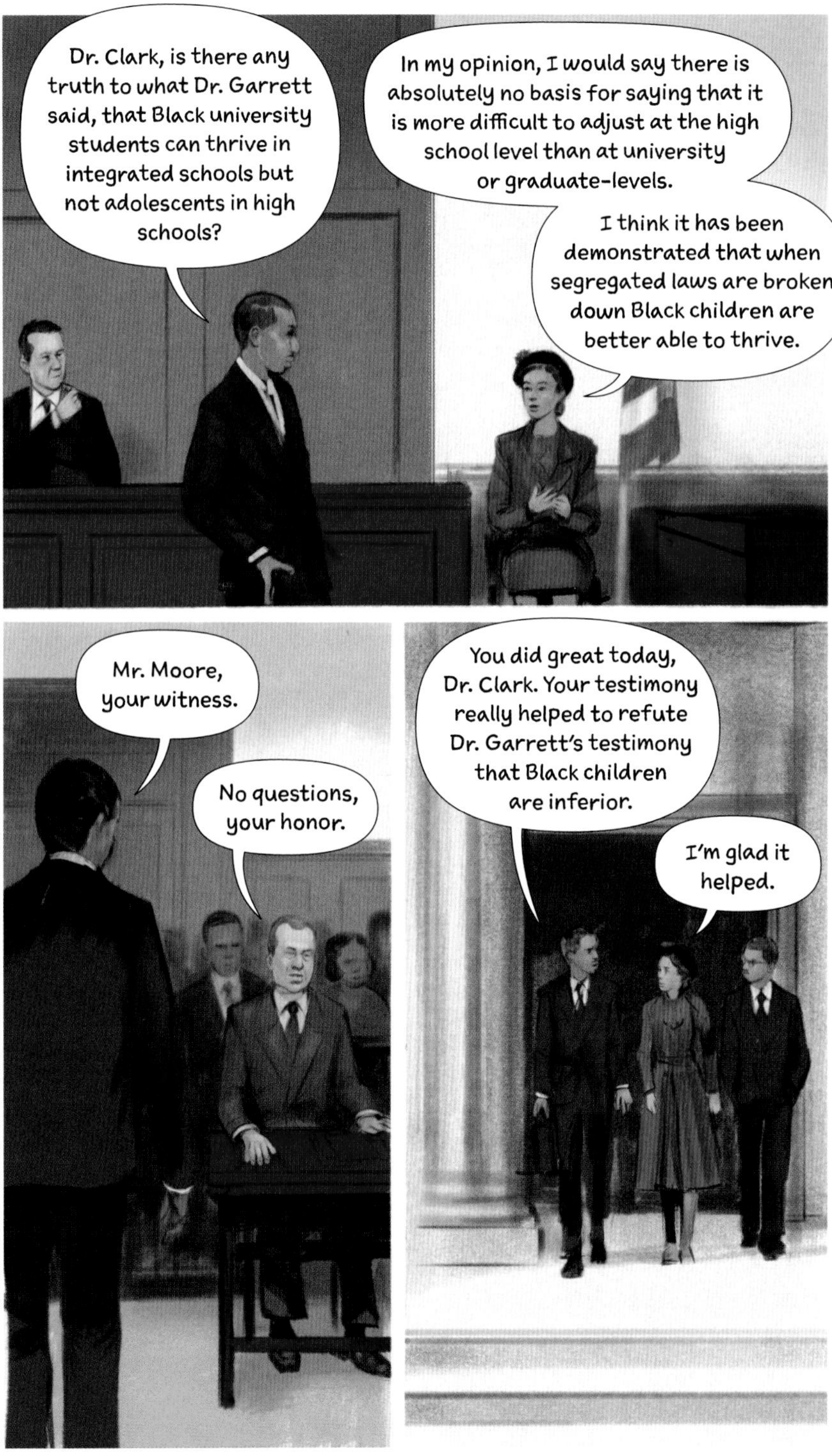
Dr. Clark, is there any truth to what Dr. Garrett said, that Black university students can thrive in integrated schools but not adolescents in high schools?
In my opinion, I would say there is absolutely no basis for saying that it is more difficult to adjust at the high school level than at university or graduate-levels.
I think it has been demonstrated that when segregated laws are broken down Black children are better able to thrive.
Mr. Moore, your witness.
No questions, your honor.
You did great today, Dr. Clark. Your testimony really helped to refute Dr. Garrett's testimony that Black children are inferior.
I'm glad it helped.

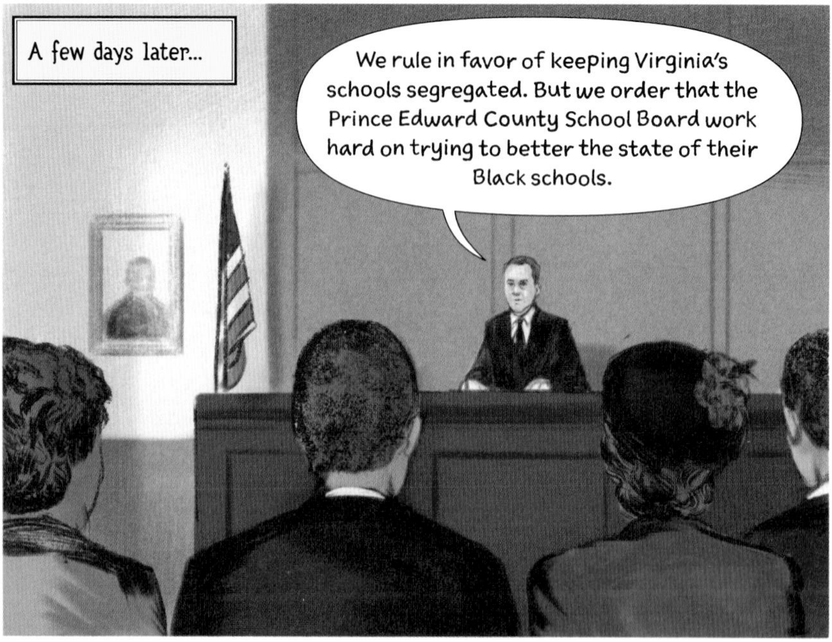
A few days later...
We rule in favor of keeping Virginia's schools segregated. But we order that the Prince Edward County School Board work hard on trying to better the state of their Black schools.

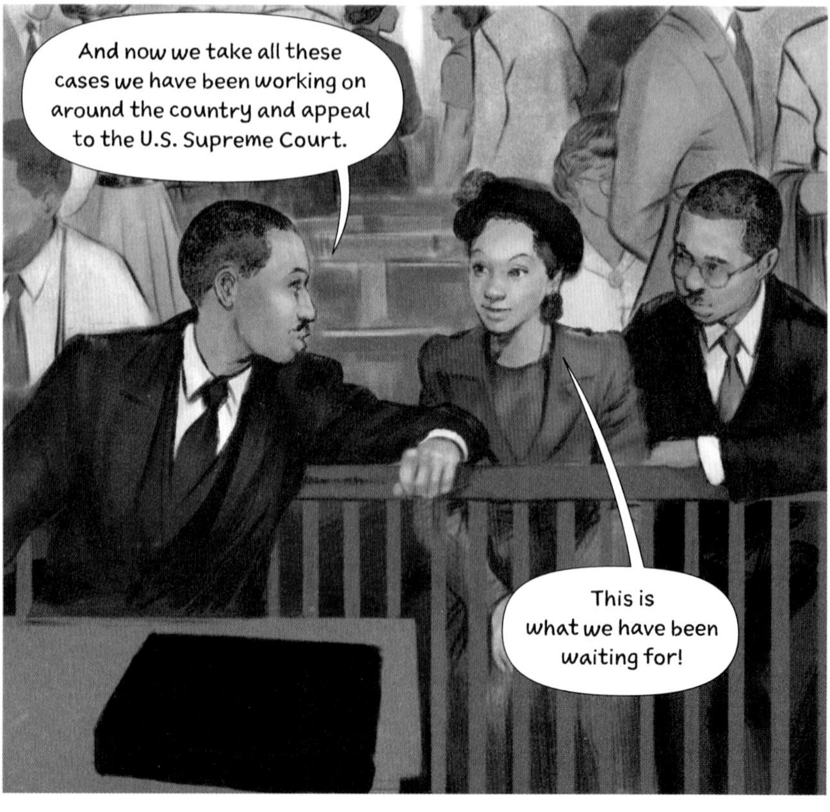
And now we take all these cases we have been working on around the country and appeal to the U.S. Supreme Court.
This is what we have been waiting for!

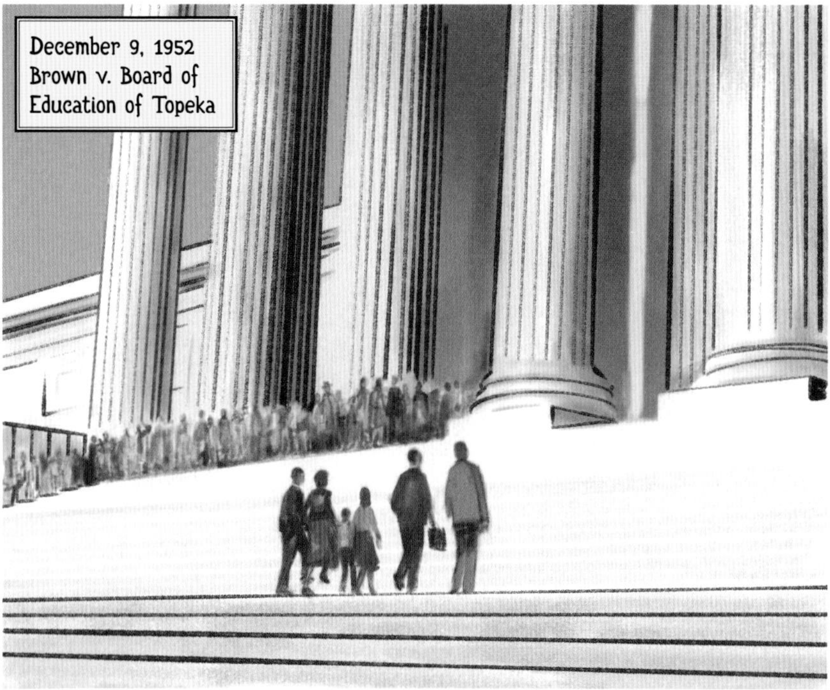
December 9, 1952
Brown v. Board of
Education of Topeka

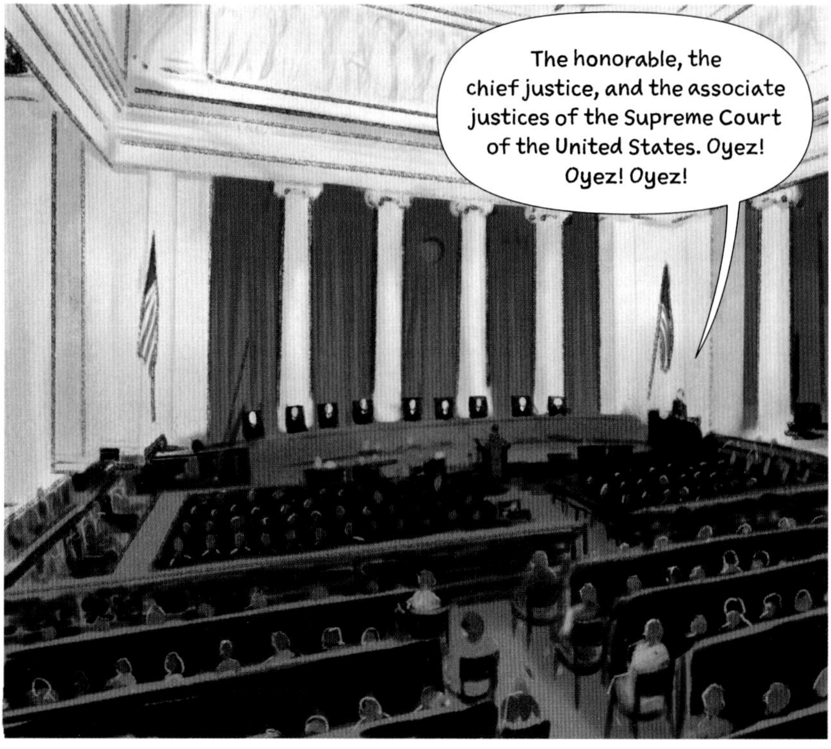
The honorable, the chief justice, and the associate justices of the Supreme Court of the United States. Oyez! Oyez! Oyez!

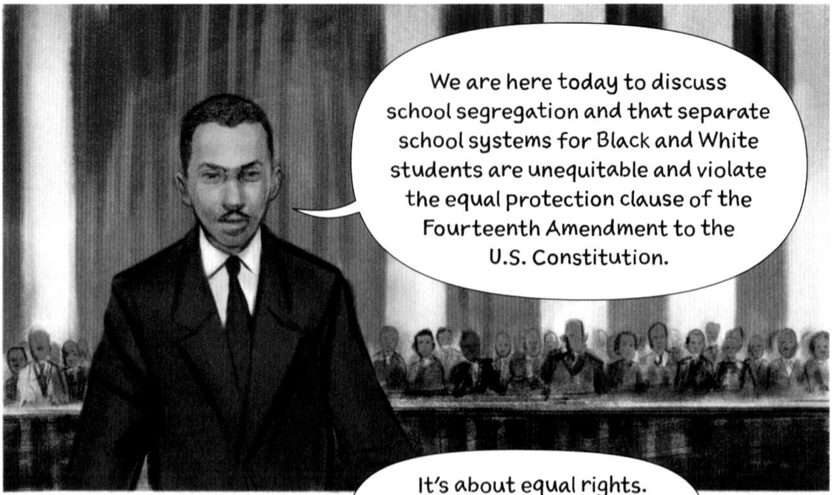
We are here today to discuss school segregation and that separate school systems for Black and White students are unequitable and violate the equal protection clause of the Fourteenth Amendment to the U.S. Constitution.

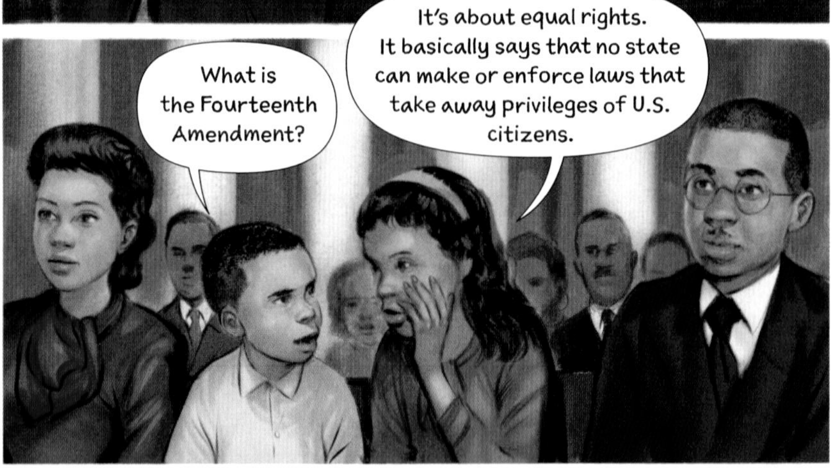
What is the Fourteenth Amendment?
It's about equal rights. It basically says that no state can make or enforce laws that take away privileges of U.S. citizens.

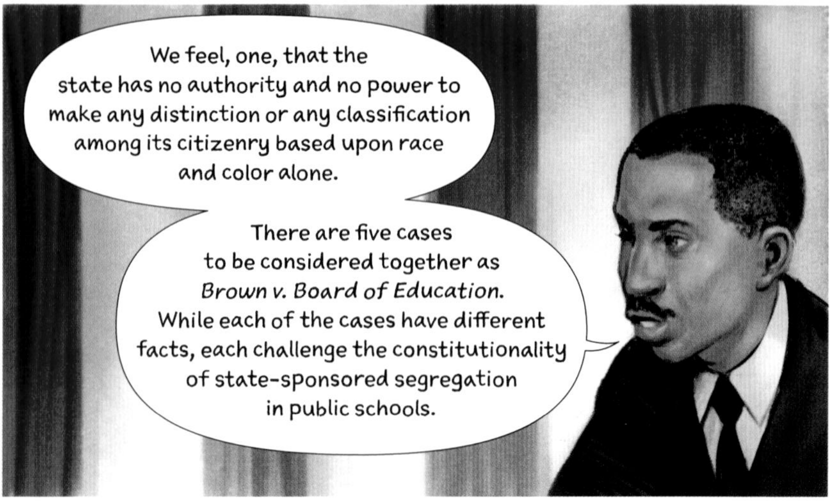
We feel, one, that the state has no authority and no power to make any distinction or any classification among its citizenry based upon race and color alone.
There are five cases to be considered together as *Brown v. Board of Education.* While each of the cases have different facts, each challenge the constitutionality of state-sponsored segregation in public schools.

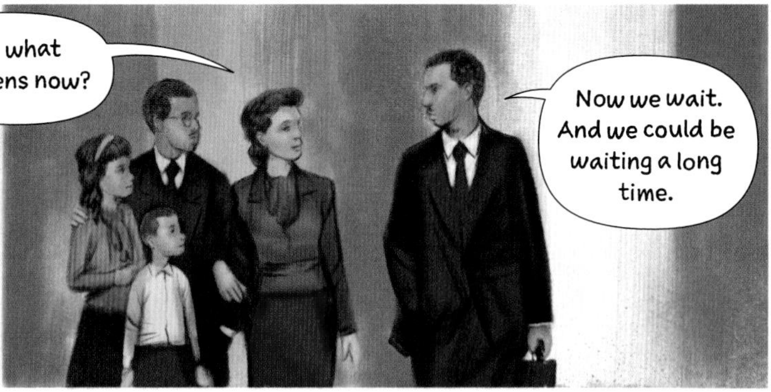
So, what happens now?
Now we wait. And we could be waiting a long time.

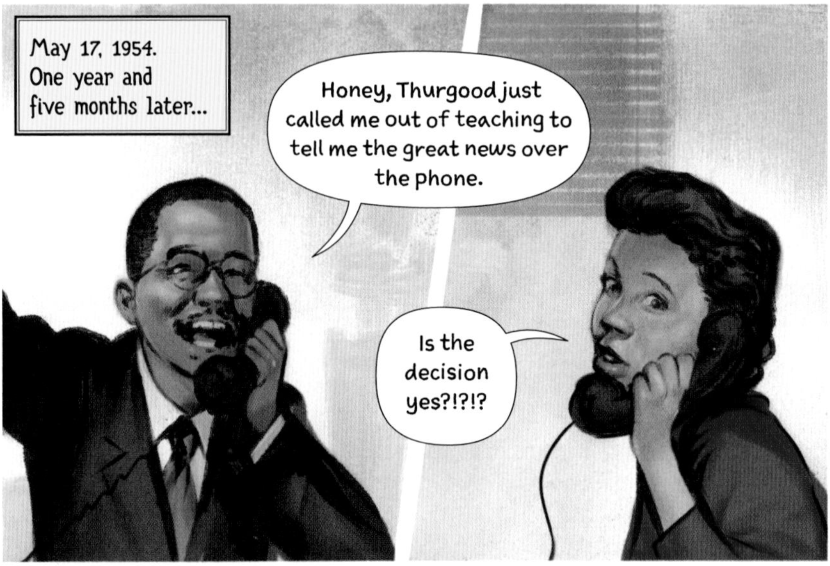
May 17, 1954. One year and five months later...
Honey, Thurgood just called me out of teaching to tell me the great news over the phone.
Is the decision yes?!?!?

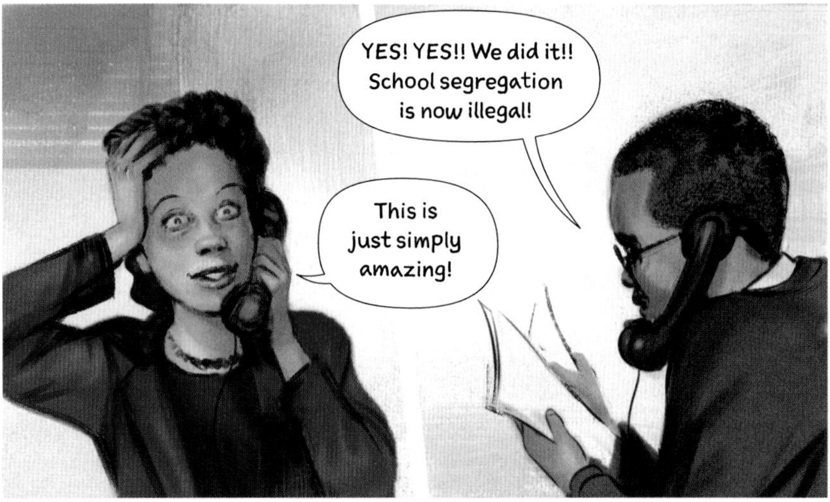
YES! YES!! We did it!! School segregation is now illegal!
This is just simply amazing!

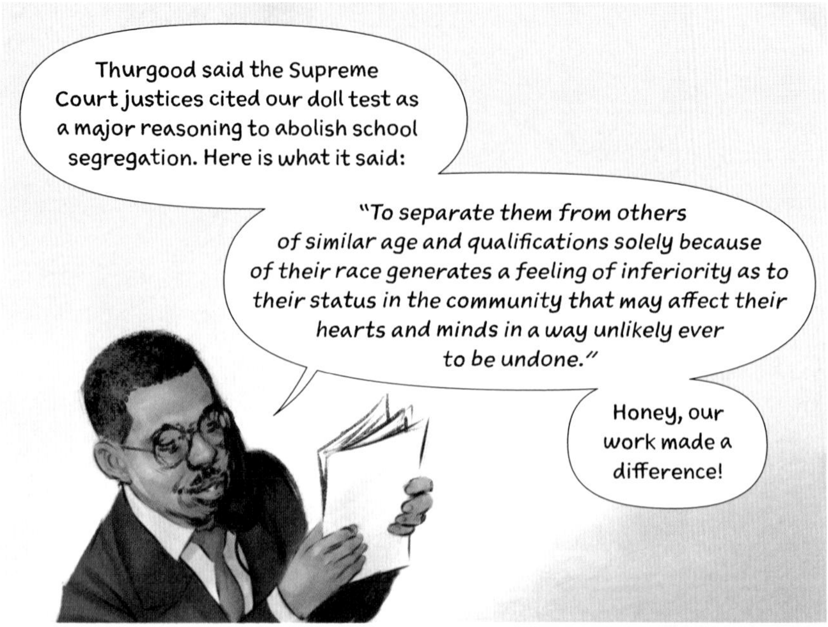
Thurgood said the Supreme Court justices cited our doll test as a major reasoning to abolish school segregation. Here is what it said:
"To separate them from others of similar age and qualifications solely because of their race generates a feeling of inferiority as to their status in the community that may affect their hearts and minds in a way unlikely ever to be undone."
Honey, our work made a difference!

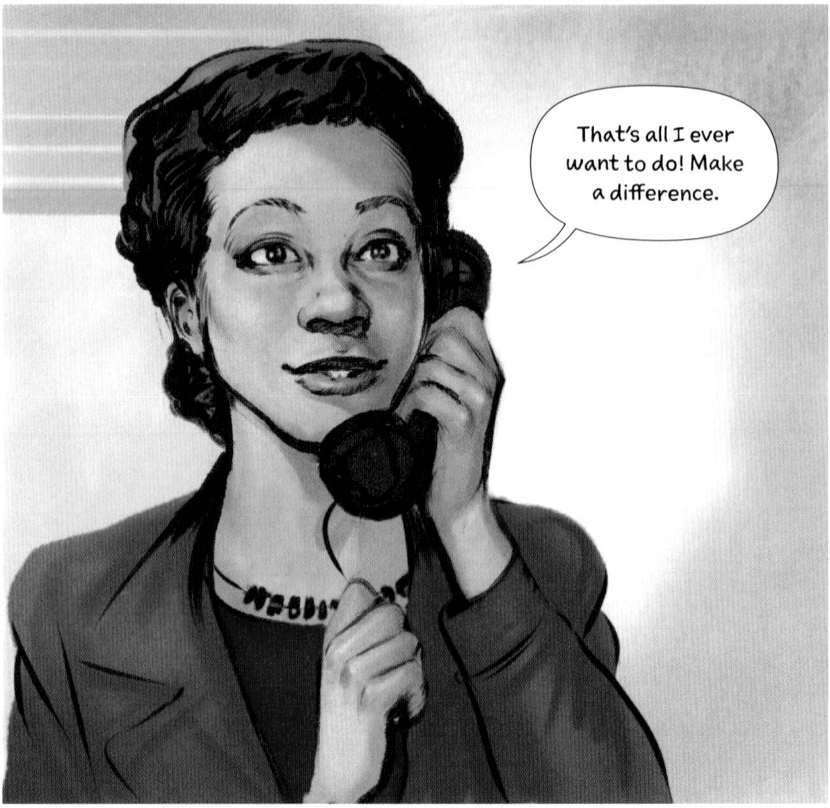
That's all I ever want to do! Make a difference.

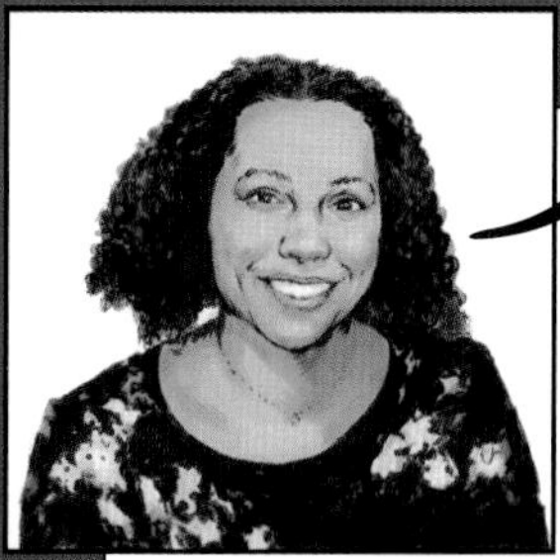

DID YOU KNOW

Hedgepeth-Williams Case

There were many cases that were important leading up to the *Brown v. Board of Education* case desegregating schools. One of these important cases was called the Hedgepeth-Williams case. In 1944, two mothers decided to bring a lawsuit against racial segregation to the Trenton Public Schools. Trenton is a small city (population 124,000 people in the 1940s) in New Jersey that, at the time, had schools segregated by race. Two Black middle school students, Janet Hedgepeth and Leon Williams, tried to enroll in the local all-White school called Junior High No. 2. They were famously told by the principal that Junior High No. 2 was "not built for Negros." Instead, they were informed that they needed to go to the all-Black school called the New Lincoln School. The New Lincoln School was one of four school buildings in the city that were built exclusively for educating Black children.

The New Lincoln School had a great reputation for educating its Black students, but the issue was physical distance. Unfortunately, the New Lincoln School was located 2.5 miles away from Janet and Leon's homes. There were no school buses in those days, so that would mean that they would have to walk 5 miles each day to get back and forth to school. This seems like an impossible feat to do daily given all the time and energy needed to walk 5 miles. Janet and Leon's mothers, Gladys Hedgepeth and Berline Williams, decided to bring a court case against the Trenton Board of Education to challenge the school's refusal to let

Janet and Leon into the school based on their race. This became known as the *Hedgepeth-Williams v. Trenton Board of Education* case.

The lawsuit went all the way up to the New Jersey Supreme Court. On January 31, 1944, the court decided in favor of Janet and Leon. Ultimately, they decided that Junior High No. 2 was unlawfully discriminating against the students based on their race. This was an important case for desegregating schools in America, as this case was referenced in the *Brown v. Board of Education* case that was decided May 17, 1954.

Trenton started to move toward desegregating schools.

New Lincoln School

Janet, Leon, and 200 other Black children were admitted to Junior High No. 2. And in 1946, White students started to enroll in the New Lincoln School. The principal of the New Lincoln School prior to desegregation was Patton J. Hill. Mr. Hill continued as principal of the New Lincoln School during desegregation, which made history. He was one of the first Black principals in the nation to serve White students.

The Junior High No. 2 school building still exists in Trenton today. The Hedgepeth-Williams Case was so iconic that Junior High No. 2 is now renamed the Hedgepeth-Williams Intermediate School.

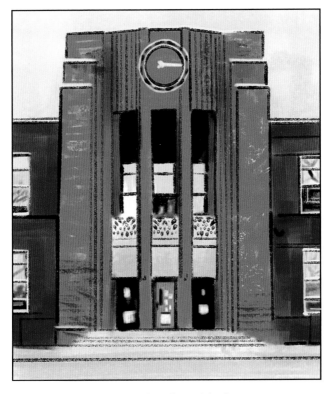

Hedgepeth-Williams School

Identity and Self-Love Journey

The Clarks' research centered on these questions: how do children's identities develop, how do they see themselves, and, ultimately, how do children find self-love and know their worth? This exploration of self-love led to the whole country hearing about their research and influencing the desegregation of schools. This activity is a journey about how you see yourself, and also, what you love about being *you*, and getting to the core of what the research showed. Below are some reflection prompts. There are a variety of activities you can do with these prompts, such as: (1) use them as writing prompts for a journal reflection activity, (2) use them for story sharing with friends or family around a dinner table, or (3) draw/paint/sing or make a creative response to the questions.

These reflection prompts are purposefully broad questions so you can really go deep and explore the various thoughts and emotions connected to the reflection prompts.

Identity and Self-Love Journey Reflection Prompts

- What does identity mean to you?
- How do you define yourself?
- How do others define you? In what ways are other people right? In what ways are other people wrong?
- What would people find out about you if they really knew you?
- What do you love most about yourself?
- What do most people love about you?
- How do you want to share or offer your talents to the world?

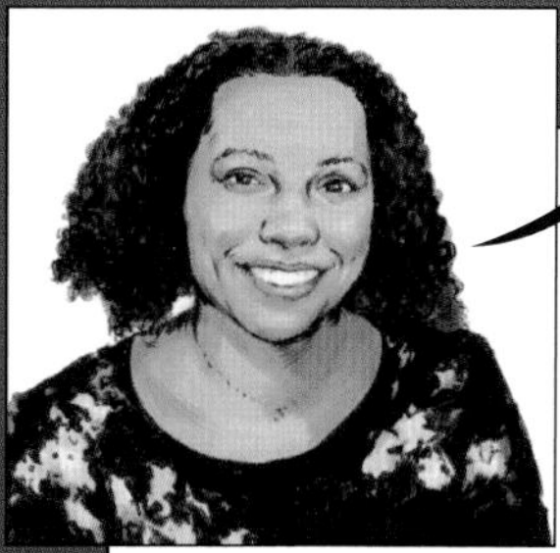
DID YOU KNOW

Black is Beautiful Movement

Dr. Mamie Phipps Clark's research was about children seeing, and ultimately loving, their Blackness. Yet, on January 28, 1962 in Harlem, the same place where Dr. Clark would build a legacy center called Northside (see Chapter 6), more Black history was being made. At the Purple Manor jazz club, documentary photojournalist Kwame Brathwaite and his brother, Elombe Brath, created and hosted a historical fashion show. The fashion show was called *Natural '62*, and the purpose of the show was to uplift the beauty of Black people and go against the mainstream idea in media that Western beauty was the ideal.

The fashion show consisted of female models called Grandassa Models. These women exuded beauty with their deep, rich skin, natural hair styles, various body types, and dresses made from African cloth. These models and displays of their African and Black American beauty went against the traditional norms of beauty that people would see in magazines then, and sometimes, even now. This event was actually a protest to *Ebony* magazine, as Mr. Brathwaite and the other creators of the event argued that you could not find ebony women in the magazine. This event was considered the spark to the birthing of what would be called the *Black is Beautiful Movement*.

The message of the movement, which continues today, is that Black beauty should be valued not only in media, but more importantly, should be valued, respected, and honored among Black people. It is a movement to counteract the internalized negative views of Blackness by Black children, as found by Drs. Mamie and Kenneth Clark

For some, the Black is Beautiful Movement in 1962 was the first time that Black children heard they were beautiful. The hope of the movement is the continued message that Black children are worthy, intelligent, and valued.

TRY THIS

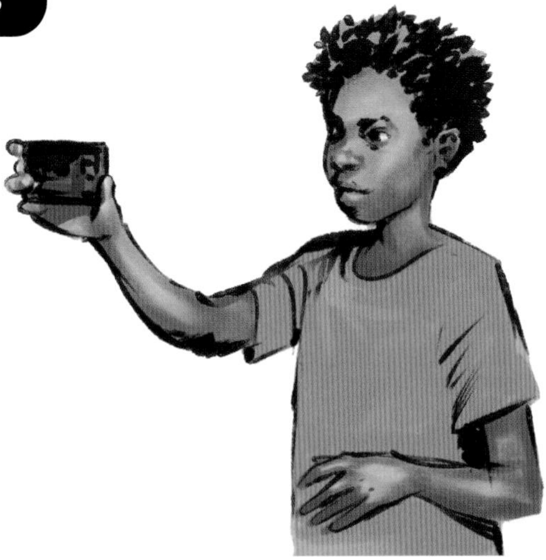

Picturing Black Joy

This activity is created with the idea of uplifting Black joy, and it is an activity for everyone. We have seen through Dr. Mamie Phipps Clark's work the importance of advocating and remembering the greatness of Blackness that can often get lost in our world today. In this activity, the concept of photovoice will be used. Photovoice is a method of answering a question or prompt with taking a photo.

The prompt for this activity is: *What does Black joy mean to you?* Using a smartphone or some other type of camera, take a digital photo that answers this question for yourself. If you don't have a camera, consider drawing a picture or thinking of an image that means Black joy to you. If you have an Instagram account, please share your photo and tag @picturingblackjoy (Instagram) or #picturingblackjoy. This allows an opportunity for us, as a collective, to make a photo album of all things Black joy. Further, this Instagram page will live on as a living archive that continues to spread the message of Black joy and love to the world, just like Dr. Clark did through her psychological research and championing of children.

CHAPTER 6

Northside Center for Child Development

Dr. Mamie's Legacy: Northside Center for Child Development

Dr. Mamie Phipps Clark's research studies exposed the negative effects of racial segregation in children and helped desegregate schools in the United States. Her research in racial identity development truly changed the lives of children all over America. But her work didn't stop with the Black Doll/White Doll studies and the *Brown v Board of Education* decision. In some ways, that was just the beginning of her pursuit for civil rights and social justice for Brown and Black kids. Combining the mind of a scientist, the dedication of a civil rights activist, and the compassion of an advocate for children, Dr. Clark was an unstoppable force!

Dr. Mamie Phipps Clark,
Northside Center
Executive Director,
1946-1979.

Mrs. Kate Clark Harris,
Northside Center
Executive Director,
1979-2007.

When she couldn't find a job teaching at a college, Dr. Clark started working with children in New York City at Riverdale Children's Association as a psychiatrist. She loved the work but wanted to make a difference for children in her own neighborhood of Harlem. She wanted there to be a place where children could get all the services they might need, a place where they could come to be psychologically evaluated, diagnosed, and gain further support if needed.

Her lifelong dream of making a difference came to fruition when she founded the Northside Center for Child Development in Harlem, NY, in 1946.

With a modest loan from her father, Mamie set up the Northside Center and never looked back. Dr. Mamie Clark's dream still exists almost 80 years later. The Northside Center started out with a $936 loan from Dr. Clark's father and served 64 children. Now it is a $25 million operation, serves 4,000 children every year.

The Northside Center initially was just an outpatient mental health clinic for children. Now it also serves as a special education school along with a Head Start program. Head Start is a preschool education program that is nationwide in the U.S. to provide free early childhood education to children in low-income neighborhoods. Dr. Clark, along with other well-known psychologists Edward Zigler and Urie Bronfenbrenner, was part of a panel of experts and committee members to initially design Head Start programs for the country. The President and the U.S. government asked Dr. Clark for her help and expertise, as she clearly understood this work from creating and building the Northside Center.

Dr. Thelma Dye, Northside Center Executive Director, 2007-present.

Dr. Clark's continued vision to deliver services to children and families in Harlem has grown to a large scale. The Executive Director, Dr. Thelma Dye, in 2021 attributed Northside's success to Dr. Clark being a visionary. Dr. Dye explained how Dr. Clark, "always said the children should be surrounded by beauty." This is why, even today, the hallways are adorned with children's art and artists of color. A library is situated in the school with books that speak to children of color. This concept is more common in today's libraries, but it was a unique idea back in the 1940s and 1950s when Dr. Clark created these spaces at the Northside Center. Even today, Dr. Dye expressed that, "I feel her always throughout the agency...you can certainly feel her love of children and love of Northside. It permeates."

The Northside Center's success is also attributed to Dr. Clark's approach to services. She was known to say that mental health is "not a psychological problem, it's a sociological problem." This means that all of society must let go of the stigma around mental health and understand that psychological services can be helpful for all. Because of Dr. Clark's expertise, visionary abilities, and love for children, her dream lives on at the Northside Center in Harlem.

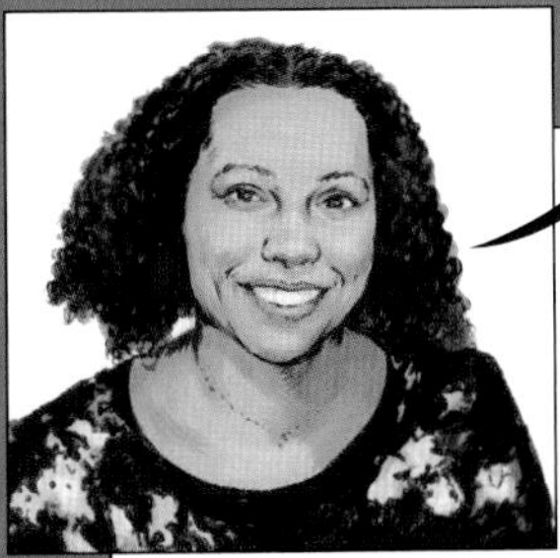

DID YOU KNOW

Little Rock Nine

Dr. Mamie's work building and running The Northside Center, along with the Black doll/White doll experiment, continues to help a large number of children. Dr. Mamie also advocated for children on a smaller scale. In particular, she helped Minnijean Brown, who was one of the Little Rock Nine.

The "Little Rock Nine" is a nickname that was given to a group of nine Black high school students from Little Rock, Arkansas. These nine students were the first to racially integrate the all-White Little Rock Central High School in 1957. This was the first step in desegregating schools after the *Brown v. Board of Education* decision. The nine students were Ernest Green, Elizabeth Eckford, Jefferson Thomas, Terrence Roberts, Carlotta Walls, Gloria Ray, Thelma Mothershed, Melba Pattillo, and Minnijean Brown.

The nine students faced verbal and physical violence from some of their fellow White students, parents, and community members. The violence toward these high school students was on such a large scale that the governor at the time, Orval Faubus, had the Arkansas National Guard purposefully block the doors so they could not enter the high school. The President of the United States, Dwight Eisenhower, even had to get involved with this situation.

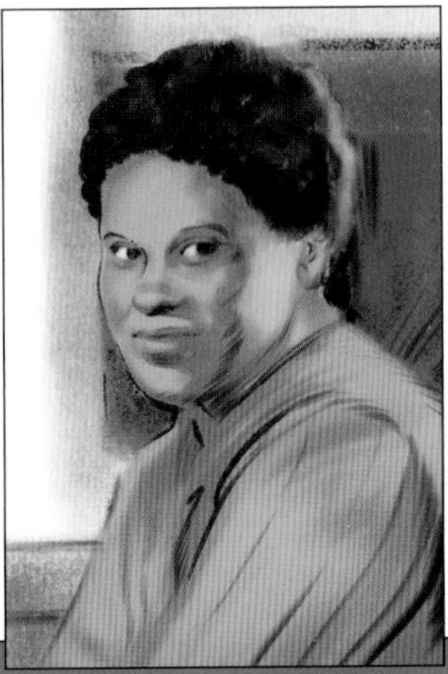

As you can image, school for these nine high schoolers was not easy at all. Minnijean, along with the other students, was harassed for months. Just five short months after school started, Minnijean experienced violence at the hands of a group of White girls who threw a bag of heavy combination locks at her. Minnijean was hurt and upset, and she called the girls "white trash." She was immediately expelled from the school for saying the comment, but the girls who hurt her and harassed her were never punished for their actions. After Minnijean was unjustly kicked out of the school, White students held signs that said, "One down... eight to go."

After learning about what happened to Minnijean, Drs. Mamie and Kenneth convinced her family to send Minnijean to New York, where she would have an easier time with racially integrated schooling. Minnijean lived with Dr. Mamie, Dr. Kenneth, Kate, and Hilton. She completed 11th and 12th grades in New York City and went home to Arkansas during the summer months. She attended the New Lincoln School, which was in the same building as The Northside Center, so Dr. Mamie drove Minnijean to school every day. On the day of Minnijean's high school graduation, Dr. Mamie had a dress specially made for Minnijean that she designed herself.

Minnijean continues to live a fruitful life. She studied at universities in the United States and Canada, earning her bachelor's and master's degrees, eventually working in the field of social work. She married and had six children. Most of the Little Rock Nine are in their early 80s, but they have received prestigious awards for their courage over the years. In 1999, President Bill Clinton awarded them the Congressional Gold Metal. There is even a statue of Minnijean and the whole Little Rock Nine group on the grounds of the State Capitol in Little Rock, Arkansas, today.

Explore Your Community's Needs

Dr. Mamie Clark really saw the needs of her community in Harlem. She understood that Black and Brown children and children with special needs require supports and advocates. She met the call for the community's needs by building the Northside Center, which still exists today.

Being an advocate means understanding the deep needs of a community. You probably have an idea of some needs within your community. For example, maybe there is a group of people in your community, like those that are experiencing homelessness, that don't have services. Maybe there is a lack of green space for children, and there is a need to build a park or community garden. Whatever it is, it is important to understand the needs of the community you live in.

Start to survey people around you about what they think are some needs of the community. You can do this by having conversations with fellow students in school, teachers, librarians, custodial workers, bus drivers, and shop owners. You can also poll your class to get everyone's thoughts on the needs of the community. You can send people you know a Google Form or even have them fill out an index card sharing what they think is an important need in the community. In short, this is a great activity of being a great listener and hearing what people want to share about their viewpoints on the community. This is the starting place to becoming an advocate and champion, just like Dr. Mamie Phipps Clark.

How to Be a Champion

BY DR. KIRA BAKER-DOYLE

Hey you, reading this—congratulations! By reading this book, you just took one step toward being a champion for change, just as Dr. Mamie Phipps Clark was a champion for civil rights!

Yes, it's true, learning about the history of change-makers like Dr. Mamie Phipps Clark is one way to become a champion yourself. Actually, there are a number of simple (and fun) ways that you can help to make a change in the world. Who knows, maybe one day they'll be writing graphic novels about you!

So, what else can you do to become a champion for change? Here are a few ideas:

Believe: Although Dr. Mamie Phipps Clark and her colleagues helped to make the world a fairer place, there is still a long way to go. Sometimes it can feel overwhelming to think that you can make a difference. But the first step to being a champion is to believe that you can! Anthropologist Dr. Margaret Mead once said, *"Never doubt that a small group of thoughtful, committed citizens can change the world; indeed, it's the only thing that ever has."* And it is true; any move you make, big or small, can make a difference. It all starts with believing that *you* make a difference.

Harness Your Superpower: You already have inside you a superpower that can help you be a champion. Do you know what it is? It's what you love to do. Dr. Clark loved math and learning about psychology. She harnessed her superpowers to help make a change in the world. What do you love? Food? You can help to feed others or learn about the causes of hunger and poverty. Music? You can use your songs to send a message about important issues in the world. Sports? You can learn about issues of fairness and participation in the sports world. Medicine? You can find opportunities to care for others in need or learn more about what causes health inequalities. By starting with what you love doing, you will have fun and feel excited about what you do.

Always Ask Why: Asking "why"' is a crucial part of becoming a champion. It is important to understand the root causes of problems so that you can help to solve them. Dr. Clark was curious about how children in the 1950s perceived racial identity, and her research led to major legal changes. When you ask questions, you start on a journey that can lead to big changes. For example, you may be curious about why your school has a certain rule that seems unfair to you. Ask your friends, teachers you trust, and other caring adults about their thoughts about the rule. Sometimes just asking why sparks change.

Be the Change You Wish to See: Change starts when people get inspired by others. Many people attribute the idea of *being the change you wish to see* to Mahatma Gandhi, a 20th century Indian leader and activist whose writings about non-violent civil disobedience and social justice inspired civil rights leaders, such as Dr. Martin Luther King, Jr. If there is something you would like to see changed, you can be that inspiration in your everyday actions. For example, if you are tired of seeing trash on your street, pick it up when you pass it by—or better yet, organize a clean-up party. A simple action like this helps people take notice of the issue or problem and can lead to bigger changes. After you have a clean-up party, talk with your party mates about *why* they think the area has an issue with trash, and think together about more ways you can work together to address the problem.

Build Your Super Team: The truth is, champions never champion alone—you need your super team! Those are the people that also care about you and the issues that are important to you. Remember that each person has their own superpower—so that means, together, you've got a whole lot of superpowers. Rely on each other and the superpowers that you bring. Remember how lawyer Thurgood Marshall reached out to Dr. Clark and her husband for their expertise when he was working on the *Brown vs. Board of Education* lawsuit? Although Mr. Marshall had his superpower in law, he needed Dr. Mamie Phipps Clark's help with her superpower in research and math. Think about who can help you, and what super skills they can bring; you don't have to champion alone!

And finally....

Tell Your Story: Stories are one of the most powerful change agents in the world. When we hear stories, we connect with them, we feel for others, and we imagine new possibilities. If you want to be a champion about an issue that is important to you, share the story of what made that issue important to you. You can share stories in many ways—through music, poetry, pictures, videos, writing, and more. Keep in mind that using social media can sometimes make us confuse popularity with change. Just because a post is popular does not mean it will make lasting change. The more important thing is to build meaningful relationships with others through your storytelling. Through those relationships, you can build your super team and get started on championing some real change!

So, go forth and champion some change with your super-powers and super team—you can do it! Believe!

Kira Baker-Doyle is an associate professor of curriculum and instruction at the University of Illinois at Chicago.

TIMELINE

Howard University

APRIL 20, 1882
Harold Hilton Phipps, Mamie's father, is born in St. Kitts in the British West Indies.

1896
Plessy v. Ferguson is a U.S. Supreme Court decision that "separate but equal" is allowed in schools.

JULY 24, 1914
Kenneth Bancroft Clark is born in the country of Panama.

1882 1896 1914
1892 1913 1917

AUGUST 18, 1892
Katie F. Smith (to become Katie Phipps), Mamie's mother, is born in Hot Springs Arkansas.

OCTOBER 18, 1917
Mamie Katherine Phipps (to become Mamie Phipps Clark) is born in Hot Springs, Arkansas, in her home at 302 Garden Street. Her father delivered her into this world.

Young Mamie Phipps (front left)

Dr. Harold Phipps and Mrs. Kate Phipps

JUNE 19, 1913
Will Norman is lynched by a mob of 4,000 men in Hot Springs, Arkansas.

JUNE 2, 1934
Dedication of the Hot Springs Confederate Monument was held on the spot where Gilbert Harris was lynched.

SPRING 1934
Mamie graduates at the age of 16 from the Langston High School.

FALL 1934
Mamie starts Howard University on a merit scholarship.

Mamie Phipps as May Queen

APRIL 14, 1938
Mamie and Kenneth have a secret wedding.

MAY 1938
Mamie is crowned the May Queen at Howard University. Her marriage was still a secret, as the May Queen is not supposed to be married.

JUNE 1938
Mamie graduates with her bachelor's degree from Howard University.

FALL 1938
Mamie starts her groundbreaking master's research project on racial identity development.

1934   1938
1922   1935   1939

AUGUST 1, 1922
The lynching of Gilbert Harris occurs in Hot Springs, Arkansas.

NOVEMBER 1935
Mamie joins the historically Black sorority Alpha Kappa Alpha (AKA).

JUNE 1939
Mamie graduates with her master's degree from Howard University.

1939
Mamie and Kenneth start conducting the doll tests in the Northern and Southern parts of the country.

Dr. Kenneth Clark conducting a doll test

1940–1942
Mamie and Kenneth receive the Rosenwald Fellowship in order to conduct their doll test.

JULY 12, 1940
Kate Miriam Clark (to become Kate Clark Harris), Mamie and Kenneth's oldest child, is born.

Kate Miriam Clark at 12 days old with her parents

JANUARY 31, 1944
The *Hedgepeth-Williams v. Trenton Board of Education* case is decided in New Jersey stating that it is unlawful to discriminate against students based on their race.

1947
The Northside Testing and Consultation Center changes its name to the Northside Center for Child Development.

1940 1944 1947
1943 1946

JUNE 1943
Dr. Mamie Clark is the first Black, female graduate with a PhD in Psychology from Columbia University.

SEPTEMBER 30, 1943
Hilton Bancroft Clark, youngest child of Drs. Mamie and Kenneth, is born.

FEBRUARY 8, 1946
The Northside Testing and Consultation Center opens its doors for children in Harlem at 226 W. 150th Street in the Dunbar Apartments.

Mamie and Kenneth in 1941

U.S. Supreme Court

JAN 15, 1954

Dr. Mamie is named the Bob Hope Woman of the Week.

MAY 17, 1954

The *Brown v. Board of Education of Topeka* case decision is rendered by the U.S. Supreme Court, making racially segregated schools illegal.

Minnijean Brown with the Clark family

FEBRUARY 1958

Minnijean Brown, one of the Little Rock Nine, was expelled for calling names toward fellow White students who racially harmed and tormented her. Drs. Mamie and Kenneth Clark took Minnijean into their home, where she finished going to school in New York for 11th and 12th grades.

1954 1958
1952 1957 1960

FEBRUARY 25, 1952

Dr. Mamie Phipps Clark testifies against her PhD professor during the *Davis v. County School Board of Prince Edward County* trial.

DECEMBER 9, 1952

Brown v. Board of Education of Topeka case is argued in front of the U.S. Supreme Court.

MAY 11, 1957

Dr. Mamie Phipps Clark is named by Alpha Upsilon, Omega Psi Phi Fraternity as Mother of the Year.

SEPTEMBER 25, 1957

Nine Black students, known as the Little Rock Nine, are the first to racially integrate Little Rock High School in Arkansas.

1960

Dr. Kenneth Clark becomes the first tenured Black professor at City College in New York.

Soldiers from the 101st Airborne Division escort Black students to Central High School in Little Rock in September 1957.

1966

Dr. Kenneth Clark becomes the first Black president of the American Psychological Association.

AMERICAN PSYCHOLOGICAL ASSOCIATION

1978

Mamie, Kenneth, Kate, and Hilton all start a consultancy business called Clark, Phipps, Clark, and Harris, Inc. helping schools and businesses to racially integrate successfully.

1983

Dr. Mamie Phipps Clark received the Candace Award for Humanitarianism from the National Coalition of 100 Black Women.

AUGUST 11, 1983

Dr. Mamie Phipps Clark dies of lung cancer at the age of 66. She even planned her own memorial service before her death.

1966   1978   1983
1973   1979   2005

1973

Dr. Mamie Phipps Clark receives the American Association of University Women Award.

APRIL 21, 1973

Dr. Mamie is named to the Board of Directors for ABC Network.

1979

Dr. Mamie Phipps Clark retires as Executive Director from the Northside Center. Her daughter, Kate Clark Harris, becomes the new Executive Director of the Northside Center.

MAY 1, 2005

Dr. Kenneth Clark dies at the age of 90.

Drs. Mamie and Kenneth Clark at The Northside Gala

2007
Kate Clark Harris retires as the Executive Director of the Northside Center. Dr. Thelma Dye becomes the new Executive Director.

Black Lives Matter protest against St. Paul police brutality

JULY 13, 2013
A social movement called #Blacklivesmatter starts as a platform to bring to light racial injustices that occur in the United States.

MARCH 2020
The COVID-19 pandemic effects the world and schools close down. During this time, the inequities that still affect Black children in U.S. schools became more apparent.

JUNE 9, 2020
George Floyd was unlawfully killed by police in Minnesota. His death sets off an international outcry for the injustices toward Black people in the U.S.

2007 2013 2020
2009 2017 2022

JANUARY 20, 2009
President Barak Obama is inaugurated as the first Black president of the United States.

AUGUST 17, 2022
Hilton, Dr. Mamie and Kenneth Clark's son, dies at the age of 79.

2017
Columbia University established the Mamie Phipps Clark and Kenneth B. Clark Distinguished Lecture Series which "recognizes the extraordinary contributions of a senior scholar in the area of race and justice."

President Barak Obama

Bibliography

Abbott, S. (2006). Mamie Phipps Clark, a Hot Springs woman who "overcame the odds." *The Record 2006, Garland County Historical Society.* p.15–21.

Adesina, P. (2020, August 3). *The birth of the Black is Beautiful movement.* BBC Style. https://www.bbc.com/culture/article/20200730-the-birth-of-the-black-is-beautiful-movement

Arkansas Gazette. (1922, August 2). *Negro lynched by Hot Springs mob.* https://encyclopediaofarkansas.net/media/harris-lynching-article-11909/

Avilucea, I. (2021, April 14). *Trenton school officials lead tour of Hedgepeth-Williams ahead of May reopening.* The Trentonian. https://www.trentonian.com/2021/04/14/trenton-school officials-lead-tour-of-hedgepeth- williams-ahead-of-may-reopening/

Banks, J. A. (2007, July 17). *Remembering Brown: Silence, loss, rage, and hope*, 1954. BlackPast. https://www.blackpast.org/african-american-history/remembering-brown-silence-loss-rage-and-hope/

Blakemore, R. (2022, January 11). *How dolls helped win Brown v. Board of Education.* History Stories. https://www.history.com/news/brown-v-board-of-education-doll-experiment/

Brathwaite, K. (2023). About. https://kwamebrathwaite.com/about/

Cherry, K. (2021, February 19). *Experiment ideas of psychology assignments.* VeryWell Mind. https://www.verywellmind.com/psychology-experiment-ideas-2795669/

Christ, M. K. (2020, November 16). Hot Springs Confederate Monument. *Encyclopedia of Arkansas.* https://encyclopediaofarkansas.net/entries/hot-springs- confederate-monument-13208/

Clark, K. B., & Clark, M. K. (1939). Segregation as a factor in the racial identification of Negro pre-school children: A preliminary report. *The Journal of Experimental Education*, 8(2), 161–163. http://www.jstor.org/stable/20150598/

Clark, K. B., & Clark, M. K. (1939). The development of consciousness of self and the emergence of racial identification in Negro preschool children. *The Journal of Social Psychology*, 10, 591–599. https://doi.org/10.1080/00224545.1939.9713394

Clark, M. P. (1976, May 25). *Oral history transcript.* Columbia University Library Oral History Research Office.http://www.columbia.edu/cu/lweb/digital/collections/nny/clarkm/transcripts/clarkm_1_1_1.html/

Cross, W. E., Jr. (1991). *Shades of Black: Diversity in African-American identity.* Philadelphia: Temple University Press, 1991.

Cross, W. E., Jr. (1995). The psychology of Nigrescence: Revising the Cross model. In J. G. Ponterotto, J. M. Casa, L. S. Suzuki, & C. M. Alexander (Eds.), *Handbook of multicultural counseling* (pp. 93–122). Sage Publications.

Dunhill, H. (2020, July 7). *Kate Harris on her front-row seat during the Brown v. Board of Education.* Sarasota Magazine. https://www.sarasotamagazine.com/news-and-profiles/2020/07/kate-harris-sarasota/

Dye, T. (2021, November 19). Transcript from interview with Dr. Lynnette Mawhinney.

Ely, M. (2022, January 28). *The fashion show that helped launch a movement.* Brooklyn Public Library. https://www.bklynlibrary.org/blog/2022/01/28/fashion-show-helped/

Encyclopedia of Arkansas. (2022). *Pythian Bathhouse.* https://encyclopediaofarkansas.net/media/pythian-bathhouse-8561/

Fenwick, L. T. (2022, May 17). *The ugly backlash to Brown v. Board of Ed that no one talks about.* Politico. https://www.politico.com/news/magazine/2022/05/17/brown-board-education-downside-00032799/

Ferdman, B. M., and Gallegos, P. I. (2001). Latinos and racial identity development. In C. L. Wijeyesinghe & B. W. Jackson III (Eds.), *New perspectives on racial identity development: A theoretical and practical anthology* (pp. 32–66). New York University Press.

Grant, T. K. (2022). *The road to school desegregation.* National Geographic Kids. https://kids.nationalgeographic.com/history/article/the-road-to-school-desegregation/

Helms, J. E. (1995). An update of Helms's White and people of color racial identity models. In J. G. Ponterotto, J. M. Casa, L. S. Suzuki, & C. M. Alexander (Eds.), Handbook of Multicultural Counseling (pp. 181–198). Sage Publications.

Hochschild, A. (2012). *The second shift: Working families and the revolution at home.* Penguin.

Horse, P. G. (2005). Native American identity. *New Directions for Student Services,* 109, (61– 68).

Hunter, L. P. (2022, October 12). *Mamie Clark's unsung contribution to Brown v. Board.* Black Perspectives.

Izzo, C. (2013, May 23). *Trenton City Museum marks closing of New Lincoln School exhibit with ceremony.* The Times of Trenton. https://www.nj.com/mercer/2013/05/trenton_city_museum_marks_clos.html/

Kalman, A. (2019, October 2). *Children lead the way: A gallery of youth-made climate-strike signs.* The New Yorker. https://www.newyorker.com/culture/culture-desk/children-lead-the-way-a-gallery-of-youth-made-climate-strike-signs/

Kim, J. (1981). *Processes of Asian American identity development: A study of Japanese American women's perceptions of their struggle to achieve positive identities as Americans of Asian 6 ancestry.* Doctoral Dissertation University of Massachusetts Amherst. Available from Proquest. AAI8118010.

Kim, J. (2001). Asian American racial identity theory. In C. L. Wijeyesinghe & B. W. Jackson III (Eds.), *New perspectives on racial identity development: A theoretical and practical anthology* (pp. 138–161). New York University Press.

Lakritz, T. (2020, June 3). *Powerful signs from Black Lives Matter protests across the US.* Insider. https://www.insider.com/black-lives-matter-photos-protest-signs-2020-6/

Lancaster, G. (2017, August 18). *Lynchings hidden in history of the Hot Springs Confederate monument.* Arkansas Times. https://arktimes.com/arkansas-blog/2017/08/18/lynchings-hidden-in-the-history-of-the-hot-springs-confederate-monument/

Leyens, J. (2011). *Three centuries of African-American history in Trenton: Significant people and places.* The New Yorker. https://www.trentonlib.org/wp-content/uploads/2020/04/Trenton'sAfrican-AmericanHistoryManual2015.pdf/

Library of Congress Collections, Manuscript Division, Kenneth B. Clark Papers, Boxes 1-13; 212-230, OV 1-OV 10

Lloyd, S. M. (2006). *A short history of Howard University.* Howard University. https://medicine.howard.edu/about-us/mission-vision-and-core-values/short-history/

Markowitz, G. & Rosner, D. (1996). *Children, race, and power: Kenneth and Mamie Clark's Northside Center.* Routledge Press.

Mawhinney, L. (2014). *We got next: Urban education and the next generation of Black teachers.* Peter Lang.

McNeill, L. (2017, October 26). *How a psychologist's work on race identity helped to overturn school segregation in 1950s America*. Smithsonian Magazine. https://www.smithsonianmag.com/science-nature/psychologist-work-racial-identity-helped-overturn-school-segregation-180966934/

Poston, W. S. C. (1990). The biracial identity development model: A needed addition. *Journal of Counseling and Development*, 69(2), 152–55.

Robbins, E. (2022, September 1). *Time tour: Jones School*. The Sentinel-Record. https://www.hotsr.com/news/2022/sep/01/time-tour-jones-school/

Rockquemore, K., & Laszloffy, T. A. (2005). *Raising biracial children*. Rowman Altamira.

Rothberg, E. (2022). Dr. Mamie Phipps Clark. *National Women's History Museum*. http://www.womenshistory.org/education-resources/biographies/dr-mamie-phipps- clark/

Sameth, M. (2015). A Civil Rights Pioneer Returns to Hastings. Hastings Historian. Retrieved from https://hastingshistoricalsociety.org/2021/06/18/minnijean-brown-of-the-little-rock-nine/

Science Buddies (2022). *Steps of the scientific method*. https://www.sciencebuddies.org/science-fair-projects/science-fair/steps-of-the-scientific-method/

Spofford, T. (2022). *What the children told us: The untold story of the famous "doll test" and the Black psychologists who changed the world*. Sourcebooks.

Steele, J. (2022). *Children come first*. Trenton Public Schools. https://www.trentonk12.org/PattonJHillsLegacy.aspx/

Stone, M. R. (2013). *"Somebody better put their pants on and be talking about it": White therapists who identify as anti-racist addressing racism and racial identity with White clients*. Smith College. https://scholarworks.smith.edu/cgi/viewcontent.cgi?article=1682&context=theses/

Sue, D. W. (2001). *Multidimensional facets of cultural competence*. The counseling psychologist, 29(6), 790–821.

Trenton Division of Planning. (2014). *City profile report: Trenton 1792–2042* https://www.trentonnj.org/DocumentCenter/View/260/City-Profile-Report---2014-PDF/

Wenatchee Valley College. (2023). Summary of stages of racial identity development. https://www.wvc.edu/students/support/diversity/Stages%20of%20Racial%20Identity%20Development.pdf/

Photo Credits

Page 112: Howard University, Sdkb, CC BY-SA 4.0 <https://creativecommons.org/licenses/by-sa/4.0>, via Wikimedia Commons; Mamie Phipps Clark's parents, Deluxe Studios, public domain; Young Mamie Phipps, public domain

Page 113: Mamie Phipps Clark as May Queen, Scurlock Studio Records, Archives Center, © National Museum of American History, Smithsonian Institution; Kenneth Clark conducting test, © The Gordon Parks Foundation

Page 114: The United States Supreme Court, Joe Ravi CC

Page 115: Mr._&_Mrs._Kenneth_Clark_and_children._1958_(cropped): Charlotte Brooks, photographer, LOOK Magazine Photograph Collection, Library of Congress, Prints & Photographs Division, [Reproduction number e.g., LC-L9-60-8812, frame 8]; National Guard escorting students, The U.S. Army, Public domain, via Wikimedia Commons

Page 116: Dr. and Mrs. Clark at Northside Gala, Njames0343, CC BY-SA 4.0 <https://creativecommons.org/licenses/by-sa/4.0>, via Wikimedia Commons

Page 117: Black Lives Matter protesters, Fibonacci Blue from Minnesota, USA, CC BY 2.0 <https://creativecommons.org/licenses/by/2.0>, via Wikimedia Commons; President Barak Obama, Official White House Photo by Pete Souza, Public domain, via Wikimedia Commons

Key Terms, People, Civil Rights Cases, and Organizations

14th Amendment: A part of the U.S. Constitution that talks about equal rights and that says no U.S. state can make or enforce laws that take away privileges from U.S. citizens

American Psychological Association (APA): A professional organization of psychologists

Black doll/White doll experiment: A psychological experiment where Drs. Mamie and Kenneth Clark explored how Black children understand their racial identity

Brown v. Board of Education of Topeka: A court case that made racial segregation illegal in U.S. schools

Charles Houston: A prominent Black lawyer who worked on demolishing Jim Crow laws and founding the NAACP Legal Defense Fund. He also trained Thurgood Marshall.

Colored/Negro: Terms used to describe Black people back in the 1800s and 1900s

Davis v. County School Board of Prince Edward County: A case in Virginia where Dr. Mamie Phipps Clark testified about the doll test. This case was one of the cases leading up to the *Brown v. Board of Education of Topeka* case.

Doctoral program: An education program where someone becomes a PhD and is then referred to as doctor.

Hedgepeth-Williams v. Trenton Board of Education: An early case in New Jersey that decided it was unlawful to discriminate against students based on their race

Horowitz's Investigation: Named after Leonard M. Horowitz, this was a psychology assessment about people's motivations. This was the basis of Dr. Mamie Phipps Clark's research.

Integration: The act of including everyone into a group no matter their differences, such as race, gender, sexual orientation, religion, age, ability, etc.

Jim Crow South/Jim Crow Laws: These were state and local laws, found in the Southern part of the United States, that reinforced racial segregation. The term "Jim Crow" was a negative term to describe Black people.

Lynching: An unjust practice where Black men, women, and children were killed just because they were Black

National Association for the Advancement of Colored People (NAACP): A civil rights group focused on supporting and providing justice for Black people in the United States

One-room schoolhouse: Schools in the 1800s and 1900s that combined all ages and grades into one classroom

Pythian Hotel: A local hotel in Hot Springs, Arkansas, where Black people were allowed to go. Dr. Phipps, Dr. Mamie Phipps Clark's father, had his medical practice in this building.

Racial housing covenant and redlining: These were systems and laws that were put in place to purposefully keep Black people out of living or buying homes in White neighborhoods. Ultimately, this continued the concept of racial segregation in very subtle ways.

Racial identity development: A field of study that looks at how people understand their racialized selves, and how they feel about the race they are

Robert Carter: A legal assistant to Thurgood Marshall in the NAACP. He was the initial person to advocate for Drs. Mamie and Kenneth Clark's research during all the school desegregation cases they were working on. He later became a New York Supreme Court judge.

Rosenwald Fellowship: The two-year long scholarship where Drs. Mamie and Kenneth Clark received monies in order to do the doll test.

Second shift: The task of doing both household and childcare duties after working a full-time job.

Segregation: The act of excluding and keeping a group separate based on their differences, such as race, gender, sexual orientation, religion, age, ability, etc.

U.S. Supreme Court: The highest court within the United States. The judges that sit on the court decide if cases follow the U.S. Constitution or not.

Thurgood Marshall: The first Black person to sit on the Supreme Court. Prior to this high position, he was most notably known for being one of the lead lawyers of the *Brown v. Board of Education* court case representing the NAACP.

Lynnette Mawhinney, PhD, is an award-winning scholar, educator, and author of several books, including *Lulu the One and Only* (Magination Press). She lives in New Jersey. Visit lynettemawhinney.com and @lkmawhinney on X and Instagram.

Neil Evans is a Welsh illustrator. A lifelong comic art fan, he drifted into childrens' illustration at art college and has kept a foot in both camps ever since. He lives in Wrexham, North Wales.

  The art for this book was created with Apple Pencil in Procreate, with the help of hundreds of historical reference photos.

The American Psychological Association works to advance psychology as a science and profession and as a means of promoting health and human welfare. APA publishes books for young readers that aim to make navigating life's challenges a little easier. It's the synthesis of psychological science with narrative nonfiction that makes APA kids books distinctive. Visit maginationpress.org.

Robert Carter: A legal assistant to Thurgood Marshall in the NAACP. He was the initial person to advocate for Drs. Mamie and Kenneth Clark's research during all the school desegregation cases they were working on. He later became a New York Supreme Court judge.

Rosenwald Fellowship: The two-year long scholarship where Drs. Mamie and Kenneth Clark received monies in order to do the doll test.

Second shift: The task of doing both household and childcare duties after working a full-time job.

Segregation: The act of excluding and keeping a group separate based on their differences, such as race, gender, sexual orientation, religion, age, ability, etc.

U.S. Supreme Court: The highest court within the United States. The judges that sit on the court decide if cases follow the U.S. Constitution or not.

Thurgood Marshall: The first Black person to sit on the Supreme Court. Prior to this high position, he was most notably known for being one of the lead lawyers of the *Brown v. Board of Education* court case representing the NAACP.

Lynnette Mawhinney, PhD, is an award-winning scholar, educator, and author of several books, including *Lulu the One and Only* (Magination Press). She lives in New Jersey. Visit lynettemawhinney.com and @lkmawhinney on X and Instagram.

Neil Evans is a Welsh illustrator. A lifelong comic art fan, he drifted into childrens' illustration at art college and has kept a foot in both camps ever since. He lives in Wrexham, North Wales.

  The art for this book was created with Apple Pencil in Procreate, with the help of hundreds of historical reference photos.

The American Psychological Association works to advance psychology as a science and profession and as a means of promoting health and human welfare. APA publishes books for young readers that aim to make navigating life's challenges a little easier. It's the synthesis of psychological science with narrative nonfiction that makes APA kids books distinctive. Visit maginationpress.org.